THE BLUEBIRD HOUSE

THE BLUEBIRD HOUSE

Rae Ellen Lee

Five Star • Waterville, Maine

This novel is a work of fiction. Names, characters, places and incidents are either the product of the author's imagination, or, if real, used fictitiously.

Five Star First Edition Women's Fiction Series.

Published in 2002 in conjunction with
Alison J. Picard Literary Agent.

Set in 11 pt. Plantin by Al Chase.

Printed in the United States on permanent paper.

Library of Congress Cataloging-in-Publication Data

Lee, Rae Ellen, 1945–
The bluebird house / Rae Ellen Lee.
p. cm. — (Five Star first edition women's fiction series)
ISBN 0-7862-4022-9 (hc : alk. paper)
1. Buildings—Repair and reconstruction—Fiction.
2. Middle aged women—Fiction. 3. Trials (Murder) Fiction. 4. Divorced women—Fiction. 5. Young men—Fiction. 6. Montana—Fiction. I. Title. II. Series.
PS3612.E348 B57 2002
813′.6—dc21 2001059223

In memory of
Wesley "Spike" Moore, alias Posthole Augerson
(1906–1991)
who told great stories, some of them true

ACKNOWLEDGMENTS

I am grateful to my agent, Alison Picard, for believing in this project and to my editor, Russell Davis, a man willing to take a gamble. He kept reading, found a diamond in the rough, then helped polish it with a great deal of enthusiasm.

Special thanks to my favorite population on the fringe: Kathryn Hamshar, Sherry Gohr and Sam Irvin, and Penny and John Bews, collectively and individually, for their friendship, for telling me stories, and for reading my drafts with so much love. I am especially grateful to Penny and John for providing a quiet retreat on the river where I could write and test recipes. I also appreciate Linda Allen, singer-songwriter, who led The Artist's Way workshop that gave me the courage to write fiction again.

Members of two writing groups insisted on metaphors with muscle and asked questions that kept me writing answers. Thank you Kit Axelson, Sue Erickson, Ann Melton, Veronica McNamee, Colleen Schwartz, Cary Deringer, Scott Brown, Robin Holbert, Joan Kraft, and Mary Lu Perham. You've been more help than I can say. Thanks also to Nancy Lee for teaching the excellent fiction writing course at Simon Fraser University, Vancouver, B.C. Thanks to both Anna Klocke and Karen High, back east, who provided helpful comments on an early draft. All your voices echo in the canyon where the old buildings of Snowshoe lean toward the sun.

Special thanks to Keith Leatherman of Helena for information and stories that I warped and shaped into the

Snowshadow Hot Springs Resort and the career of one main character. And thanks to Dusty Dunbar, member of The Saddle Bags, for sharing tales of her ride in Montana's 1989 Centennial Cattle Drive.

Thanks to Ellen Baumler at the Montana Historical Society for help with research on the subject of mining camp prostitution in the early part of the twentieth century. Dave Barnes, a jeweler and friend in Helena, provided helpful information on gems. Roslyn Cameron of the Charles Darwin Research Station in the Galápagos Islands supplied me with the exact quotation by Mr. Darwin about the importance of reading poetry and listening to music. Daniel Lee, trained as a chef, helped me with the mountain man recipes. And Christine Metcalfe, my Austrian friend, offered guidance in lettering the map and capturing the spirit of the German language. If any errors are found in the novel, they are entirely my doing.

Lastly, I am grateful to Tom Lee for his constant support and encouragement, for editorial suggestions that always ring true, and for helping me to renovate a former brothel in an old Montana mining camp—so long ago.

What Darwin Said About Music

". . . If I had to live my life again I would have made a rule to read some poetry and listen to some music at least once every week . . . (for) the loss of these tastes is a loss of happiness, and may possibly be injurious to the intellect, and more probably to the moral character, by enfeebling the emotional part of our nature."

The Autobiography of Charles Darwin,
1809–1882, New York: W.W. Norton, 1958

Snowshoe, Montana
1902

CHAPTER 1

Two weeks after my accident, I am released. Even with good insurance, the hospital has its limits. A steady stream of patients had arrived with various illnesses, not one of them as bizarre as my reason for being hospitalized.

Alone now in our cavernous house with my pets I move slowly, and only when I must. My body's bruised condition and the stiffness of my joints regulate my movements. I rest. I read. I watch *Days of Our Lives.* At other times, I stare out the picture window in the living room over the Prickly Pear Valley. I sit silently, watching the afternoon light change on the Big Belt Mountains. When the moon rises you cannot see it move unless you look away and then look back again. That's the way the light changes on the mountains, except when the cloud shadows gallop soundlessly across the rock on their ghost legs. When the cloud shadows race along the face of the steep mountains I always think of immense dark leaves let loose, fleeing ahead of a storm—until they reach an unseen line of fences and the outer limits of their freedom.

I study the horizon to the north, with its odd, shallow dip like an antique washbasin. The Missouri River once passed through that basin, until the mountains lifted and the river took an elbow turn to the east toward the Great Plains. When the uplift occurred, I suppose that, too, was nearly imperceptible.

I've read that there are no accidents in life, that things happen for a reason. My accident must mean something, and that is what I ponder while I rest and stare out the window. Maybe I'm being reminded that *I* have never been the dominant creature, not once, not in any situation. A heavy, oddly centered anger sometimes seethes and roils underneath the faded purple hoof print, and it isn't anger at the animal. Instead, I've been thinking about love, about how I don't really love Bradley, and how by staying with him all these years I haven't loved myself. Like some slow geologic event, I had barely noticed it happening.

I can recall no joy in our marriage that was unbearably good, the way I've heard other women, like Myra, talk about their relationships. Years ago I read *Total Woman.* Other women were reading it, too, but we never talked about what the book did or didn't do for us. I even wore *Wind Song* perfume for a while, but nothing I tried seemed to make me more of a woman or Bradley more of a man, or our marriage any more like the song of the wind.

We've been married twenty-six years. I remember the night I met him at a dance at the University of Montana, where he was taking business management and I was studying biology. I loved to dance. He knew the steps and danced smoothly, confidently. But we only danced one other time after that—at our wedding reception. Mom and Dwight were pleased that I'd done so well at college, landing a man with a secure future in business. Boy, was I surprised that first year of marriage, and bewildered, too, at how little there actually *was* to being married. But then my two beautiful boys came along and kept me busy. When they went off to grade school I got a job as a biological technician at the state water quality lab and found that my college studies were good for something besides landing a husband.

When Bradley's in town and at home in the evenings, he reads war stories, works on the computer, talks on the phone or golfs with his associates. I've heard his subtle reprimands about my cooking and housekeeping so often I no longer listen. He says, "Molly, if you'd get rid of the dog and cat the house wouldn't need to be cleaned so often." But the house is never what I'd call dirty, even though I no longer spend all my free time cleaning. And I do love my pets. He's probably jealous.

Years ago I began to notice that after Bradley was home a few days from his business trips I'd develop flu-like symptoms. When he'd leave again, I'd recover. In case my symptoms meant something besides an allergy to Bradley, I went to my doctor. After several tests, he found nothing wrong with me physically. Then he asked if I'd ever considered counseling. Later that week I arranged free sessions with a counselor through the employee assistance program at work. It didn't take the counselor long to tell me, rather bluntly, "You're a caretaker and it's making you sick." She didn't say I should leave my husband, but I figured that's what she meant. The weird part was, I couldn't do it. Bradley needed me. He still needs me.

But how important will the words loyalty and faithfulness be when I'm in a rest home someday? I don't think they'll matter much. What I'll want when I'm old is a deep well of memories to drink from. Yet who am I without Bradley?

And then, without bidding, I relive the details of my afternoon in the woods, and once again, I hear the sound of my bones snapping like twigs under the weight of the wild animal. He was the dominant creature, in control and forceful. I was his prey. And after he charged, after time had stopped, I was left behind, abandoned to my silence and pain. My helplessness swims over me, pulling me under.

CHAPTER 2

What can it hurt if I rob the food chain of a few stems and shoots? Pushing my way through willows and alders, I take care to step over the occasional mound of frozen moose droppings. Chickadees flit from branch to branch, chittering like Gregorian crickets, as my boots chuff along the frosty ground. *Chick-a-dee-dee-dee.* Occasionally I hear a bird's faraway clear whistle—*fee-bee.* It's a perfect Montana spring day—just right for hunting and gathering—and I'm determined to take a little wilderness home with me to our modern, oversized house in Helena, the house that Bradley built.

A clump of red-osier dogwood bushes stops me. A long wine-colored branch, straight and round as a fishing pole, will give me two or three pieces for the face of my window shutters. The frames are built. Now is the best time to gather the stems, before the bushes sprout leaves. At midday, the air is chilly in the shade of the firs and pines where the dogwood branches grow long and straight. The pruning shears snap cleanly through a stem, and I add it to the growing bundle on the ground near my feet, pleased that soon I'll be able to replace one boring set of beige, pleated drapes with a bit of color from the wild. Cascading all around me is the chatter of birds, like the sound of a stream filled with miniature waterfalls. At home, when I look at my finished shutters, I'll think of today and of chickadees.

I wipe my wet, cold nose on a sleeve then reach up for a perfect branch. Suddenly the woods fall silent. A slight breeze stirs the tips of the fir branches; otherwise, there are no bird sounds, no movement. Nothing. Curious about this strange hush, I turn my head.

At first only a puff of breath, behind me and off to my right. Then a small cloud, like steam from a radiator and a loud snort, an announcement. I hold my breath, my heartbeat. When I turn my head further, I see a looming dark form, too close and slightly out of focus. Where did he come from? Another grunt, this one louder, angrier. A hoof strikes frozen snow. I must keep calm. I've seen bigger. I will put something between myself and the beast. The bush in front of me doesn't offer much of a barrier, but moose don't see well. If I move slowly, he might not notice me. I step sideways with the right foot, then bring the left foot along. I do this again, and then sink down, moving under the branches, around to the other side. Maybe the moose will get confused and think he's seeing things. I take another slow step. I'm almost there. The bush is now between me and the moose.

I don't know if I hear a pause before the moose lunges, or how I know he's coming at me through the bushes. Dropping to my knees with a lurch, my glasses fly off my face and catch in a low, red stem—a stem just right for twig shutters. Now crouching to shelter my internal organs, I clasp my hands over the back of my neck to protect my spinal cord. Or is this what you're supposed to do when you meet a grizzly? Oh, God. Please help me.

It happens so quickly, so inevitably—the furious snorting, the pawing, the crashing of brush over my head and the one step, heavy as a logging truck, onto my back, crushing me into the ground. I hear bones break with a dull, muffled snap, then my ears are filled with the thundering vibration of hooves pounding frozen ground. In the seconds before I pass out, I smell the musty, acrid exhaust of the large, unwashed animal.

When I come to, the pain in my back bites like the jagged, rusty teeth of an old crosscut saw. I must cough, but when I do the pain surges. The ground spins me around. Bushes blur. I wipe my mouth and see blood on a sleeve, a sleeve on an arm I am barely able to move.

My car is somewhere out near the gravel road. But which way is it to the road? I pass out again. The cold wakes me up. The road. I must reach the road. I can hear Bradley, if I live to hear him again, saying, "What in the world were you doing out in the woods alone?"

As I drag myself onto all fours, some broken branches fall away from me while others cling to my clothing like claws, or fishhooks. The relentless pain in my back and chest sears like hot coals, and I am dizzy again. Not far away, the creek trickles past between ice-bound banks. If I listen carefully maybe I can hear the direction the creek is moving. The loudest trickles should come from downstream, not upstream, and the creek flows downstream toward the road. But the slope of the ground appears level, except for patches of snow, broken branches and the mounds of frozen moose shit I now see everywhere.

Groaning, I drag my pain, as if it is contained in a basket, forward on arms so weak they feel as if they belong to a stranger in a dream. Pieces of branches, now like broken wings, dangle from my jacket. Other branches hide the creek from me, but I believe I'm crawling toward the road. Every time I move the pain strikes, hot and forked as a lightning bolt. My legs trail along behind. Moving ahead is too painful. Oh God, please don't let me die out here. Cold and numb, I inch my way forward, my hands freezing.

Wait . . . a sound . . . a car on the road. Without my glasses, I reach toward the invisible noise, toward a blur of brush. Moving forward again, slow as a glacier, I realize it will take hours, days, for me to reach the road. I will die from my wounds. I'll freeze to death tonight a short distance from help. Using my elbows, I crawl toward a slant of afternoon sunlight in a clearing. Finally, finally, I flop a leaden arm over a bank of snow. But is it the edge of the road?

"Wake up, wake up," a man yells. "Jesus, what happened to you?"

I open my eyes to a gray wool hat and a face so near that I can see individual wiry hairs in his brushy, walrus mustache. I close my eyes and groan. My teeth rattle against each other. "Moose . . . help."

"Hold on. I never found a half-dead person before. Gotta get you into the truck."

With more gratitude than I have ever known, I give in again and let the darkness reclaim me.

Curled in the fetal position on the seat of an old pickup truck, I am wrapped in a dirty blue blanket smelling of stale beer. The pain, like knives, stabs at me, over and over and over. My head rests against the man's thigh that smells of oil and sawdust. My feet bump against the door handle. During the few moments I am conscious, the truck rattles and shakes and hammers the bumpy, icy road. I doze and, moaning, wake up to the engine roaring in my ears. Soon white snowy silence. Then I hear a growling rumble as the man shifts down and the jarring clatter of loose tools and beer cans on the floor. *Am I worse off now than when I lay in the woods?* But I don't care. All I want is to stay alive, to sit on a mountaintop one more time with the sun on my face, to hear birds singing. Drifting off again, I dream that Bradley cannot find me, that this strange mountain man takes me to a deserted old building in a long-ago place in another century, and hides me there.

CHAPTER 3

"Can you tell me your name?" a female voice asks.

"Molly Binfet," I groan. "It hurts. My back."

My jacket is cut away, then my shirt and bra, and I'm exposed under bright lights. Now they're cutting off my jeans.

"We're going to take some X-rays, Mrs. Benefit," the woman says, "Then we'll give you something for the pain. Can you tell us who to call for you?"

I mumble Bradley's name and our phone number, then hear footsteps receding from the bright glare. The words benefit and insurance float through my head. If I could, I'd smile. I suppose she's going to call Mr. Benefit. I groan again into the darkness.

"You have four broken ribs and a punctured lung, Mrs. Benefit," I hear a male voice saying, a warm hand touching my shoulder.

Where am I? I open my eyes to a doctor no older than my sons.

"You're lucky for two reasons," he says. "The moose wasn't full grown. We can tell that by the hoof print on your back. And he didn't step on your spine. You'll be all right in a few weeks."

"Thank you," I whisper, then try to explain, "my name is Binfet, not Benefit."

"Okay. Mrs. Binfet." The young doctor pats my inert hand. "The pain shot we gave you should make you more comfortable." He leaves the room.

A nurse says, "We took down the name and address of the man who brought you in." She takes my hand. "He stayed around long enough to make sure you'd be all right. Mr.

Binfet will be here pretty soon."

A wave of pain sweeps through my chest. The kindness of the man with the mustache, the nurse's caring hands on mine, something, everything, builds a fist of emotion in my chest. I drift into an unknowing and welcome drugged state.

I dream I am living a fable, oblivious to some lesson I'm supposed to be learning. I fall into an abyss, deep and sweet, not sour, as you would expect a dark empty space to be. Still falling, eyes closed, the warm sunshine caresses my face and I'm floating in clean blue sky. Now enfolded in pallid fog, I am sluggish, slow in my nothingness, overcome with a new understanding: it's no use to pretend. I hear praise and chanting far away, and thoughts of forgiveness, of how important it is to forgive myself.

"Molly?" the familiar voice whispers. I open my eyes. Bradley is standing by my bed. He's wearing a suit and tie.

"I hate to see you like this," he says, touching my arm, then moving away toward one of the chairs in the room.

He seems awkward. It must be a shock for him, unaccustomed as he is to seeing me helpless when I'm always so healthy, always serving him and his needs, meeting his unspoken wishes. I look blankly at him, unable to think of anything to say. Each breath sears my chest and my back. If only I didn't have to breathe.

After a few seconds he says, "I don't know why you were in the woods alone. What were you thinking?"

"Bradley," I whisper. "I'm so tired . . . sleep . . . remember to feed Al and Chug. And please, bring my spare glasses."

"Sure," he says, bending to kiss my cheek. "I'll be back in the morning with the boys after I pick them up at the airport."

In what seems like minutes, for I've completely lost track

of time, first Scott, then Jeremy are walking into my room.

"Hi, Mom," Scott says, kissing me on the temple near my teary left eye.

"Hi, honey. I'm so glad to see you." My voice, soft and weak, sounds hollow, as if coming from someone else, from an invalid. "Jeremy. How are you, sweetie?"

"Well, gee, Mom. I'm good. What about you?"

"I'll be all right."

Bradley comes over to my bed and takes my warm hand in his cool, smooth hand. We look at each other a moment, the way two parents look at each other when they find themselves unexpectedly in the company of their adult children, children they made together and raised. With so much that could be said, it seems useless, even unnecessary, to try. And since I'm weak and not up to talking much, I ask questions of my sons, encouraging long answers with my eyes. "Jeremy, how do you like working at the new restaurant? Scott, how's Jessica? Sorry she couldn't come with you." I adore listening to my sons talk, hearing their voices. They're both sometimes a little too much like their father to suit me, but I can overlook this tendency, at least in them.

Jeremy, always the most outspoken, says, "Mom, imagine what it's like to answer the phone and hear Dad say, 'Your mom's been attacked by a moose.' "

I smile a weak laugh, and the boys laugh a little awkwardly, concern in their eyes and voices. "It wasn't the moose's fault," I say.

After a couple more visits to the hospital, my sons return to their lives in Seattle. My days settle into a routine of groggy rest, hospital meals, more rest, and a parade of curious hospital employees. Each time a new nurse or doctor comes to gawk at the bruise on my back, a bruise in the perfect shape of a moose's hoof, I close my eyes and see a looming, dark object, hear the crashing of brush, the breaking of branches and bones.

One day, before the bruise has a chance to fade away, I ask to see it. Two nurses bring in large mirrors and position me and then the mirrors so I can see the object of everyone's attention. The hoof print is still purple and ugly—about five inches long and four inches wide on my white back beneath the left shoulder blade. The perimeter of the bruise is turning pale yellow, like tired leaves in autumn, the color of my helplessness. I am a marked woman. For the first time, I spill tears about my encounter with the moose.

"You go ahead and cry, dear," one of the nurses says. "You've been through a lot."

At that moment, I really want to tie one on. From the depths of my hollow core I want to howl in pain, untamed, to tap into sounds from some other world. I want to wail until I'm finished with my feelings of wasted time, of squandered chances—until I'm rid of my longing and melancholy. But after the first heaving sob, my injured ribs hurt so much the urge to cry vanishes.

Bradley comes to visit every evening, although he doesn't have much to say, and I'm increasingly annoyed when he walks into the room. I want to be alone. In an attempt to entertain him, I suppose, I say to him one evening, "Bradley, would you like to take a look at my bruise? It looks like a hoof print." For some reason, I want him to see the bruise, too. Everyone else has wanted to.

"No, Moll. It would hurt me to see it. When I think about what that moose did to you, I want to take up hunting."

We both know he doesn't hunt, that he wouldn't know how to use a gun. He couldn't even kill a rabbit.

"It wasn't the moose's fault," I say, staring at the dark window of my room.

"They want to keep you a few more days. They're watching you for signs of pneumonia," Bradley says, looking at me intently. "Then you can come home."

"Well, since I'm not out of the woods yet, as they say, I'd like to stay here as long as they'll let me. I enjoy being waited on. And I'm getting involved with the people on *Days of Our Lives*. They're my new friends." I say this to irritate Bradley, who hates television.

"I'll cancel my out-of-town appointments for next week. I can stay home and help you."

Why is he being so considerate now, when everything about him irritates me so—from his average height to his average build, from his angular clean-shaven face to his trimmed and receding brown and gray hair? Come to think of it, there's nothing about Bradley that's not average. I've never really thought of him like that before.

"Thanks, but I want to stay here a little longer," I say. "When I take a deep breath the pain still surprises me, and I can't move around very well on my own."

"Of course. Whatever you want. Our insurance will cover it."

It's true. We have good insurance of every sort—one of the benefits of being married to an insurance man. There must be other reasons, but right now, they fail me.

My friends at work come to see me at the end of their days at the lab. They take turns joking about my "lost-time accident." Myra brings me a bouquet of daffodils and pussy willows. Gary, my lab partner, brings me a stuffed toy moose.

"I feel sorry for the poor moose that stepped on you," he says. "After all, there you were, stealing his favorite foods from his own private dining room."

"I've been trying to tell everyone the same thing," I say. Leave it to Gary to understand.

"Now, Molly, I want you to apologize to Harry, here," Gary says, setting the moose on my night table. The stuffed moose, about a foot high, brown and furry, with a long moose face complete with a dewlap, strikes me as much cuter than the real thing.

"I'm sorry, Harry," I say, and mean it. Then I tell Gary, "You know, it's a good thing I'm not a petite little woman. I might not be alive." I can say things like this to Gary that I might not say to anyone else.

"Yes, but you still have that rusty red hair to live with. It didn't turn completely gray when the moose stepped on you."

I knew I could count on Gary. He's one of the most wonderful men I know. He's funny, sensitive, good-looking, smart, and when we talk, he never looks at my breasts. He's gay.

CHAPTER 4

Strangely calm, I walk the familiar path from the stove to the breakfast nook where Bradley is sitting. Warm spring sunshine streams in the windows this Saturday morning, illuminating the two glasses of orange juice on the table. But when it is time for me to speak, I stand frozen, gripping the back of a chair for support.

"Bradley, I need to talk with you."

"Doug is waiting at the club," Bradley mumbles, newspaper in one hand, a fork filled with scrambled eggs in the other. "I'm already late. Can we talk later?"

"I want a divorce," I say to the newspaper.

The newspaper drops onto the plate of scrambled eggs and toast. Bradley's mouth droops open and his fork stops in mid-air, then falls to the table. The way he brings his mouth together reminds me of a fish out of water. He stares at me without speaking. If his piercing gaze continues he will bore a hole through my head or extinguish me.

Finally, he says, "You're still upset about the thing with the moose. Life will get back to normal for you pretty soon."

"I don't want it to be normal, not like it's been. When I had all that time to think I realized I don't want normal any more." Breathe, I tell myself.

"Molly, please. Be reasonable."

"All my life, I've been reasonable, Bradley. It's my specialty. I'm sick to death of it. Life's been passing me by and nothing happens to me except normal and reasonable. One year is no different from the next. At least this year a moose stepped on me."

"You don't know what you want, but I can't believe you want a divorce. Life's been good. I thought it was as good for you as it's been for me."

"Something happened. The moose changed me, made me realize how angry I am. It's like I've been treading deep water and you've been standing on my shoulders, but you're too heavy and my head keeps going under. I'm drowning." I begin to cry. "I'm sorry, Bradley. I really am. It's probably all my fault."

He stands up, leaving his breakfast untouched. Moving toward me, he stares through me, all the way out to the street. Putting his arm around my shoulders, he says, "Molly, I love you. You'll be all right. I'll meet Doug now on the course. You and I haven't done anything fun for a long time. We'll go out to dinner tonight. Would you like that?"

I do not answer. I'm watching birds flit from bush to bush outside the window of the breakfast nook. Bradley moves away from me. How like him to treat this as if I'm having a bad hair day, to invalidate my feelings. I'm finally catching on, and now it's too late.

"I'll be home by five to get ready," he says, picking up his golf hat.

I hear the happy chirping of the birds over the sound of Bradley's footsteps. The back door opens and closes, the garage door rises and, for the last time, I hear Bradley's car back out of the garage.

By the time Bradley returns from playing golf, I'm gone. I take a few carefully chosen clothes and my pets to Myra's place, a few miles east of Helena, where she and her husband, Jim, have a small ranch with some llamas. I'm staying in their mother-in-law cabin. The hardest thing I do after leaving Bradley is to call Jeremy and then Scott, and announce my decision to leave their father. One at a time, I listen to their astonishment ("First the moose, now this?!"), then their denial that this could be happening, and I hear them convince themselves that it's all the moose's fault. I hear myself apologizing to each son. They're both sure I'll change my mind.

"I don't think so," I say to each one. Now is not the time to argue.

On my first day back to work after my run-in with the moose, I spend the morning trying to straighten out some data integrity problems that occurred in my absence. This doesn't go well, and I begin to wish I were anywhere but here. But when it's time for our break, Myra escorts me into the lunchroom, where a dozen or so of my coworkers clap their hands as I enter, officially welcoming me back. Everyone eats donuts and exchanges banter. I choke back tears.

"Gary, who cuts your hair?" I ask one day after the others have left their cubicles. Gary wears a hairstyle I like.

"Whalen at the Wild Mane Corral."

"Does he cut women's hair?"

"Well, I've seen one or two in there. No-nonsense types, or maybe they were lesbians," he says, smiling.

"Great, I'll fit right in, an androgyne coming out of the closet. You won't mind if I get my hair cut like yours, will you?"

"Please do. People will talk."

On Saturday morning men are talking loudly and laughing as I enter the barber shop, but they become quiet when I sit down to wait. I toss my shoulder-length red and gray hair one last time. Bradley had insisted I wear my hair long.

Three barber chairs face those of us waiting for haircuts. A clod of dried manure decorates the footrest of one chair. Like the piece of manure, I don't exactly feel welcome here, but then I don't really care. As soon as a barber becomes available a customer stands up and saunters over to his chair. Musical barber chairs. I've made an appointment with Whalen so he's expecting me, but he hasn't yet acknowledged my presence. Hair flies, clippers race up from earlobes, and no one looks at me. Testosterone, the dialect of the Old West, is still spoken here, and when I arrived, I wrecked the dynamics of the place. I'm at least as macho as Gary is, and if he can withstand a visit to this barbershop, then so can I.

Looking back at me from the mirror above the barber chairs is the kind of woman men don't turn around to look at twice, but they might look at me once, and smile. Nonthreatening, that's me. I don't look like someone who could steal another woman's husband, nor do men become nervous with me like they might around someone who is drop-dead gorgeous. It's a good way to look—sort of ordinary, with good posture holding up a body that's only slightly overweight. And I'm tall. I can look eye-level at most men. I've seen how a short woman always has to look up at others from her observer-inferior position. I've also noticed how young men, with their short hair, seem so unfettered and free. Maybe that's why I want my hair cut short.

Whalen signals to me. Time to climb aboard. Still a little sore from my moose encounter, I step through several inches of black, gray and brown hair to the barber chair. I sit with my best posture to face the men waiting their turns, but they look everywhere but at me. Whalen takes my glasses, whisks a cape around me and cinches it around my neck.

"Well? What'll it be?" he asks, as if I'm at a bar.

"I want my hair cut like Gary's, my friend who works with me at the state lab. Remember him?"

"Oh, yeah. He's been coming here for years. That'll be about an inch, inch and a half all over, shaped, of course, and a bit longer in the back."

"That's it."

"You got it," he says, adjusting the height of the barber chair downward so he can reach my head. "My, you're a tall drink of water."

I say nothing. I don't tell him that besides sitting tall in the barber chair, my arms are so long I usually wear men's shirts, and that one of my feet is a whole size bigger than the other.

He presses his hand flat against the side of my head and pushes it sideways. Snip, snip, snip. Hand on the other side, more quick, confident clips. At a beauty parlor the beautician says, "Would you please bend your head?" But Whalen pushes my head forward, and I don't mind.

"How about the back, here? A little shorter?"

Because I talk with my hands, I extricate my right hand from under the cape. In reaching to feel how much hair remains at the back of my neck, I whack Whalen in the crotch. He says nothing, but scoots backwards suddenly, as if he's line dancing.

"Oh, excuse me." I say. Then, to convince him I mean it, I say, "I'm sorry." Whalen pretends nothing happened. Snip, snip, snip.

"Just so there's no hard edges and my ears are partially covered," I say, placing my arm back under the cape where it can't get into any more trouble.

"What style is in with guys now?" I ask.

"Men want the Julius Caesar look. Boy does it look dumb, with the bangs cut straight across the forehead. Especially on a cowboy. But that's what they want, so that's what I give 'em."

He combs what's left of my hair back on the sides, then wisps a few hairs down over the tops of my ears, steps back, admires his work. I've never had a faster haircut.

"What do you call my new haircut?"

"Modified shag. Haircut of the stars."

"Want your eyebrows, ear and nose hairs clipped?" the adjacent barber asks an older man with a thin gray mustache and a fringe of hair around the base of his bald head.

"Sure," the mustache mumbles.

Will Whalen ask *me* that? Is this a standard question at a barbershop? I'm suddenly aware that I should have depilated my mustache weeks ago. I'm relieved when Whalen reaches for a mirror to show me the back of my hair. He stands back while I extricate my hand from under the cape. Wow. I smile at my younger, sassier self. The word *haughty* comes to mind, a word I've never used on myself before. With a noisy, oversized hair dryer, probably a Black and Decker, Whalen blows hair clippings off my head and face, then vacuums loose hairs off my neck. Everything happens much faster in a barbershop than it does in a beauty salon.

"That'll be $10.00," he says, whipping off my cape.

And it's cheaper.

I leave the barbershop and walk to my car a block away feeling victorious, pounds lighter, and free as a chickadee. As soon as I'm sitting behind the wheel, I adjust the rearview mirror to examine my new hairdo. Yes! Now I look more like a person, less like a gender. Slightly dazed, I roll down the window and fill my lungs with the clean May air. What would my mom have said about my haircut, about my leaving Bradley, about anything? She would have hung her head and prayed for me. Poor Mom. She always asked herself how in the world she ended up with a daughter like me. Even when I was a stick-in-the-mud matron and a dutiful wife, she'd sigh and shake her head. I never knew what I wasn't doing right. Why is it I've always disappointed everyone I've ever lived with? What will it be like to live alone, with no one to disappoint? A feeling of relief wells up from deep inside me, just below my rib cage, and I smile as the tears form and stream down my face at the simultaneous joy and sadness of my question.

CHAPTER 5

Chug fills the passenger side of my new, used silver and white four-wheel-drive Toyota pickup truck on our first drive out of town since my wreck with the moose. Her head nearly touches the roof and her haunches and fur spill over the bucket seat. We look like one-half of the *Montana Double Date* postcard of two guys and two dogs sitting in the front seat of a truck—except there's only the two of us. Not only is Chug my date, but she's the best date I've ever had. She's demanding in her own slobbery, snuffling sort of way, but she is a dog and she's direct and honest about her needs.

The winding gravel road along the creek is graded and smooth, and I drive with care through the mismatched plaids of shade and shadow. Alders and brush, Douglas firs and lodgepole pines crowd the left side of the winding gravel road. A creek washes past close to the right side. And, as I shift down again to slow for yet another curve, the light of the southern sky is as bright as the shine from a pot of gold.

In the last month, the red-osier dogwoods have leafed out, reminding me of the window shutters I started and never finished, reminding me that I no longer have windows to decorate. I slow the truck to a crawl as I drive past the woods where the moose ended my outing that day and, as it turns out, my marriage. The snowbanks have melted next to the road where the man named Dewey picked me up that day and drove me, moaning and half-dead, to the hospital.

"Do you see a moose anywhere, Chug?" She turns to look at the woods, too, then turns back to me, curious. "Me neither," I say. And I didn't expect to see one. In fact, I'm not sure what I'd do if I did.

When I come to the sign near a collection of large log buildings, I can hardly decipher the weathered lettering, but this must be my destination—the Snowshadow Hot Springs Resort. I pull into the parking lot next to a giant fir tree and park next to a vaguely familiar pickup truck, battered and dented, with one tire elevated on a pile of dirty snow.

"Wait here," I say to Chug. She pants and looks at me with hopeful eyes. I know that in my absence she'll lick all the partly opened windows. A German shepherd lies near the entrance to the main building, gnawing on the hairy shank of a deer's leg. Chug barks her deep, loud *hurrumph* at the dog, who ignores her. As I skirt the shepherd and the snowbank, the shepherd stops chewing, fastens his eyes on me, and tightens his teeth around his bizarre prize.

Grabbing hold of an antler handle, I pull on a massive wood door and step into a small pine-paneled room with coat hooks lining both walls. I open a second door, this one with a boomerang-shaped piece of branch as a door handle, and find myself in a bar. I stand quietly, in awe of the scene in front of me. I raise my hand to shield my eyes from the glare of light bouncing off the mirror behind a long bar, reflecting past bottles of booze, a jar of pickled eggs, and packages of peanuts, pretzels and jerky. Then I see it. Lording over the far end of the bar is an enormous moose head whose shiny eyes appear to be watching me, watching everywhere at once. A mountain lion prowls on a shelf. Almost no piece of wall is bare, but is decorated with heads of elk and deer wearing oversized antlers. A black bear, its mouth open and showing yellow teeth and a dusty red tongue appears ready to attack. All the creatures are fixed safely behind blank stares. If I had a pair of binoculars, I'd reach for them.

"Dewey? Dewey Slocum?" I say to the only person in the bar, a man bent over the pool table, wearing a blue denim shirt and jeans, complete with buns. With his back to me, though, I can't see if he's wearing a walrus mustache.

The man turns around. "Hey! You survived," he says, putting down the cue stick. No question, it's him. "I didn't hear you come in." He extends his hand to shake mine. "You know, you didn't tell me your name that day."

"Molly. Molly Binfet."

"So, Molly Binfet, you been out matching wits with that moose again?"

Today this man named Dewey looks nothing like the psychotic mountain man I thought he might be that day he saved my life. Except for the oversized mustache, I couldn't remember much of his appearance at all. His thinning sandy brown hair has a hint of gray, especially in his beard. Laugh lines edge his eyes, blue as sky, and he continues to hold my hand in his callused hand, big and warm, not like Bradley's cool, soft office hands.

"No, actually I haven't been in the woods since," I say, retrieving my hand. "I came up here to thank you for rescuing me. You happened by . . . uh . . . your timing saved . . . anyway, I'm really grateful." Breathe, I tell myself. Don't get all emotional.

"Glad I happened by that day and found you. Not many people on the road in the afternoons. Let me buy you a drink," he says. He walks toward the bar with a slight limp.

"It's a little early for me to have a drink, but I would like some herb tea."

"Well, I'll have to take a look, see what I can find. Have a seat." He motions to several tall, mushroom-shaped wooden barstools with fake leather seat covers.

I climb onto one of the barstools and study the interior decoration some more. A sign at the end of the mirror behind the cash register reads: *WE RESERVE THE RIGHT TO SERVE*

REFUSE. I read it again and smile. Everything in the bar seems designed to put a person in a relaxed, anything-goes, frame of mind. You can even take a dip in one of the hot springs pools, visible beyond a window wall on one side of the bar.

"Eureka," Dewey says, returning through a pair of swinging doors. He offers me a box of assorted herb teas and a mug of hot water. "Last weekend someone asked for a cappuccino, and they were out of luck."

I drop a chamomile tea bag into the mug.

"As you can see, Snowshoe's at the end of the road," Dewey says, glancing at my left hand, resting on the bar. The last time he saw me I was wearing a wedding band, but he wouldn't have known that because I was wearing gloves.

At that moment, Chug lets out a huge *hurrumph,* deep and low, from my pickup.

Dewey looks surprised. "Did you hear that?"

"It's my Saint Bernard, Chug. She's calling me, telling me she's ready to leave."

"But you just got here. Bring old Thug in here. No one else around."

"Her name is Chug," I say, laughing. "You know, the sound bison make? She has a nasal problem and snuffles like they do, so I named her Chug. She's not as big as a buffalo, but she's pretty big."

Dewey grabs another beer out of a cooler behind the bar as I leave to rescue Chug from the truck. She's totally thrilled to see me. Holding her collar, we detour around the German shepherd and back to the front door. Once inside the bar, Chug stops and sits, looking around at the wildlife on the walls. She's never been in a bar before and seems bewildered by the decor.

I squat down next to her. "Come on, girl. It's okay. They won't hurt you."

Glancing once more at the mountain lion, she follows me over to the lineup of bar stools where Dewey waits with his Coors. I introduce them and climb back onto the tall stool. We sit, Dewey and I, facing each other, our knees almost touching. Chug sits on the floor beside us, panting in the warm bar, glancing up every few seconds at the fixed stares of the wild animals. She practically mops the floor with her tongue as Dewey leans slightly to pet the top of her head.

"What do you do here, Dewey?"

"Oh, I do about everything, more or less. Hell, the day I found you lying beside the road I was on a beer run. Beer companies won't deliver up this far. Say the road's too dangerous. And, let's see, I swim around in the pools with a big brush a couple times a week, scrubbing the sides. In winter we rent out inner tubes for some white-knuckle fun, so I have to keep the luge course packed down. And I cut those 32 oz. stone-age steaks we serve. Broil 'em to order, remove my apron, then serve 'em." Dewey motions toward a spacious dining room off the side of the bar opposite the pools. On the end wall of that room hangs a pair of long snowshoes, the old-fashioned kind with honey-colored wood and dark brown leather, laced with cobwebs. They're affixed to the pine paneling in a V shape, as if their owner, his toes pointed out, had walked up the wall and stepped right out of them.

"Nice snowshoes," I say.

"Belonged to my granddad. The resort's been in our family for a few generations now. Gramps used those snowshoes to travel around in the hills up here in winter."

"Oh, so they don't call the town Snowshoe for nothing."

"You got it," he says. "But back to what I do here. After the restaurant closes, I'm the bartender. I swear nobody visits at home, only here in this bar. 'Course I know everybody in Snowshoe." He takes another swig of beer. "Let's see. Oh, yeah, and I'm also in charge of keeping the place warm in winter, hell, year-round. Takes a lot of firewood. You ever been up here in the winter, Molly?"

I've been looking at his blue eyes, thinking about the laughter in his voice and how weird it is not to see a person's mouth when they speak. And there's something else. He's unpretentious. That's it. But now I realize he's waiting for me to speak.

"What? Uh, no, I haven't."

"Well, it's another world, let me tell you. Snow up to your eyeballs, cold as a moose. Oh . . . excuse the reference."

"That's okay. I don't hate moose," I say, glancing toward the moose head at the end of the bar. "I was in the wrong place that day for one particular animal."

I watch Dewey in the mirror for a while, noticing how his upper body seems too big for the rest of him. And I watch the woman sitting next to him on the barstool. She looks pretty good, if I do say so myself, with her sassy new haircut. Of course, the mirror *is* hazy. That alone can lop ten years off a person's age.

"Where do you work, Molly?"

"I'm a biological tech for the state. At the lab, I work with a hydrologist named Bo. We call him Bo Knows Water." We're part of a team and we analyze water samples, stuff like that, and do support work for agencies involved in mining reclamation.

"Really," he says, and takes another glug from his Coors. I wonder what his non-response indicates. I can only guess that residents of old mining towns might not appreciate my line of work.

"Well, I need to be on my way," I say. "I think I'll take a drive up the road and see the town before I head back to Helena."

"Don't blink or you'll miss it."

"I'll keep my eyes open," I say, sliding down off the high stool. "Thanks again, Dewey. Thanks for everything."

"Hope you'll hurry back," he says, shaking my hand again.

After saying goodbye, Chug and I circle around the German shepherd, and continue our date. We drive into the little town of Snowshoe, past dilapidated cabins and sheds and rusty, unidentified mining equipment. About an eighth of a mile from the Snowshadow Resort, I turn onto a side road toward a second row of old buildings along the creek. My truck creeps along as I roll down my window, now smeared where Chug has licked it. I don't want to miss anything.

In front of the first derelict structure, I bring my truck to a stop as quietly as possible. Loud noises don't seem appropriate here next to this silent, ghostly husk with its false front, its faded yellow door and two broken front windows, one on either side of the door, like eyes.

"Stay, Chug." I open my door, step out onto the sandy soil into the silence, and walk toward the old structure. NO TRESPASSING. The sign is tacked onto the wall in the shade next to the door. A remnant of a different blue-gray sign dangles from the edge of the porch roof. I can't make out the words. Twigs and feathers spill from the broken face of a birdhouse under the eave of the porch. The porch floor slopes nearly as much as its sagging roof, and even though it's early May, piles of snow cling to the ground on the building's shady north side. The roof peak, buckling in the center, causes the entire building to appear out of perspective, warped, and ready to cave in on itself.

About fifty feet behind the two-story affair, a creek murmurs past in a gathering of low voices. A log cabin, no more than a hut, sits about seventy-five feet away, and a larger log shell hugs the ground behind the first cabin near the edge of the creek. An outhouse stands between the two log cabins. A pair of warped old work boots, their soles split apart, dangle from a nail on the side of the tiny building. A giant cottonwood tree with a thick, corrugated trunk reaches over the top of the two-story building. A fragment of shed leans out over the creek. Tumbleweeds and howling wind are the only things missing in this scene out of an old *Death Valley Days* television show.

I'd heard about Snowshoe, Montana, and that the town had had its moments in history—like me, with my streaked reddish-gray hair and failed marriage. Bradley and I had enjoyed our moments too, but that was many years ago.

A jumble of debris and rust, old logs and boards cover the lot across the alley from where I'm standing. Some of what I see could actually be buildings: a woodshed, maybe an outhouse. A stack of logs with a rusted stovepipe emitting a curl of smoke from its top could be the sign of a dwelling. Dozens of chickens begin to fan out in all directions from a shed, pecking and scratching in the dirt. A small, stooped man emerges from the chicken shed, shuffles over to a stack of wood rounds, picks up an axe, and begins to chop wood.

"Hello!" I yell, ready to wave, maybe even visit with the old man.

He rests his axe on the ground and looks over at me. When I wave, he looks away and swings his axe, and he doesn't look my way again. I continue to watch as he stoops, picks up a piece of wood, splits it, and stoops for the next one. Maybe he thinks I'm casing the joint. This ridiculous thought somehow reminds me that my life is so much more amusing and filled with possibility, now that I'm not with Bradley.

My eyes move to the sides of the sheds and lean-tos. A watermark shows about two feet up from the ground. On every structure in sight, the wood is light-colored above the mark, dark below it. I've heard about how some years in June the creek overflows its banks. I remember the front page headlines and photos several years ago, during what the hydrologists called a one-hundred-year flood, of Snowshoe residents being rescued from their rooftops by helicopter. But that shouldn't happen for another hundred years.

Eerie and silent, except for the guttural croaking of a few ravens and an old geezer chopping wood, Snowshoe awakens in me a need of some kind, a longing I can't quite identify. I don't want to leave.

As I back my truck around in the narrow road, chickens squawk and run out of my way. Driving slowly again, as if in a horse-drawn buggy a century ago, I retrace my route back to the main road, past abandoned, mongrel cars and trucks parked haphazardly on the side of the narrow road. Some of their doors have been left open, as if the drivers had slammed on their brakes, flung open their doors, and ran indoors, never to come back out. It's as if Snowshoe has stayed the same as it's always been, while every place else has grown newer and bigger.

Like most people I know in Helena, I'd never taken the time to drive the sixteen miles, half of it gravel road, to visit the little old mining town. It isn't on state maps, so I suppose it's easy to forget that there was once a town here, that one still exists. Now that I've seen Snowshoe, tucked back in time up here in the mountains, I'm feeling a bit unhinged, almost intoxicated. Of course, these feelings could be the result of breathing the thin air so close to the Continental Divide. Or maybe I can relate to the brooding message of lost hopes and dreams given off by the decaying old buildings.

What a strange contrast to Helena, where government employees and businessmen drive around in new sport utility vehicles talking on cell phones. Probably no one living in Snowshoe has one; you couldn't talk on a cell phone and keep an old junk car on the gravel road. Anyway, people up here are probably busy feeding chickens, chopping wood, and trying to keep their cabins more or less upright in the standoff between time and weather. Unpretentious. That's Snowshoe.

I stop again at the Snowshadow, obviously the largest, best maintained cluster of buildings in all of Snowshoe.

"Well, hello again," Dewey says, looking up from his solitaire game at the bar. "Glad you came back so soon. Grab a stool."

"Hi yourself," I say, mounting the same stool I sat on before. "I really like Snowshoe. In fact, I find it downright enchanting."

"Whoa, now. I've heard Snowshoe called a strange little town with an undertow. I've heard that said . . . but enchanting? That's a new one." Dewey places a red queen below a black king on one row of his solitaire game.

"I'm looking for a little place to buy and wondered if you'd know of anything for sale. I'm interested in a place I saw along the creek, a two-story building with a false front."

"The one with the faded yellow door, a couple log cabins next to it?"

"Yes. That's it."

"One of the old brothels," he says, shaking his head. "You looking for a weekend getaway?" He sifts through his cards, picks up a black jack and places it under the red queen.

"No, I might want to live up here."

"By yourself?"

"Not exactly. I have Chug, you know, and a cat." I look up at the sign above the cash register, *WE RESERVE THE RIGHT TO SERVE REFUSE.*

"You'd certainly dress up the town. I don't know, though. Snowshoe isn't a place for a woman alone. But I can tell you this: the old guy who owns the place stopped by a couple weeks ago. He drove up to see if his buildings made it through the winter. Said he never comes out here anymore, ought to just sell the place. Could have been just talk. Hear it all the time. But he is getting up in years."

"Do you have his name? Maybe I'll call him."

"I'll write it down. Number's in the phone book. But Molly, I think you'd be biting off more than you can chew with that particular place, in this particular town."

CHAPTER 6

The old two-story brothel stands forlorn and forsaken, the same today in the late May sunshine as it did the first time I saw it. On one side, the boards are scorched brown by the sun; on the opposite side of the building, the wood is bleached a shiny silver dollar gray. The broken windowpanes at the front of the building seem to mark holes into the heart of the old girl's lost soul.

But some need other than wanting to save the building, something other than being a caretaker in need of a new project, is operating in me—memories of summers spent at my grandparents' ranch on the Big Hole River and my love, from those early days, of being in the country. After Daddy died, my mom and her new husband, Dwight, pulled their trailer around every summer delivering the word of God as mobile evangelists while I stayed on the ranch. Unlike Mom and Dwight, Grandma and Grandpa were easygoing and fun to be around. But when Mom and Dwight saw how ranch life had turned me into a tomboy, they became concerned for my future and sent me to a class called White Gloves and Party Manners, where I learned to set a table for an eight-course meal. Most people in Montana don't know what to do with that many courses—there's beef or chicken, sometimes a fish, potatoes and vegetables, maybe a salad—so even thirty years later when I entertained Bradley's business associates, I set everything on the table at the same time except dessert.

I had felt my grandparents' love like the warm summer sun on my tan skinny arms. Grandpa and I caught trout in the creek, and Grandma and I picked wild strawberries in the field. I still miss my grandparents. The creek at the ranch, too, had been a constant in my life, like a pulse. Of all the places in the photo album of my childhood memories, the creek is one of the most important. Now I'll have a creek in my own back yard. If only Mr. Leonard will turn loose of this place.

As if on cue, Mr. Leonard drives up in his tan four-door sedan. He stops and sits in the car, not moving. When he opens the car door, one leg appears and he pauses. His foot touches the ground, then he pulls himself upright, still clinging to the car door.

"Mr. Leonard. Hi, I'm Molly. I'm happy to see you." I shake his hand. He nods but says nothing, removes his hand from mine and looks at the creek, then the cabin, then the ground. We've talked on the phone a couple of times, and it was like talking on the phone to my cousin in Alaska. There was quite a delay between the time I stopped talking and the time I received a response. And even though he agreed to meet me out here, he's been noncommittal about selling.

Mr. Leonard takes a few shuffling steps toward the creek and stops.

"Brought my family up here on the weekends," he says. "In winter the kids went sledding on the mine waste heaps. Lots of snow up here in the winter and the tailings made good runs. You know about the snow, I suppose. In the summer, we'd come up here to relax and listen to the creek. Sometimes it feels like yesterday. But then the kids grew up, even the grandkids. The place flooded that one June, of course, then a couple years ago my wife died. I don't know. Sure hate to let go of the place."

We walk another ten feet or so in the direction of the creek. He stops and raises his right arm toward the two-story.

"Never did anything with that old building. Tried to keep the kids out of it so they wouldn't fall through the floor. Now the family doesn't care to bring their kids out here. Seems like all young people want to do these days is stay home and play video games."

"I'd fix the place up and live here. Have you thought about what you want for it?" I know he'll start high, if he'll sell at all, and we'll have to negotiate. I'll have to be tough.

"Seems kind of quick. I've had the place for thirty years. All those good times. And you should know, the kids said the big building's haunted; they heard noises, even voices, more than once."

"I'm not afraid of . . ."

"$5,000?"

"Well . . . that sounds fair enough," I say, trying not to wear my shock. Does he mean that as the down payment? No, I'm not going to ask. "Can we meet at the courthouse this week one day at lunch time to start the paperwork?"

"Maybe I could come out some time and see the place all fixed up. But I need some time to think. I'll call you in a week or so."

"Mr. Leonard, I do hope you'll decide to sell. You'd be welcome out here any time." I grab his hand and pump his frail arm, but he pulls his hand free to wipe away a tear.

As the tan car creeps away from the weather-beaten brothel, the sun glows luminous red on Cinnamon Peak. I hold my breath for fear the old man will stop, that he'll decide not to sell the place, that he'll turn his car around and come back to tell me so. Finally, when I hear his car turn onto the main gravel road toward the highway, I allow my breath to escape.

During my week of waiting for Mr. Leonard's decision, the time at work and at Myra's moves much too slowly. I file for divorce, and Bradley is served with the papers.

He calls me at work. "Molly, please don't go through with this."

"I'm sorry, Bradley," I say, then hang up, take sick leave and go home to my cabin at Myra's to cry.

The phone rings several times that afternoon but I do not answer. I have nothing more to say to Bradley; nothing will ease the distress for either of us. I'm going through with it. Around four o'clock I decide to face the music and pick up the ringing phone.

"I can meet you tomorrow at noon at the courthouse," Mr. Leonard says. "No sense in me keeping hold of that place any longer."

I can't speak.

"Hello?" he says.

"I'll be there, Mr. Leonard. Thank you so much. What did you say the price was, again?"

"$5,000. Is that too much? That's more than I paid for it, of course, but I thought the value might have increased some."

"The price is fine."

"There's something I have to tell you before I can sell it to you, and if you want out of the deal after you hear this, I'll understand. The refrigerator in the cabin is very old. Works fine, but it doesn't have a handle. We opened it with a screwdriver. It's still there somewhere. You see, for a while one summer we had the refrigerator on the porch and stored canned and dried foods in it. Had a cooler we used indoors. One night a bear ripped open the refrigerator and helped himself. Never did find the handle."

"Thanks for telling me about what happened, Mr. Leonard, but I'm not afraid of wild animals," I say, relieved. At this point, a hungry bear is no obstacle to me. "I'll look for you tomorrow at the courthouse."

★ ★ ★ ★ ★

"That's like the one-night stand method of buying a place to live, Molly," Gary says to me at work. "You don't even know what's inside the buildings."

"The cabin has a refrigerator," I say, not mentioning the missing handle or the bear. "Besides, for that price it doesn't matter what's in them."

Anyone who lives in Gold West Country will understand what can happen to a person during the warm, sunny days of May after the long cold blizzard that is winter. We can't be held responsible. Marriage proposals are made, then rescinded when June rains come. Babies are conceived in strange positions in stranger locations, and to the most unlikely couples. People go out for a drive and come home with a brand new pickup they can't afford. Still others survive a moose stepping on them and then get a divorce. And now, for the price of a used car, I'm buying a pile of old boards and a couple of log cabins on a creek in a run down old mining town. What is it I've heard about the architecture of dreams?

CHAPTER 7

Suddenly behind me I hear squawking, screeching noises and a flapping of chicken wings at the exact moment the old green cabin door, yielding to my weight against it, pushes open against the linoleum flooring with a hideous scraping noise. After my breathing settles down, I check the nest behind a pile of firewood in the corner of the porch. Two eggs—a small price to pay for the chicken droppings on the porch floor. Tomorrow morning I'll cook the eggs here in my own little bed and breakfast. It's Friday evening and I'm moving in. The papers have been signed, and thanks to a loan from my 401K at work, Bradley could not interfere.

Inside the cabin, I flip the light switch and an amazing thing happens. The lights come on. The power company has granted my wish. Electricity is such a nice touch in a wilderness setting. Dust and dirt, very old dirt, everywhere—on the cracked linoleum top of the wooden counter, in the white porcelain sink with its single faucet, and on the small woodburning cookstove. I wipe my hand along the surface of the simple wood table that sits with two chairs in front of a wide low window. From my standing position, all I can see when I look out the window is the ground. You have to be sitting down in order to view the outdoors. I guess the miners were tired when they came home from work. Instead of standing around looking out their windows, they wanted to sit down and rest.

On the log wall behind the open door are two empty shelves above a row of coat hooks. About six feet in front of me is a ladder with round wood rungs leaning against a small loft—my sleeping quarters under the peaked roof. Beneath the loft is enough space for a couch and chair. The former owner and his family must have been on unusually friendly terms to spend weekends in such a tiny space. Maybe, in fact, it was a better experience for Mr. Leonard than it was for his family. These things happen.

Mr. Leonard came out earlier in the week to turn the water on, and now I can scrub the wood table and linoleum-covered countertop using cold water from the faucet. If I want hot water, I'll have to heat it on the wood stove. But with Chug and Big Al waiting impatiently in the truck, I'm only going to clean the place enough to sleep here tonight. Tomorrow's another day.

When I sweep the floor, some dirt falls into the crack around a square that has been cut in the floor, like a trap door. Oh well. Less house is more, and 320 square feet of living space is plenty for me right now—and also less to clean. In fact, the cabin is about the size of the master bedroom in the house I left behind in Helena, the house that had confined me.

Up in the loft, I wield my hand-held vacuum on the spider webs and dust covering the rafters overhead and I run the vacuum over the mattress that will be my bed. What *are* those stains? When I place the four-inch foam cushion from the canopy of my truck on top of the mattress, and roll my sleeping bag out on the cushion, my new bedroom will be almost inviting.

By the time I go out to my truck to let Big Al and Chug loose, black clouds are scudding across the sky and night is overtaking the canyon. Chug runs around outdoors sniffing, her nose to the ground, before she stops to squat. When I open the door so she can go inside the cabin, she stands near the door, looks around the one room, glances up at the loft, then studies me as if waiting for some answers.

"Like your new doghouse, little girl?" I ask, hugging her head to let her know everything is okay.

After a few more trips to the truck and back with food and other household items, it's bedtime. I help Big Al climb the ladder to the loft. His claws are sharp and he's motivated, so he doesn't need much assistance. I turn out the light and, by the dim glow of my flashlight, I slip into my silk pajamas. As is her custom, my big dog turns in circles and finally settles down to guard the front door.

"Good night Chug. Goodnight Big Al." I adore having my animals indoors with me at night. Bradley wouldn't allow them in our bedroom.

As I drift off to sleep with Al purring on my chest, my head is filled with many unanswered questions. Will a mouse run across me in the night? Can Al climb down the ladder to use the kitty litter box? If I have to go to the outhouse in the night, will a cougar jump me? And worse. Mr. Leonard had mentioned voices in the brothel. Will they come after me?

Booming, cracking thunder awakens me in the night. Flashes of lightning illuminate the inside of the cabin while pellets of hail, then rain, pound the tin roof, inches above my head. Now I hear other noises. Inside the cabin, something knocks over the woodbox, spilling kindling onto the floor. Toenails scratch linoleum. I hear growling. My God! A bear has broken into the cabin. I fumble for my flashlight. In the beam of light, I see that Chug has cornered Big Al, who is puffed up to twice his normal size. His back is arched, and dangling from his teeth is a mouse, or at least a mouse-like tail. And the cat can't defend himself from the dog because his mouth is full.

From my bed in the loft I yell, "Chug! Back off!" She slouches over to the table. Al leaps from rung to rung back up the ladder to the loft, where he sits near my makeshift bed crunching his first mouse.

At least the roof isn't leaking.

When I awaken late Saturday morning, I'm a little groggy, and stiff, too. My bed isn't exactly a Sealy Posturepedic. Al looks over at me, stretches his big front paws forward, and arches his head and yawns, grinning like a boy who has laid his first girl. I can see the remains, tiny bits of fur and blood, on the floor nearby. But now I must get to the outhouse. Al beats me down the ladder, and as I grab my robe and dash past him to the door, he's sitting in front of his empty food dish. Either mousing is labor intensive or it's not nutritionally satisfying.

After building a warming fire in the cookstove and eating a breakfast of boiled eggs with a bagel, I'm sitting in a lawn chair on the front porch drinking coffee, holding Big Al and petting Chug's head. I smell decaying wood, chimney smoke and chicken manure. Birds are singing from the thousands of acres of national forest all around us, land free for exploring. The bright sunlight and the constant sound of the creek sweeping past, banks full, mesmerize me, until I think about the creek and how it's even higher after last night's rainfall. Will it crest soon and flood me out?

"You like it here, girl?" Chug snuffles once and hangs out her giant Saint Bernard tongue.

On each side of the porch entrance are courses of horizontal logs extending up about three feet from the floor, low enough so I can see over them to my queendom. When the sun rises high enough in the sky to reach into the canyon, it streams onto the porch. I'll buy pots of geraniums so my cabin will look like a little Swiss mountain hut.

To the right I can look up toward Cinnamon Peak with its rocky red dome at the top and ribbons of avalanche chutes streaming down the mountain's side, like crepe paper streamers from the top of the May Pole when I was in grade school.

I can see the upper edge of a clearing that must be the luge course above the Snowshadow Resort. Or maybe it's an old mining adit—one of those horizontal passageways the miners built into the mountainsides to access the ore. Their open doorways, framed with timbers, are all around here in the mountains. Sometimes people out snooping in the hills simply disappear. I've seen the news stories in the *Independent Record*: *MAN PRESUMED VICTIM OF ADIT.*

As I sit here, my view straight ahead is not idyllic. The elf-like old man who lives across the alley and owns the herd of free-range chickens also has several free-range junk cars, pieces of rusted equipment, and an ancient full-size pickup truck with a snowplow blade on the front. The bed of the old truck is full of garbage bags. Ravens land on the ripped bags, berate each other, and fly off carrying bits of unidentifiable trash. I'm curious about the old man who was so unfriendly the first time I visited this place. Guess I'll have to ask Dewey about my neighbor.

A small cottonwood tree grows up through the roof of an old car that sits rusting beside the geezer's woodshed, its wheels gone, windows broken out. The car speaks to me from across the road, pulling me back to lazy childhood afternoons on the ranch when I sat in a rusted old Buick under a giant cottonwood tree by the river. I wore an old lady's hat grandma had given me to play with, and sometimes I carried a stolen cigarette in my shirt pocket, one grandpa had rolled and set aside for later. Grasshoppers leaped up and down in front of me as I picked my way through waist-high grass. The car looked sad and lonely, sitting there with no wheels. One door was missing but I always entered through the other door, although it was dented and difficult to open. I'd turn the handle with both hands, put my right foot up on the side of the car for leverage, and pull hard. The door creaked open on rusty hinges. Then I'd turn, jump up, scoot backwards onto the seat, and swing my legs into position under the steering wheel. Birdie, the ranch dog, would jump up on the seat next to me through the open door, the way Chug does now, and she'd sit looking ahead through the dirty, cracked windshield. We pretended to motor along through the endless meadows that stretched away from the car in every direction. The river flowed on one side of us until it disappeared around a distant bend. For a little while I was big, and even though the drive ahead of me was long and dusty I had unlimited summer afternoons to reach my destination.

Now the trip ahead of me is long and hopeful and scary, and I'm in a hurry. I'm in my fifties. Sometimes I feel as if I have one foot in a rest home. What is it some brilliant philosopher said about never being too old to be who you always wanted to be? If he's right, who am I—a river running near but out of sight, running away from who I've accidentally become. And anyway, who is it I've always wanted to be?

A few more hours of cleaning and I'll snoop around inside my old brothel and find out exactly what it is I've acquired, for so little money. Grandpa used to say, "When something happens that's too good to be true, guess what? It probably is." But I don't care. I have something of my own now, something that's not Bradley's.

Light-headed, I step onto the creaking porch boards and reach for the knob on the faded yellow door. Next to the door, one of the broken windowpanes opens into the silent two-story building like an adit, while the rest of the window reflects the decrepit buildings and cars across the alley. Will I find a dark mystery inside? A coffin with secrets? Or will I find a light switch to illuminate the interior, bright like a mind on fire before it's been diminished by chance?

It's been quiet in the canyon all day. I've heard no one, but now I think I hear voices coming from inside the old building. I turn the knob and yank hard on the door. The knob pulls off and I stare at the black round orb in my hand as I lurch backwards off the porch into the sky. I am falling now through a pale yellow pastel shimmer, through the smell of warm pitchy resins from the pines and firs all around the canyon. And then, with a heavy thud, I hit the ground.

I'm glad Bradley cannot see this, my latest clumsy act. We're separate now. The stitched seam that held us together gave way. The fabric pulled apart. I couldn't repair it, and now I don't want to. Instead, I want to cry and heal the loss of time, of all that was missing for so many years. I don't need a man in my life now, and certainly not in my bed. I don't need the trying and failing, the making do like Grandma did with her wringer washer. Bradley will have to find another skirt.

Lying here, I am not uncomfortable. And no one is around to see me on display in the road near the edge of the porch. A bird sings off in the distance, a bird whose song I think I heard moments before the moose attack, before I smelled the acrid fur and heard the departing hooves. I'm getting good at having accidents. But this time nothing hurts. My right hand brushes back and forth in gentle swimming strokes on the ground, collecting individual grains of sand on my outstretched fingers.

It's late afternoon and the sun is setting behind the towering west wall of the canyon. I'm cold now, and although I no longer hear voices, I don't want to be alone next to this spooky place when night overtakes the canyon floor. Not yet. Like a centipede, or a baby, I maneuver onto all fours and push myself upright. I'll wait to explore the building tomorrow through the back, through a door that's already open.

On Sunday morning, I rise early. We had a quiet night, with no nighttime adventures—no mice, no wild scratching noises, no mouse parts. Instead I dreamed that Robert Redford paid me a huge sum of money for the brothel and that I lived in the building as a ghost. He spent over $100,000 renovating the structure, including mirrors on every wall, funhouse mirrors, and an elegant Sundance-looking deck off the back of the building out over the creek. He knew I lived in the building as a ghost, and he talked to me about his latest film projects. He told me this old mining town was a perfect setting for a film, and he said, "You could be a character in it."

On our way to the brothel, Chug and I walk past Big Al, who is lying on a large dark-colored boulder embedded in the yard next to the cabin. The top of the boulder is dished just right for the curl of my very large cat who looks like the Norwegian Forest Cat on the poster at the vet's office.

At the back entrance to the two-story building, Chug stops. "I'll stay here," she says, studying me. She's made her decision. It's her job to guard the door. "Okay, Chug. You make sure nothing breaks into the building."

I enter the lean-to back porch through an open door, push loose boards aside and step over empty wooden dynamite boxes. After crossing the threshold, I stand on spongy, rotten floorboards in the musty fecal air, *eau de mouse turds.* What a filthy mess. Dewey was probably right when he said I might be biting off more than I could chew. At least this morning I hear no voices.

The tops of the thin four-by-eight wallboard panels lean forward into the room from all sides, as if they're bowing at the waist, as if they could let loose and bury me in a coffin of dust, spider webs, nest material and mouse droppings. A bird flies out from behind a wallboard. More scratching noises. I duck down and grope my way along the back wall, where the floor feels more stable. A piece of old newspaper, folded over, pokes out from the wall. An article on its face is titled *How to Change a Hotel Into a Brothel and Break All Ten Commandments in One Night.* An amazing demonstration of upward mobility. I believe this was the best little whorehouse in Snowshoe. And, while the building is not National Register material like some of the brothels in Butte, the place deserves more attention than it's received for the past few decades.

Putting the piece of newspaper in my shirt pocket, I head for a narrow, enclosed corner stairway, pausing at the dark entrance to consider the cobweb snares and spiders lurking in the corners. I climb the steep, rickety stairs, unsuccessful in my attempt to stay away from the corners, until I emerge into a shaft of daylight streaming onto the second floor. Above my head, between two rafters, is a gaping hole in the collapsing roof. On the floor lies more debris: old magazines, rusting cans of chewing tobacco, rotten clothes, and other anonymous objects—all decomposing. If the madam who ran this place could see it now, she'd probably say its condition is lewd and indecent. I dust the spider webs off my sleeves and shoulders and keep moving.

Three small rooms occupy the east end of the upstairs space at the front of the building—rooms that must have been used by *the girls.* One room is larger, maybe eight by ten feet, while the other two are smaller, about six by eight feet. Not much to cleaning a room that size. The rooms are partitioned off with smooth pine boards, many of them missing. Rough-sawn lumber covers the rest of the upstairs walls. I creep along the end of the north wall, stepping from one floor joist to the next. Some joists are hidden under warped, spongy boards while others are exposed. In no one spot is the floor securely fastened to the joists. The beams are two feet apart so I pause, gauge the distance, and then step. Suddenly a beam buckles and splits apart out in the center of the floor. I scream as I leap to the next joist, one with boards on it, and the entire building creaks and shudders, adjusting to the loss of the beam. I think of Bradley, of the hopelessness of *us,* of how my life had come to mean so much less to me than this crumbling building does now. I must adjust to the loss of all those years, the loss of the marriage itself. Yet what I remember at this moment is how skilled he had become at pretending to listen to me speak. I know what he'd say right now, though. He'd say, "Look at this mess you've gotten yourself into. What this place needs is a can of gasoline and a match!"

Any fool would agree that I'm in big trouble. I could slink back to the stairway and slither down through the cobwebs to the first floor, but since I'm already this far, I'm going to continue so I can see inside the closest of the three rooms. I hesitate, then step from joist to joist. As I approach the door of the largest room, I hear the scratching sounds of something scurrying across the floor. A tall, vertical double-hung window brightens the room, but I see nothing that could have caused the sound. Just inside, folded and stuck between a two-by-four and the wall, I find a handful of pages out of a yellowed magazine. On the first page is a quote:

> "*What Darwin Said About Music: . . . If I had to live my life again I would have made a rule to read some poetry and listen to some music at least once every week, for the loss of these tastes is a loss of happiness, and may possibly be injurious to the intellect, and more probably to the moral character, by enfeebling the emotional part of our nature.*"

Who put this here? The building was, after all, a brothel, not a civic center. Still, the quote holds truths, and I want to give these pages a place of honor in the cabin. Maybe I'll take them with me to the outhouse to read. Yes, I want poetry and music in my life, not just scratching noises.

CHAPTER 8

My truck sits between the brothel and the cabin, springs sagging, overflowing with debris from the past century: bags of rusted cans and odd chunks of metal, gloves, broken bottles, branches and dried grass, part of an old leather work boot. Myra and Gary and I cleaned only a small patch of ground around the blacksmith shop, but my hands are blistered from all the raking and shoveling. And I still tire easily, even though it's been three months since the moose stepped on me. Tomorrow it's back to work, where I can rest up physically if not mentally. Myra left for home to be with Jim, and Gary had declined coming to the Snowshadow with me. He picks his watering holes with care.

The sun is setting on Cinnamon Peak as I trudge into the Snowshadow's parking lot. The German shepherd gnaws on something over near the Dumpster. Nearby, six or seven burly ravens feud over some decomposing item. The object of the squawking, ripping and tearing is half a loaf of moldy Wonder bread.

Entering the hot springs pool, a blast of steam fogs my glasses. I grope through air that smells only slightly of rotten eggs. Of course, the fact that the mineral content in the hot springs here isn't high also reduces its healing benefits for a person's aching bones and muscles, but, to me, hot water always feels like a miracle.

From the pool I squint, trying to see through the steam-drenched window-wall into the bar. I'm half-blind without my glasses, but I detect a dozen or so vague, ghostly outlines sitting hunched on the barstools. Who are all these people? I didn't expect a crowd, just Dewey, maybe one or two others. Every now and then someone in the bar glances toward the pool. I close my eyes. Bradley always said that in Montana you were only safe living in the cities, small as they were, because so many cretins lived out in the hills hiding from the law. He was convinced that even in the open on the ranches the people had so little contact with the twentieth century that they, too, were dangerous. Now I'm the one who is on parole. And for the moment, I'm happy to be sitting here in hot water with several potential cretins on the other side of the window.

Dressed now in a clean shirt and jeans, I enter the bar through a door from the dressing room. Walk tall, I tell myself. One beer and I'll leave.

"Molly! Come on over. Grab a stool," Dewey hollers. Every man on every barstool sets his drinks down in unison and turns to stare at me. Am I that strange looking? Did I forget my pants? I glance downward. All covered. The background music for this scene of frozen, frowning faces is an old song on the jukebox: *if you don't love me like I want you to, I'm gonna haul off and die-eye over you.* What was it Darwin said about making it a rule to hear some music at least once every week?

I wish Dewey hadn't called attention to me. These men must be a few of the other thirty-eight-odd residents of Snowshoe. A dark, bearded man with a hawk nose peers out from under Fuller Brush eyebrows. I should give him the name of my barbershop so he can find some help for those unruly hairs. Another man, round and red-faced, wears a red plaid shirt with black suspenders holding up frayed black twill pants, cut off just above his boot tops. I approach one of two remaining empty barstools, and everyone goes back to talking, drinking, and acting like no one came in. I do not take the stool at the end of the bar near the stuffed moose head. I choose, instead, the other vacant stool at the end of the bar near the cash register. I'll work up to sitting near the moose, but not tonight. I'm five-foot-eight inches tall, and the stool is high even for me. I step on the rung with my left foot and swing onto the seat cover like I'm mounting a horse, and when I do this my hiking boot nicks an old man in the butt. He doesn't flinch. He doesn't turn around. Nothing. I'm grateful for the way these western men handle awkward situations. I guess to their way of thinking, if they don't acknowledge something, well then, maybe it didn't really happen.

"Excuse me," I say to the old guy. "I'm sorry."

No response.

"Herb tea?" Dewey yells.

"Sure. Chamomile lite draft, no foam."

Finally the old man, wearing a stained, gray Jimmy Stewart-style hat, turns his spare, hunched form away from his bar stool neighbor, both hands on the edge of the bar for leverage. His neck is recessed into the top of his khaki-colored shirt, and I am reminded of a snapping turtle I once saw on my grandparents' ranch. He smells like smoke, both cigarette and wood, and he's wearing blue bib overalls not much bigger than rompers. Without turning, he looks at me sideways, up and down, from under his hat. I smile at him. He grunts and turns back the other way.

Dewey sets a mug of beer on the bar, looks at me and smiles.

"Gum!" Dewey yells at the old man. "Yoo-hoo, Gum! Turn up your hearing aid." The old man fiddles with a knob on one of his shirt pockets, a knob attached to a wire attached to a hearing aid the size of a small home appliance suspended from his right ear.

"Gum, this is your new neighbor, Molly," Dewey says pointing at me.

The old man turns again, hunched, hands on the edge of the bar, no neck.

"Molly, this is Gumboot Charlie."

"Hello," I say offering my hand. It's what we do at work, shake hands when we meet someone. It's a friendly, non-threatening thing to do. Gumboot looks at me long and hard, saying nothing, not extending his hand. I think maybe he needs to hold onto the bar with both hands or he'll fall off his stool, which is nearly as tall is he is. I take my hand back, grab the handle of my beer mug and look at Dewey, whose gaze is fixed on Gumboot.

"What the hell happened to your hair?" the old man croaks, glancing sideways at me again.

"Jesus, Gum," Dewey says. "What kind of thing is that to say?"

"Well, she looks like a boy, for Christ sake."

I snort my beer and nearly choke. A boy! It would take an old coot, ancient as dirt, to say a thing like that about a fifty-one-year-old woman. Wait until I tell Gary at work.

"Thank you, Mr. Gumboot," I say.

Dewey sighs and looks relieved. I guess he feels lucky. One more bar room brawl, stopped before it started. Dewey delivers a beer to the moose head end of the bar.

"So, how long have you lived up here in Snowshoe?" I ask Gumboot.

Dewey returns to stand in front of me on the other side of the bar, a towel flung over one of his shoulders like a scarf. We watch Gumboot. He clears his throat and fiddles with his hearing aid again.

"Moved over from Twodot in '16," he drawls, gravel in his old voice. "Run away from home."

"Tell us why you ran away," Dewey says. He turns to me and says, "This is too good."

We both lean in toward Gumboot. I glance at our hazy reflections in the mirror behind the bar, at Dewey's broad back, and, for the first time, I notice a bald spot the size of a shiny silver dollar on the top of his head. Someone hollers for a beer. Dewey yells, "In a minute."

The jukebox plays a country and western tune: *some girls don't like boys like me, ahhhhhhhh but some girlsioooooo.*

"Well, things was a little dull one day," Gumboot begins, pausing to adjust his hat. He looks at each of us, one at a time, as we watch him and wait for him to speak. He sits a little taller on the barstool, and begins. "My cousin, Gertie, and me got to branding gophers, just for practice. Hell, the brand was just two dots. We shot the gophers first with a twenty-two, so they'd hold still. Built a little fire back of the church. Next thing you know the wind kicked up, like it's prone to do over there along the Musselshell, and the goddamn church caught fire. Should of know'd better. Hell, I was twelve at the time. Pa lit into me pretty good. Person can't live a thing like that down, least not in Twodot. So I run off the next day."

Dewey slaps the bar and says, "I love that story," then leaves to deliver a beer.

Not one of Bradley's business associates ever told a story this good.

"Did you come straight to Snowshoe?" I ask.

"It was easy to end up in Helena from anywhere, them days. Caught a freight wagon. Got up here and went to work in the mines. Worked in the woods off and on. Done some gold panning on the side."

Dewey returns and tells us, "The guy who wanted the beer is a realtor, asking about properties along the creek. Them developers are snooping around everywhere these days. You got your place in the nick of time, Molly."

"Just another entremanure, trying to turn a buck," Gumboot says.

Should I inform the old guy the word is *entrepreneur?* I glance around. No one bats an eyelash at the word, so instead I say, "Gumboot, do you know anything about the brothel on my place? Was it still in operation when you moved here?"

"Oh, hell, yeah. The Bluebird House, it was called. Never went there myself. 'Course I heard about it."

"Oh, of course," Dewey laughs. "Ha, ha, ha."

"Your Grandfather sure knew about the place, Dewey," Gumboot says, his tone becoming more serious. He clears his throat. "Operated for a couple years after I arrived. Flu got the madam in 1918, then the girls left. Silver prices had went to hell anyway. Things weren't too pretty around here for a while."

Things still aren't too pretty around here, I'm thinking. And the old brothel does look something like a colossal birdhouse in the way it's constructed.

"Do either of you know a good carpenter?" I ask. "I'm afraid my old building's going to fall in on itself if I don't do something with it before winter." My beer glass is about half full and I take another swallow.

"Let her fall," Gumboot says. "Getting to be an eyesore, if you ask me."

I sputter and snort my beer again, spraying it onto my clean sleeve. I can't believe he said that, when his own place is such a junkyard. It's the worst place in town, and he says *my* building is an eyesore. Calm down, I tell myself. Just act like nothing happened.

"I want to save it," I say, trying not to sound defensive. "It has potential."

"For what? You gonna open it up for bi'ness again?" Gumboot says.

I'm thinking, wouldn't you love that, you old coot? I say, "Maybe I'll live in it. The cabin's not really big enough."

"You should get out of there while you still can. That place'll eat you alive. It's bad luck. Ain't no place for a woman alone."

"Do either of you know a carpenter?" I ask again, ignoring Gumboot.

"Well," Dewey says, "there's always Ben Weigland, living up in the mountains like a hermit. My age. Traps in the winter, does odd jobs in the summer. 'Course he was accused of a murder here about twenty years ago. Made headlines. You probably heard about The Bacon Rind Murder. Ben got himself acquitted on lack of evidence, but most of us know he did it. Wasn't far from his cabin. He tied a hiker to a tree and stuffed bacon in his shirt and pants. Wild animals got to him. A couple of his friends went looking for the guy the next day, found what was left of him."

"I do remember that. They never did find out who did it," I say, glancing at the hands hugging beer mugs up and down the bar. Anyone here could have murdered that guy up in the woods twenty years ago. Guess I'd better start locking my door at night.

"He's a weird duck," Gumboot adds, throwing back a shot of straight whiskey. "Heard he even has skunks for pets. Nice kid growing up, too. Don't know what happened to him."

"You guys have been real fun," I say, swallowing the rest of my beer. "But I need to get up early for work."

"Hurry back, Molly," Dewey says.

Gumboot studies me with his rheumy eyes. I can't read his expression. I'm guessing he's curious, but who could tell.

I use the indoor plumbing one last time, then retrieve my sack of dirty clothes from a locker in the women's changing room. Walking home under the glow of stars, an umbrella of galaxies above the mountains, I kick a fist-sized rock out of the road and begin to skip. I'm as close to the top of the world as I have ever been in my life.

Locking the door behind me, I greet the animals, brush my teeth, put on my pajamas, and climb the ladder to my nest in the loft. Lying up under the roof of my cabin, I stroke Big Al's fur and wonder about the gruesome unsolved murder. And then I think about Gumboot's age. By adding and subtracting a little, I determine he's ninety-one years old. And what a maddening old prick he is, too, but I have to hand it to him—living up here alone, chopping his own wood, climbing on and off that bar stool. We don't have to be pals, but I'd at least like to be on a neighborly basis with the old coot. Besides, he knows things about my place, I know he does.

Will I be living up here when I'm ninety-one? Probably not, but one of these days I'll qualify for some senior discounts. Maybe I'll be able to get a deal on a new pair of snowshoes.

CHAPTER 9

Chug's huge sad eyes follow my every movement as I open my ancient Kelvinator refrigerator, using the screwdriver. She's sprawled by the door, head on paws, waiting for me to take her on her evening W-A-L-K. I had mentioned it, now she'll hold me to it. From the refrigerator, I pull out an assortment of green, orange, and red items to toss together a quick salad. I won't take time to throw together a tofu stir-fry tonight. Feeding myself after work is so simple these days, now that I don't have to worry about Bradley's craving for red meat. Chug sighs and watches me eat my dinner. I adore knowing what a date most desperately wants.

Chug and I cross the creek on a rickety log bridge. The creek is flowing bank high, the water nearly touching the undersides of the log stringers. It's been warm and sunny since the rainstorm my first night in the cabin over a week ago. Snow melt is tumbling out of the mountains and gathering velocity as it rushes downhill toward the Missouri River and the Atlantic. I hope we won't suffer another one-hundred-year flood, only ten years after the last one.

The old abandoned railroad bed is overgrown with robust young alders now leafed out. The level trail follows along the creek toward Cinnamon Peak. Chug ambles beside me, head lowered, tongue flapping alongside her lower jaw like a red flannel mop. Where boulders, trees, logs or shrubs intrude into the path, Chug walks behind me, snuffling. Now and then a robin takes flight from a tree or shrub on our side of the creek and wings its way over to an aspen or cottonwood tree on the other side. I see a flash of blue wing, my first bluebird of the season. So, they *are* up here—probably the mountain bluebird.

Beyond the town, we pass a steep hillside, once squandered by mining. A few years ago the steep slope was reclaimed and planted with grasses and small trees. The landscape architects did a good job of designing the hillside to resemble one of the vertical trails made by a snow avalanche. Below us on the road across the creek, a rusty old jeep is crawling along the road. No one appears to be driving the vehicle, but when I squat down for a better view into the jeep, I see Gumboot's hat poking up above the steering wheel. Where would he be going this evening?

As Chug and I walk along, I think about Gumboot and old men in general. Like other men, like *all* dangerous animals, I think they're best kept at a distance. But old men, except when they act cocky and all knowing, seem in some ways superior to other men. If they've paid attention, they can be downright enlightened. My grandpa was like that. Or they can be old S.O.B.'s—grizzled and grumpy and crafty. Gumboot has survived ninety-one Montana winters. He must be wise about something. If you aren't somehow friendly to the rhythms of the long, frigid nights and the cold, bright, too-short days, you can easily end up as winterkill. Yet Gum seems mysterious. For all the stories he shares, it's as if he's hiding something captured and defined for all time in its current state. Like a fossil. I want to know him better, but his unexpected remarks scare me into wanting to keep my distance.

As Chug and I turn and hike along a splashing side stream, an odd thought occurs to me. How many women do you suppose the old man has slept with? Then I wonder, is this a natural curiosity on my part or am I becoming perverted? After all, I did buy an old brothel.

We zigzag through an area of ground disturbed by

dredging, and follow the stream uphill under a dark canopy of lodgepole pines. Whenever I'm outdoors, I enter a goofy rapture state, and now the smell of pitch, with its vague but pleasant hint of turpentine, envelops me and I begin to feel euphoric, as if under a spell. Beneath the dense canopy of the lodgepoles, however, the ground has no grasses or shrubs and it's appearance is sterile, almost spooky. I hope the scenery changes soon. We aren't following a trail, so there's no telling where we're going, except that we're on our way up a creek. When it's time to head home, we'll retrace our route. At least with so little green stuff to browse, moose shouldn't be a problem up here. Chug stops for a drink in the creek every few minutes, and this gives me a chance to catch my breath and drink water from a plastic flask in my day pack.

Suddenly a large hawk-like bird swoops down at me. I duck and raise my arms to protect my head. A few seconds later it dives on me again, this time with its talons extended. The creature misses my head by mere inches.

"Chug, let's go," I yell, and take off running uphill, one hand gripping my water bottle, the other one over my head as the shrieking bird takes aim on me again. I can tell it means business. I've logged a few miles hiking, but nothing like this has ever happened before, not with a bird.

The screeching pterodactyl flies off. I glance over my shoulder as Chug and I slow to a trudge and continue on, panting. Up ahead, beyond a line of trees, is a brightly lit area. When we reach the line of trees, a meadow opens up in front of us—a silent, shallow dish of marshy pond, reflecting sky and trees. Somewhere on the other side of this open-hearted sanctuary, a trickle of stream must keep it filled. To my immediate left, the creek we had followed trickles from a beaver dam of sticks and mud, gathering volume and speed in its downhill tumble. But in the marsh itself, all movement in the landscape has stopped to renew itself. Here it is restful, luxurious and peaceful. Next to the log where I'm sitting, a congregation of elegant pink monkey flowers bow their heads as I think about what Darwin said. Certainly this place qualifies as poetry.

I can smell the sedges and spireas, and behind me, the warm pitchy aroma of pine trees. Flamboyant dragonflies flit over the edge of the marsh, catching the slanting sunbeams in their iridescent wings. At the ranch on the Big Hole, I watched dragonflies for hours. Grandma called them darning needles. Because of their metallic wing colors, I had thought they were related to peacocks. One alights on the right knee of my jeans for a second and flits off over the pond, where water striders are zipping around the mirrored surface. Grandma called them Jesus bugs but always wondered how they could walk on water. How I wish I could tell her what I learned in college about these bugs, about the hairs that cover them and trap the air that holds them above water, about how they row with one pair of legs and steer with another as they skate around searching for food. For some reason, I think of Dewey and how he limps when he walks.

What a vast, sweeping place of endings and beginnings. Moose habitat, no doubt, although I see no dark, looming objects. What I do see and hear and feel are mosquitoes. Dragonflies eat mosquitoes but they're no match for this population. I search through my day pack for the bug repellent. If a moose or a hawk doesn't finish me off first, using bug repellant probably will. It's bad for you. I splash it on my hands, neck and face, and rub some on my long sleeves. In spite of the flitting, skittering and buzzing of insects, the scene is what I would imagine a mirage to be like.

Chug jerks her head to bite at a black fly, then catches sight of something at the side of the marsh that wasn't there before. A growl begins low in her throat. Her eyes are focused on a huge brown object about a hundred yards away. The thing glances our way for a few seconds, then looks down at something. All my life I've heard tales of huge, hairy ape-like men, or men-like apes, living in the woods. Maybe this is one of them, a Bigfoot. I keep an eye on the brown object as I grab my pack, ready to swing it onto my back and make another run for it. When it looks up toward us, I see that it has a hairy face, and I see it's a man. He lifts his arm to wave. I wave back and he rises to full height. While the man is not a Bigfoot, he's pretty darn big, and he's moving in our direction. I'd leave, but I don't want to be rude. Chug growls, deeper and louder. She never growls at anyone or anything, and her behavior alarms me. I grab her collar, big around as my own belt, and I know if she decides to she could drag me over into Jefferson County.

"Hello," yells the man, his voice deep, almost hollow sounding.

"Hello," I yell back.

"Is your dog dangerous?"

"She can be. I wouldn't come too close." I've always thought of Chug as a very large pussycat. Now I'm not so sure.

"This is Try Again Meadows," the man says, continuing to walk toward us.

With a ferocious growl, Chug lunges. "Stop it, Chug," I say, but not with too much authority. That way she'll know I don't really mean it.

The man stops about fifty feet away. He's at least six-foot-three, huge and bulging like Paul Bunyan. He's even dressed a bit like him in blue jeans and a brown plaid flannel shirt, worn thin. His tan-brown hair is cut like someone put a bowl over his head and he has a bushy beard. Middle-aged.

He's in his mid-forties, maybe a little older, with a big nose that might have been broken at one time and healed a little crooked. Looks like he could compete in one of those lumberjack competitions over in North Idaho, maybe chop down a huge tree, roll some logs and take home big prizes. His appearance isn't menacing, but Chug is acting almost rabid.

"Name's Ben," he says. "My cabin isn't far from here." He gestures off toward Cinnamon Peak, now beginning its red glow in the setting sun.

"I'm Molly Binfet," I say. "Nice to meet you." I'm thinking about the unsolved murder, where it took place. They say it wasn't far from his cabin. I decide to ask my question. What can it hurt?

"Aren't you a carpenter?"

He acts surprised by my question, then says, "Do a fair amount of that kind of work, when it comes up."

"Well, I need one."

"You were looking for a carpenter up here?" he asks.

Ignoring his question, I continue. "I heard that a man named Ben lives up here somewhere and that he does carpentry work. I bought a place in town near the creek, a two-story building with a false front. The one with the faded yellow door."

"Sad shape, last I saw it." He glances in the direction of Snowshoe, then back to me. "Take a lot of work to save that one. I can look at it, give you an estimate if you want. I'm not as expensive as most. Not cheap, either."

"That's fair. I think the old building needs help right away. How soon can you do it?"

"I'm a carpenter, not an emergency-room doctor, but I'll take a look tomorrow. I can be there when you arrive home from work."

"How do you know I work?"

"I can see most of the town from my cabin, and what I don't see the birds tell me."

I study his expressionless face. He's different, all right. And Chug hasn't stopped growling during our entire conversation, if that's what you want to call it.

"See you tomorrow evening, then," I say, holding onto Chug's collar.

"Watch out for moose," he says, smiling.

"Moose?"

"We have a couple in the meadows but they're mellow enough. Not like the kind you come across at lower elevations," he says, motioning toward Snowshoe.

Why did he say *we?* He doesn't even have a dog with him.

"Right now I'm more worried about a large bird that attacked me in the woods back down the creek."

"Goshawk. Probably has a nest near the trail. On your way down the hill, I'd recommend you walk around her territory. That way she'll leave you alone. And I'd appreciate it if you'd secure your dog tomorrow when I look at your building so she can't chew on me."

When I drive up to my place after work, a vintage Chevy pickup, gray and dented, is parked in my yard, but I don't see anyone around my buildings. Where is he? Chug has spent the day indoors and she'll want out as soon as possible, so I head toward the cabin. As soon as I open my cabin door, Chug jumps up on me and licks my face.

"Hi girl. Hi little Chuggie Choo. Hold still now." When I clip her leash onto her collar, she half pulls me out the door, across the porch and into the yard. After she does her business, we walk over toward the back of the brothel, making our way past the old blacksmith shop. When Ben steps out toward us and says, "Hello," Chug growls and lunges, grabbing one of Ben's pant legs. He attempts to pull his leg free while I pull on Chug's leash.

"Chug! Stop it!" I yell.

Ben says nothing as he attempts to back away. I hear a tearing noise. Chug has a corner of fabric in her teeth and she's shaking her head. I swat Chug on the nose and she lets go with one final, angry snarl.

I pull my strangely vicious pet back over to the cabin and close the door. When I return to the yard Ben is standing near his pickup, his arm resting on a fender. And this man is supposed to be a murderer? I can't see it. But Chug must see something I don't.

"I'm sorry. She's never acted like this before." I look down at his ripped pants and hairy thigh. "I'd be happy to pay for a new pair of pants."

"They're work pants. I can fix them . . . or maybe it's time to retire this pair." He smiles, then continues. "I surveyed your building over there. I'm afraid I have some bad news."

"It *can* be fixed, can't it?"

"Well, to be honest with you," he says, "it might be easier and cheaper to tear it down and start over." He speaks slowly and carefully, and his deep voice tends to crack in mid-sentence.

"No," I say. My heart is racing. I bring my hand up to my chest. Calm down, I tell myself. "Please. I want to keep the building, the old boards, even the yellow door. Can't we do something? I don't want to lose it." I'm like a child, pleading for a lost toy.

"The roof is the most urgent thing. If it isn't replaced you'll lose the building this winter. It'll cave in, the walls will smash to the ground and you'll end up with a mountain of kindling."

"That's what I thought."

"If we're lucky we have four months before the heavy snow sets in. That's plenty of time to replace the roof. What are your plans for the building? If you only want to save it from falling over so you can use it for storage, that's one type of roof. If you want to live in it or use it as a guest house, you'll want a different kind of roof."

"I want it to be my home," I say, ready to grovel. My old brothel, I realize, has become much more than a broken down old building to me.

"Well, then I'd recommend an insulated roof with metal panels to shed the snow. If I use fir decking for the first layer over the new rafters, you'll be able to look up at a nice wood ceiling from the inside."

"Okay, let's do that . . . and I'd like a couple skylights so I can watch the stars at night."

Ben reaches for a pad of paper from the seat of his truck, the kind with little squares on it like engineers use. He flips pages and scribbles some notes, using his truck's hood as a table.

"I can do that," he says. "If you'll sign me up as your contractor at one of the lumber yards in Helena I can order everything we need and have it delivered. I can bring samples of roof colors if you like, but I'd recommend a reddish-brown color to blend in with the rest of the rust around here."

"That sounds good. But how much is this going to cost?"

He pencils more notes and a few quick sketches, followed by a long list of figures on his note pad. I watch him scribble, feeling small next to this unknown mountain of a man, an acquitted murderer, the only man in Snowshoe who can save my building from falling to the ground. His rolled up flannel shirtsleeves expose muscular forearms, with soft-looking reddish hairs that look out of place. His enormous upper body looms over his paperwork. I glance away toward the thick, stealthy flow of the creek, still near flood stage. I hope I'm not getting myself in over my head.

"We'd have to do the work in phases over the next four months, including Saturdays. The roof would be first, with some nice wood trusses, followed by new joists and flooring on the second floor, then a new foundation. New joists, insulation and flooring on the first floor. New stairs. All new electrical. The wall timbers are only four-foot on center. That's the way they did it those days. Called it balloon-frame construction. It's like they didn't *intend* for these buildings to last. So we'll have to beef up the wall timbers all around, insulating as we go. Then we can talk about finish work, like the interior wall treatments, re-doing all the window sills, building kitchen counters, and so on. I think I can keep it around $50,000, materials and labor, that is if no major problems come up."

I'm stunned, a little dizzy. For some reason, I think of the nursery rhyme with the line, *And the dish ran away with the spoon*. This little reclamation project has gotten totally out of hand. It'll eat up most of my divorce settlement. I'll have to work until I'm Gumboot's age before I can afford to retire.

Ben watches me steadily, waiting for me to speak. I gulp. "When can you start?"

"Day after tomorrow. With a retainer of $2500, I can get started."

"I can write you a check, and start an account in both our names at the lumber yard." As I say this, I remind myself it would cost a lot more if a carpenter came out from Helena every day.

"Before you write that check, I'd like you to take a walk with me," Ben says.

Red chickens scatter out of the way as he begins walking. I

follow him, wondering where we're going. Maybe I should recruit Chug. He stops in the road in front of the brothel.

"Look at your wall there, on the south side. See how it's bowed out about six inches?"

"I see it." I hadn't noticed this before.

Ben walks a little farther up the alley. I follow along behind him. "Now take a look at the north wall. Same thing."

The building looks hopeless, like a busted up old birdhouse. I think about the can of gasoline and matches.

"If your building can't be saved, Molly, it'll be because I can't bring the walls into true. I'll use a heavy chain to pull them in gradually over the next couple weeks, but the old wood might be too dry and brittle to move, or if the timbers do move, they might simply split apart. A little moisture would help soften the wood. If you pray, you'll want to pray for a rainy June."

"But won't that cause the creek to rise?"

"That's a distinct possibility," he says, glancing off toward Gumboot's place across the alley, then toward the creek. "You'll want to pray carefully."

CHAPTER 10

"Gary, you should have seen him Saturday. He roped up like a mountain climber in case he slipped or one of the rotten beams gave way, and he finished ripping off all the old roofing." Gary and I are in the parking lot, saying goodbye before leaving work for the day.

"He sounds like quite a guy," Gary says. "Think he's my type?"

"I wouldn't know about that. Why don't you come out again next Saturday, if you'll promise not to make a pass at him. We could use the help."

"All right. But I suppose this time I'll end up with slivers instead of blisters."

"One or the other or both, guaranteed," I say.

"It's a date. I'll mark it down on my social calendar."

My top teeth rattle against my bottom teeth, after I turn off the highway onto the gravel road to Snowshoe. Rough as a cob. That's what the regulars at the Snowshadow say about the road this time of year. They also say that in the past year there have been thirteen single-vehicle accidents on The Snowshoe Trail, as it's called. Seems high, for an eight-mile stretch of gravel road, but then the County hasn't "floated" it with a grader for weeks. Rough as a cob. I guess that means an ear of corn *without* the kernels, all wrinkled and dried up and dusty. Okay, so I forgot to pray for rain.

Driving the sixteen miles to and from Helena every day is not conducive to lofty thoughts, but it gives me time to think about my new location in the curve of normal. What I'm doing is living on the outer edge, or the frontier, of the bell-shaped curve that represents mainstream American culture. Every day I commute into the bulge of the curve where most people live and work, where Bradley spends his time. At night, I return to my hiding cover on the outer limits.

Some people fear those of us who live on the outskirts of normal. They whisper their concerns to each other: *Are those people involved in weird cults? Are they stockpiling weapons? Are they dangerous?*

And sometimes I worry about my job, with all the talk of "reinvention." Where will I fit in if the state reorganizes our department? Will younger employees be favored?

Then I wonder if Ben actually murdered someone. And if he did tie up that hiker, whatever was his motive? Sure, he would have been physically capable of it, he's certainly able-bodied, but that's no reason to accuse him. And he *was* acquitted of all charges. I fret that he'll turn into some wild animal if I have him redo a window frame. After all, Chug doesn't like him, and she'd wander off with almost any stranger. She doesn't even realize she's *pretending* to guard the front doors of my life. Well, I'm not going to ask him about the murder. Anyway, he sure can be taciturn, unless he's talking carpentry.

The Snowshadow Hot Springs Resort is deserted this Thursday afternoon at 4:30, except for Dewey. I find him in the bar and try to pay the $2.00 to use the pools and shower.

"Naw, it's on the house this time," he says through his mustache. "When you're done with your swim, come on back for a beer."

"Thanks. I will." Dewey is consistently good-natured. He wears it like some men wear baseball caps.

In the dressing room I slip into my swimsuit, then shower and head for the hot-springs whirlpool. Sitting in the pool, I can look out the window at a clump of firs and the corner of the parking lot, where Dewey's German shepherd is gnawing on a steak bone. He has a pretty good life—all the steak bones he can chew on and only a few ravens to run off now and then. Even a dog's life is never perfect. My own life? Free and loose, almost too loose. I'm grateful I have my job and a project like the old brothel to anchor me. Of course, some rain would be nice so the two-by-fours on the old girl would straighten up. Ben tells me that as soon as the walls line up another couple inches on each side, he can build the new rafters and hoist them into place. I hope he's right. But then, rain might cause the creek to flood, and a flood might wash away the brothel. Always these trade-offs in life.

At the bar, Dewey has a lite draft waiting for me. As usual, he's nursing a can of Coors and his oversized mustache is dripping with beer. The jukebox is playing a slow country and western tune.

"So, how did your day pan out?" he asks me, before I can ask him about his day. We do this whenever I stop after work and no one else is around.

"Action packed. I placed drops of creek water onto glass plates and looked at them under a microscope. Made notes." I take a sip of beer, thinking of the tedious part of my job. "Then," I pause again, this time with a groan. "I entered all the data into a computer for analysis. We're busy right now comparing water quality during spring runoff with water quality during low-flow periods of late summer. That's the good of it."

"The water's dirtier now, right?" His half-smile is now more like three-quarters of a smile.

"Exactly," I say. He seems pleased with his summation of my job. "Actually, we're testing for increased levels of toxins in streams near old mine tailings. They're everywhere, and there's money to reclaim some of them. I enjoy the field work the most, but then it's our data that helps decide which projects to work on next. That means lots of time in front of a computer."

"Don't tell me you're one of them rabbit environmentalists, too. They're not real popular around here. If you ever smell bacon, you'd better run." He laughs.

"Ha, ha, ha," I say. "As a matter of fact I care very much about the landscape. I'm just not pushy about it." I didn't know the murdered hiker had been an environmentalist. I guess I don't need to tell Dewey or anyone else around here that I'm a card-carrying member of two environmental groups and an animal-rights organization, not to mention the Great Old Broads for Wilderness.

"All right, then. You can stay," he says, like this is a joke. We each take yet another sip of beer. "But I'll tell you another way to demonstrate that water is clean." Dewey's half-smile is now a half laugh. "A friend and I had a claim we were working. Had to take a water sample in for testing. Couldn't get a permit 'til we proved the water was clean enough. Can't remember why. When the guy told us the water test would cost $90.00, I said, 'Well, if I drink the water right here in front of you you'll know it's safe, right? You don't think I'd drink tainted water, do you?' So I drank it and smiled, and he gave us the permit to work the mine. Tasted metals for two or three days. Hell, I even sweated metals. But we saved $90.00."

"And you struck it rich, right?" I say. I already know the answer. It's my turn to smirk.

"Never found any ore worth enough to take that awful taste out of my mouth. Most of our claims were shut down soon enough. Then the hillside south of town got reclaimed. Took all summer. Lots of traffic. 'Course the road was graded every week and that was good. And the town ended up with a new water system. Business was brisk here at the bar that summer. Really kept me hopping. We could use another mine reclamation project up here, or some damn thing to increase visitation."

"What about today, Dewey? Tell me what you did today."

"Action packed. Scrubbed the pools, chopped wood, the usual. Also called the County again to request they grade the road before Gum's big party this weekend. Told them the Governor's invited, said we didn't want the Gov's limo sashaying right off the road on his way up here. Bad press for the road department."

"No kidding. The Governor's invited?"

"Naw. Gum doesn't like politicians, not that there's anything wrong with our Governor. I just told the County that so they'd get their butts up here with that grader. Let's see, then I replaced the hoses on the hot water radiators at my tepee."

"Tepee?"

"Sure. In the summers, I live in a tepee up in the trees. We rent out all the cabins, summer weekends. I like it up there. Chilly sometimes, though, even in summer, so I tapped into the hot springs to feed some old radiators I got at a building recycler's place. It's real cozy. I'll show you some time. Even got some etchings up there."

"You're really full of it, Dewey. You're about all the entertainment a person can take. I don't even read books any more."

"Thanks. But now it's my turn to groan," he says, taking a tug from his bottle. "Made a beer run today, stocking up for Gum's party. On my way back up the canyon, I met Ben on the road, heading out with a truckload of your old roofing. Like to run him off the road one of these days." His half-smile is gone, replaced by a hard, strong set to his face I've never seen on him before.

"What is it with everyone?" I say. "He's doing good work on my place and he's been a perfect gentleman." I don't tell Dewey that Chug doesn't like him.

"If you'll dance with me, I'll tell you a few things," Dewey says.

Lost in the Fifties plays on the jukebox. We dance. Dewey's chest is puffed out, much more so than my own, and it's difficult not to touch. So we do. But he's polite about it and doesn't try to press closer than what's natural. My chest on his chest feels okay, even a little more than okay. Dewey's limping gait does not affect the two steps we take to the right, the one step back, and the little turn that happens next. We aren't exactly American Bandstand material, but I don't care. I love to dance. I'm just out of practice. Bradley never wanted to go dancing, and that was one of the reasons I married him in the first place.

Next thing you know my eyes are closed. I'm warm and relaxed, and lost in the fifties. At my first dance, in 1959, I remember dancing with a boy named Tommy. I also remember how I was enjoying the dance, until Tommy said to me, "Why do you bounce so much when you dance? Are you trying to fly?" And now, here in the nineties, the warmth in my chest is taking wings in every direction.

"You're a nice height to dance with," Dewey whispers. I feel his breath and his mustache on my hair. If I were in the woods, I'd be thinking that a large insect had become tangled in my hair. My mind drifts along with the music, and I remember the saying, "You're not out of the woods yet."

Returning to reality, I say, "Thanks. But you were going to tell me interesting things?"

"Oh, yeah. 'Bout forgot, thinking how good it is to dance with you. It's like this." Dewey's voice is low, secretive, not his usual way of talking. "Ben and I went to school together.

In fact, we were pretty good friends. Before that last year of high school, we explored all over together. No one, except maybe Gum, knows these gulches and hills better than we do."

The song on the jukebox stops. Dewey seems to know what will play next and we keep dancing. "Well?" I say. "Keep going."

"Oh, yeah. Where was I?" he says, adjusting his hand on my back. "I got into wrestling big time. Won the State championship, even went to Norway on a scholarship. Nice girls there. Anyway, Ben and I were interested in the same girl here at home. Linda. While I went to school in Norway and wrestled, they spent a lot of time together. Ben got to be pretty crazy about her, and I can't say I blame him. He thought she liked him the same way, but I think she was biding her time 'til I got back."

He's quiet now, like he's reliving his return. "I'm listening," I say.

"In winter when I came home from Norway, Linda and I took up where we left off, then Ben came after me and we got in a big fight. I broke his nose. A couple weeks later someone set a bear trap in the path I kept shoveled to my truck. Covered the trap with snow so I wouldn't see it. The trap clamped shut and the teeth bit through the cheap old leather on my boot, right into my foot."

"That's just awful," I say, aware of the understatement.

"Hurt like hell. Yelled my head off 'til my dad could get to me and pry the jaws apart. Hauled me to the hospital on the front seat of his truck, sort of the way I took you in this spring. My foot was mangled pretty bad. I can see how an animal might chew off its own paw to escape a trap."

"And you think Ben set the trap for you?"

"Bingo. Don't know who else would have done it. Everyone knows about the bear trap incident, so when someone tied that guy to a tree with bacon stuffed in his clothes and then he got chewed to pieces not far from Ben's cabin, it was only natural for us to think he did it. And his grandfather shot a man around the turn of the century. If I were you, I'd be real careful around him. The man's unbalanced."

"What happened to Linda?"

"That's a topic for another dance," he says.

As I drive the short distance from the Snowshadow to my cabin, I'm filled with thoughts of the bizarre incidents I hear about every time I stop for a soak in the hot springs and see Dewey.

I turn onto the lane that leads me to my brothel, now sitting topless, its side walls winched together with chains. As soon as I pull up in front of the cabin, Chug barks from the fenced area Ben built for her. She's always so happy to see me. Ben is gone so I set her free, hug her head, and give her a steak bone. When I left the Snowshadow, Dewey handed me a sack and said, "These are for ole Thug."

Chug carries the bone in her mouth as we walk to the cabin. On the porch, lying on the seat of my lawn chair, is a carefully lettered note:

> *Molly—I found this quote by Rumi, a Persian poet: "Where there is ruin, there is hope for a treasure." Remember to pray for rain. Ben.*

CHAPTER 11

Inside the Snowshadow bar, I cannot see who is making the God-awful shrieking sounds. Gumboot sits on top of the bar, an undersized scarecrow wearing his Jimmy Stewart hat and a clean white shirt. Not one other familiar face. Dewey had said Gumboot's birthday gathering would be *one helluva party,* but where is Dewey now? Maybe I'll leave and come back later. Everyone is talking. No one is listening. And nobody's paying any attention to me. This is good. There goes that shrill laughter again, not far from where Gum sits on display. The moose head's shiny, bulbous eyes draw me further into the room.

"Excuse me, excuse me," I say, pushing through the throng of standing, talking bodies, past sharp ninety-degree elbows on arms holding drinks.

Now at the end of the bar near the moose head, I survey the room from my new vantage point. I feel a warm draft on my neck. I shiver, remembering the hot, angry, snorting moose bearing down on me that day in the woods.

On a table in front of the window wall, between the bar and the hot springs pool, sprawls a sheet cake. Wearing white frosting, the cake is bigger than the door of my cabin. Dewey had asked me during the week if he should put ninety-two candles on the cake. I had recommended he find one large candle. Now, setting in the center of the cake, more or less, burns a red Christmas candle as big around as a piece of lodgepole firewood, glowing like a campfire. I wonder if Gum will be able to blow out the fire and make a wish.

The woman shrieks again. The noise, coming from right near Gumboot, holds its own as several others join in with their loud guffaws. Gum is telling stories again. No wonder he's so popular on his birthday. As for myself, I'd rather stand here near the head of a dead moose than out in the middle of a room full of strangers.

A young man wearing a cowboy hat, standing between me and the end of the bar, turns around holding a mug of beer out toward me. "The bartender says this is for the lady by the moose head. He's moving some cases of beer and he'll be over in a minute."

"Thanks," I say, taking the beer.

The moose head above me reaches out from the wall in every direction. His face and snout is rectangular like a shoe box, one for very long shoes, and a flap of long fur, his dewlap, dangles beneath his chin. I reach up and touch the dry, stringy fur. His shiny, brown eyeballs gaze ahead out of a face full of fur in shades of tan, rust, and purplish brown. The rack of antlers rests platter-like, palms up, in a spread of about three feet in either direction.

"And thanks to you," I say, saluting the moose. "Might have been one of your descendants, kicked some sense into me."

"Congratulations," Dewey says, putting his arm around my shoulder. "I see you're on friendly terms with Dutch."

"He's got a name?"

"Every one of the mounts has a name. Laine over there bagged this one and named it."

"Dutch and I are doing fine together," I say. "Everyone else was talking to somebody; the moose was still available."

"Come on. Let's say hello to Gum and I'll introduce you to a few people."

Dewey moves among the party-goers, slapping backs, shaking hands, making room for me, until we're in front of Gum and the line-up of bodies on the bar stools.

"Cheers, Gumboot," I yell. He must have his hearing aid

on. He looks my way and raises a shot glass. I hope he won't croak out an insult about my hair again, or how my eyesore of a building is wrecking his scenery.

"Molly, this is Laine," Dewey says.

The woman utters her strange, piercing laugh and says, "Hi, Molly." She swishes her long sixties-style hair from side to side. I notice it's the color of the aged pine paneling on the walls, without any gray hairs. "Great party," she says to Dewey.

This woman shot the moose? I had assumed when I heard the name Laine, the hunter was a man. She's short and petite, not much bigger than a gun herself.

"Molly moved up here to Snowshoe not too long ago," Dewey says to Laine. "Gum's new neighbor."

"Can't imagine living next door to the old relic, myself," Laine says, "but right now he's kind of fun. People keep buying him drinks. I'm standing nearby to catch him if he falls off the bar, and he scores a free drink for me every now and then. Stick around, Molly. You might get lucky." She winks at Dewey.

"If you ladies will excuse me," Dewey says. "I'd better get back to work behind the bar."

"So, Molly, what got into you, moving up here? I live out by the highway, myself."

"It's quiet," I tell her. "I like the creek and the old buildings."

"Well, this little town is certainly unique. And people sometimes call Snowshoe a ghost town. They should see the place tonight."

"Do you come up the canyon often, Laine?"

"Used to come up quite a lot," she says, glancing toward the bar where Dewey is serving drinks.

Gumboot raises his croaking voice, addressing no one in

particular. "One of my first jobs in Snowshoe was cutting trees. Needed lots of wood around here for flumes, cabins and sheds, firewood and so on. Stayed in a camp for a while up in the hills. The cook put raisins in everything to cut down on complaints about flies in the food."

"I'll bet I've heard that story a hundred times," Laine says. "He knows about everything that ever happened up here worth knowing. And probably lots else."

"I'd like to ask him a few questions about one of my buildings," I say, "but I hardly ever see him, even though we're neighbors. And when I do he's prickly like an old porcupine."

"He's all crust on the outside, soft on the inside," she says. "Like a loaf of sourdough bread. You'll see."

"You seem to know a lot about Snowshoe, yourself," I say, sipping my beer.

"I do. Lived most of my life on the ranch out by the highway. Went to school with Dewey. We've dated off and on, when it's convenient. The day I shot the moose, we were hunting together. The moose just stood there, big and dumb as a barn door, and Dewey shot and missed the thing. Then it started running. So I shot it. I never told anybody what happened, but *he* made a big joke out of it. If I had thought Dewey missed the thing so I could shoot it, I would've had to shoot him, too."

Laine laughs her screeching hyena laugh. A tall man, also wearing a cowboy hat, hands her a drink. She hugs him, stands up on her tiptoes and kisses him on the neck. Hmmm. Laine had said she and Dewey dated *when it's convenient.* Why does this bother me? You'd think I was a teenager. I glance over at Dewey behind the bar. He winks at me. Such a sly fox.

"Chamomile lite," he says, reaching between two bodies

at the bar to offer me another beer. I gladly exchange my empty mug.

"Listen up, everyone," Dewey shouts. "In a few minutes we'll be cutting Gum's birthday cake."

Everyone cheers.

I'm ready to ask Laine about Ben, since she would have gone to school with him, too, not just Dewey, when the sound of a chainsaw tears through the smoky bar. Everyone stops talking and looks in the direction of the noise. Dewey stands ready to cut the cake with a small yellow chainsaw, the kind you use to limb trees. He stands sideways at the head end of the cake. With the chainsaw poised just above the front edge of white frosting, he dips the bar of the chainsaw into the cake and backs up, pulling the teeth of the saw through the cake. Bits of frosting fly. Good thing he's wearing a bar apron. He cuts the entire length of the cake, walks back to the front of the cake while revving the chainsaw, and cuts another long section of cake. A different kind of lumberjack contest. Laine begins her shrieking laughter again, and now everyone is laughing, wiping chunks of frosting off each other and eating it. I'm laughing and choking on my beer. I can't help it. Life is weirder and more fun than I could ever have imagined. The moose watches, and I could swear he winks at me.

After another couple minutes of spattered cake frosting, the chainsaw stops.

"Now," Dewey says, "we'll have a few words of wisdom from our guest of honor, then we'll eat some cake with our beer."

Two men, previously glued to their barstools, rise and lift Gumboot up off the bar. He rides proudly on their shoulders, grinning his toothless grin, through the cheering crowd to the cake where they set him down next to Dewey.

"The floor's all yours, Mr. Gumboot Charlie Doherty,

oldest living inhabitant of Snowshoe, Montana," Dewey shouts. "What do you have to say for yourself?"

Silence now. You can never tell what to expect from Gumboot. When I'm around him, I feel paranoid, or at least somewhat anxious. Maybe the others are accustomed to him.

"Glad you all made it," Gum says, in his wheezing, gravelly voice. "All you old faces, and a few new ones, too, like that boy over there just moved in next door to me." He points to me. I duck behind Laine, who shrieks, of course, drawing even more attention our way. A few others laugh, too, and then everyone hushes again and I come out from hiding. The men who hefted Gumboot and carried him over to the cake look me up and down. I suppose they're wondering if Gumboot knows something that they don't. "And thanks to Dewey for all the work he done to put this thing on. You're like a son to me, son." He pauses, swallows hard, and clears his throat again. "I don't have much to say. You all know I'm not much of a talker." More laughter. "I've lived ninety-two years now, most of them right here in Snowshoe. Some of them years was better than others, but I can tell you this much. Ain't no place I'd rather spent them years."

Cheering, stomping, whistles.

"Blow out the candle, Gum, before it burns the place down," Dewey yells. "And don't forget to make a wish."

Gumboot turns, puffs himself up, leans over the cake and blows out the firewood-sized candle.

He turns. "I wished for . . ." He pauses, clears his throat. "Let's do this again when I turn one hundred."

More cheering, stomping, whistles.

Then the jukebox plays while everyone eats a perfectly square piece of cake from a tiny paper plate. As deftly as Dewey cut the cake on its four-by-eight sheet of plywood, I chew on a piece of wood for quite a while before it's soft enough to swallow.

The jukebox plays *Lonely Women Make Good Lovers*. A few people begin to dance, pretty much in place in the crowded room. Laine disappears into the crowd. She finds the cowboy who brought her a drink earlier and cuddles up to him. Instead of standing alone, I begin to swim my way through the crowd so I can hide out next to Dutch, but Dewey intercepts me and extends his arms for a dance.

"Only if you take off that apron," I say.

He smiles, or at least his mustache moves up at the corners, as he removes the apron and flings it behind the bar. We dance like an old married couple, not talking, our chests plastered together, his mustache tickling my cheek, and in my hair. Two steps to the right, little steps because the room is so crowded, then one step back.

"I'm having a wonderful time, Dewey. You did a good job with the party."

"Old Gum won't be around forever," he says.

"I only wish he wouldn't make a spectacle out of me and my hair."

"He'd ignore you completely, if he didn't like you. Count on it."

"With friends like that . . ."

"Humor him," he says, moving his hand up and down my back a little, warmly, gently. Then he touches my hair. "I'll humor you, when you're ninety-two. And admit it. You're flattered when he calls you a boy."

Who can argue with that? I rest my head on his shoulder, happy to be here moving to the beat of the music, a strong chest, warm as a wood stove, on mine. I can almost feel his heartbeat, or maybe I can.

Dewey dances me toward the moose head, weaving in and

out around the other couples. "Gotta deliver a few drinks. Don't go away."

While I wait underneath Dutch's blank stare, I wish I had something to do with my hands, like hold a mug. But I misplaced my beer somewhere. If I smoked, of course, I'd have that to do, but the bar is already smoky enough. Glancing up at Dutch, I see a chunk of white frosting clinging to his dewlap. Now that I have a mission, I move toward the bar, slow swimming strokes, to retrieve a bar towel. I return and wipe the moose's fur clean.

"Hey, lady. Give me that thing," Dewey says, grabbing the towel and flinging it over several heads into the sink behind the bar.

Lost in the Fifties plays on the jukebox. Dewey must like this one. He whisks me away from my station near Dutch and we dance, my head on his shoulder again, my eyes closed. I sigh, lost and found again.

"I'd like to show you my tepee," he whispers. "It's a short walk up the hill. We'll come right back."

"Why not?" I say. What's one more curious event on a night filled with small adventures?

Dewey grabs a flashlight from behind the bar and we slip out the back door, holding hands, laughing. We walk past the covered hot springs pool, now uninhabited, past stacks of firewood, and up a rocky path through the lodgepole pines. We do not talk as we grope along in the muggy night air, following the beam of light moving along the trail ahead of us. Clouds hide the stars. A white tepee looms in front of us and Dewey throws back a door flap.

"Duck your head," he whispers.

I crouch down and enter the amazing structure, then stand up. The tepee has a canvas floor. He takes off his shoes; I kick off my sandals. An odd thought occurs to me. I haven't taken my shoes off when entering a house since I left Bradley. Dewey flashes the light around the single room. I see all the basics: a dresser, a picnic table with kitchen items on it, the radiators he said he rigged up to heat the place, and a full-size bed down on the ground. Looks like a step-up from camping. Seems to have most everything a person needs, even a few plush accents.

"Are those real furs on the bed?"

"As real as I could find," Dewey replies. "Feels the same. Come on, I'll show you."

I know I shouldn't go anywhere near the bed. I don't even want to, yet when Dewey takes my hand and leads me, I follow along like a puppy. There's something intriguing about a bed with furs on this night of beer and laughter, chainsaw sounds and cake, music and dancing close. When I walk toward the bed with Dewey, I feel like I'm floating. Maybe this isn't real. Maybe this is one of my dreams. Dewey sits down on the end of the bed. He pulls my hand. My knees give way as I sink down next to him. My hand touches the fur covering the bed. An arm, strong and reassuring yet tense, encircles me. A hand strokes my hair, my short hair like a boy's, like the hair on a person with no gender. But right now I have a gender. I feel my gender all over me, as Dewey brushes his mustache against my nose and lips, and brings his lips to mine and kisses me more tenderly than I have ever been kissed. I am kissing him back, and back, and, as Dewey brings us slowly down onto the bed the soft, plush fur bestows the feeling that what we're doing is necessary, natural, unavoidable. His hands caress my face with strokes light as butterfly wings, then a hand slips downward along the skin of my neck and, at last, to my breasts. I arch my back as he unbuttons my silk shirt, kisses my bare skin below my neck and pulls my bra down to cup a breast. His hand stops moving.

Time stops. I hear only breathing. What is happening?

"Nice tits for a woman your age," he says.

"Oh!" I growl, my face on fire. I jerk upright, adjust my bra, pull my shirt together in front and, flailing my arms, manage to stand up from my position so near the floor. "You are an animal! What a stupid thing to say. I can't believe what a fool I was, coming up here with you."

"Christ, I'm sorry. I meant it as a compliment."

I can't find the cave entrance, but I stumble forward in the dark until I bump into canvas. I scratch and claw at the wall until I locate the entrance flap, then grope around for my sandals. I can't find them, but I am so angry I don't care. I charge out into black night, blacker than inside the tepee, and stop, barely able to distinguish a dim half-light where the trees are farther apart, where the trail must lead down the hill.

Staggering barefoot over the dirt and rocks and roots on the trail, crying, I stumble toward the shrieking laughter in the bar. I trip and fall down, hard, on both knees. I scramble upright.

"Ow. Son-of-a-bitch. Stupid fool. Ow."

Close to the building I feel for the stacks of firewood and find them, adding splinters to my growing list of injuries. I move around the south side of the building. The German shepherd barks at me. I ignore him, then sob, "It's okay, doggie. Everything is fucking wonderful." I limp home to my cabin along the gravel road. I know the way now in the dark. The bottoms of my feet are cut and bleeding, I'm sure, and I still don't care. I want to reach my own front door, a door I can enter without crouching down like an animal.

On the cabin porch I step in some fresh chicken shit. When I push open the door of the cabin, I flip on the lights and Chug stands waiting for me. I crouch down next to her. She licks my face. I know she's worried, and I hug her as if

I've betrayed her honor along with my own. She follows me around the cabin, leaning against me while I run cold water into the wash pan. When I sit down to wash my filthy, bleeding feet she licks them before I can smear on the triple antibiotic and slip into clean white socks.

At last I'm in my pajamas, safely in my bed up under the roof of my cabin. Chug lies in front of the door. Big Al purrs on my chest. I pet his fur, soft as the fur on Dewey's bed. I've never felt more humiliated in my life. At the same time, I'm confused by my reaction to Dewey's remark. Tears stream down my face. My wrenching, howling sobs hurt my chest and back where the moose stepped on me.

Thunder rumbles in the distance. Lightning sets the cabin aglow for a second, and heavy raindrops begin to pound my rusty tin roof. And then I remember the note Ben left me: *Where there is ruin, there is hope for a treasure.*

CHAPTER 12

Surrounded by black, moonless night, I stand in front of the brothel. My eyes follow a beam of light slanting down from a window to its resting place on the ground in the roadway. Piano music, lively and rollicking, floats toward me and drifts over my head as I step into the light, a bright square lying prone. Men's voices, women's laughter, a sudden shrieking laugh. I am not part of the events happening indoors. I do not open the pale yellow door with its black shiny doorknob. Instead, I crouch low and make my way around the building, through the dim glow from the curtained side windows. Near the creek, next to the cottonwood tree, I stand unseen where I can watch the rear entrance of the brothel. Maybe he's in there.

Chug's snuffling awakens me from my dream. When I peer through my puffy eyes down to where she stands at the cabin door, she's looking up at me, waiting. She wants out. My God, it's 11:00 in the morning. I groan. My head hurts.

"Wait a minute, Chuggie."

My cut and bruised feet hurt on each rung of the ladder as I climb down backwards. It's still raining outside. This complicates my expedition to the outhouse. Slipping on a pair of tennis shoes, I reach for a jacket to drape over my head. Agitated, Chug waits by the door.

"Okay, okay," I tell her. "Hold on."

The door scrapes its rasping noise on the cabin floor as I

open it, but stops half way. We can barely squeeze through the opening. The rain must have expanded the wood. A chicken squawks from behind the woodpile but doesn't flap off scared. Even chickens can learn. Once outside, Chug squats and I limp toward the toilet. The outhouse door, stuck open, faces the creek that is once again running bank full. On the cold toilet seat, I assume my favorite pose, that of *The Thinker*. Big Al jumps up onto the seat next to me and waits. Thoughts of last night flood my head. Too bad the event in Dewey's tepee wasn't just another one of my strange dreams.

Stupid. That's me. Trying to be alone, trying to be a neuter with my short hairdo in a place where I'm practically the only woman for miles. It's like moving to Alaska, or to some other place that attracts more men than women. And I buy a brothel to boot. Of course a man might find me interesting. After all, I might be *convenient*. And, of course, I'd be flattered at any attention I got and act like a bimbo. Of course. Well, it won't happen again.

Lost in my thoughts, I am startled when a large form appears in front of the open toilet door. I scream and grab at my pajama bottoms to cover my legs.

"Molly! Excuse me," Ben says as he turns and steps out of sight.

"Ben, you scared me half to death."

"I came over to check the walls on the building," he says from a few feet away, not far from the old boots hanging off the side of the outhouse. "I didn't know you were out here."

"What about the walls?" I ask, as if we're having another builder–client discussion, like there's nothing at all strange about this situation.

"The rain did what I hoped. The walls aren't perfect. You can still see a slight bow in the sides, but they're pulled together enough to put the . . ."

Chug's low threatening growl interrupts and I hear Ben's heavy footsteps running away.

"Yikes!" he yells as he runs.

I use the toilet paper as quickly as possible, pull up my pajamas, and run out to rescue Ben. He's peeking out of the brothel. Chug had chased him as far as the back entrance and stopped, but she's still growling and barking. When I grab Chug's collar, she immediately calms down.

"Sorry, Ben. If you'll give me about fifteen minutes I'll put Chug in her fence and get dressed. Then if you want to come to the cabin for coffee, we can talk about the building."

"Okay," he says, panting.

The cabin door is still stuck halfway open when Ben appears with a roll of plans in hand. He's almost too big to squeeze through the doorway.

"I'll have to take the door off and sand the bottom," he says.

"I'd appreciate that," I say. "What would you like in your coffee?"

"Black is fine, thanks."

"That's good news about the walls," I say, setting our coffee mugs on the windowsill near the table.

He seems uncertain as he approaches the table and scans the small room before he pulls up a chair. "Nothing like a little rain when you need it," he says, unrolling his sketches.

I had noticed his size, of course, but now I'm surprised at the amount of space he takes up in my cabin.

"Here's a view of the building with a new roof and the two skylights you wanted. I drew a deck off the back, thinking ahead a bit."

"Ben! I love it."

He looks at me without expression, then says, "I've kept the same roof pitch, but I drew a couple different truss designs." He rolls up the first sketch and sets it aside. "Since you want the underside of the roof and the rafters to be visible, I'll stain the wood a warm honey color and use black truss plates."

My God. The work on this place is going to cost a fortune. I hope the divorce is settled before the work is done so I can pay Ben and the lumberyard.

"Both designs look good," I say, "but I like this one best."

"Okay. I'll have the materials delivered as early as possible next week. Then we'll get started."

I never can tell what he's thinking, and there's that *we* again. "Oh," I say, "do you work with someone else?"

He looks at me, that deadpan look. "No. I prefer to work alone. If you want, though, you can help me some on Saturdays, that is if you know how to use a crowbar and a hammer."

"I can learn. I like to work with wood."

"Good. There's a lot to do if you want to move into the place before winter. We'll insulate the building. You'd freeze to death in this cabin. But things will be warm and tight in the brothel."

Ben blushes. At last, some expression of *feeling*. I can't help but smile. We reach for our coffee mugs, take a drink, and look out the window toward the top of Cinnamon Peak, shrouded now in a low cloud.

He clears his throat and speaks first. "It isn't the normal way to work on an old building. I don't usually start with the roof first, but it's what we have to do in this case. I'll leave the chain up for now to stabilize the walls. We can remove it after the second-floor joists are replaced."

"I know some people think saving the old brothel is a dumb idea," I say. "But I swear I can feel the building crying *Help Me,* as if I'm its last chance."

"You might be," Ben says. "And I think I understand. When I came across that poem last week, it seemed to be about your building even though Rumi wrote it centuries ago."

"Where there is ruin . . ." I say, lifting my mug toward Ben, who finally catches on.

He clinks my mug with his, and says, "There is hope for a treasure."

Ben grows serious. "Well, Molly. Looks like I'll be around here quite a bit. I'll fix that toilet door so I won't scare you any more, and I'll sand the bottom of your cabin door before I leave today." He rolls up his drawings, rises and pushes back his chair with his thick legs, all in one motion.

I'm so happy about my building I could hug him, but I restrain myself. "Ben. Thanks so much for taking on this project."

"You're welcome, Molly. I'm looking forward to finishing what I started."

"Say, before you leave, could you tell me what this big square is here on the floor? It almost looks like a trap door, the way the linoleum's been edged with metal, but I haven't tried to open it."

"It's just as well. Sometimes we find things under these old cabins that are better off left alone."

Ben sets his roll of drawings on the table and drops down on one knee to look at the cut in the linoleum floor. He rises, picks up the ladder and leans it against the wall. "Do you have a flat screwdriver?" he asks. I reach into a drawer in the counter and hand him the screwdriver I use to open my refrigerator. The trap door is about three feet square, and he pries up one side of it. "And a flashlight, too," he says.

He holds up the square of flooring with one hand, takes the flashlight I offer with the other, and flashes the light into a gaping black hole that's been dug under my cabin. "Around the turn of the century and before, miners dug a lot of these unfinished basements."

I squat near him to look into the eerie darkness, my bruised knees under my jeans reminding me of the black hole I fell into a few hours ago in Dewey's tepee. The opening below my floor is about six feet square and six feet deep. Ben illuminates the back of the hole, where the opening of a small tunnel heads off in the direction of the creek. Along one dirt wall are shelves draped with cobwebs and covered with a layer of dirt. The shelves are empty except for a couple of dirty quart jars with no lids.

"Sometimes the miners would go half crazy with cabin fever during the long winters, so they dug for gold under these cabins along the creek. Then they'd use the holes for storage. And without a bank in town, they sometimes hid their diggings under their cabins. A few years ago a guy in town found a skeleton hunched over a rusted shovel in his unfinished basement. No telling what you'd find if you spent some time down there."

"Whatever's down there can stay put," I say. "Let's put the trap door back in place."

My rickety old lawn chair shifts under me as I look up through the broken boards of the brothel's second floor into the blue sky. Ben tells me it's no longer safe for me to go upstairs, not that it was safe before. Now, with the roof gone, nothing much except the chain is holding the walls together.

What did the madam do, exactly, in this place? How did the building function as a brothel? Did the customers come in through the pale yellow door or did they enter through the back door? Did they knock first? This must have been a small operation, for a brothel. I've read about the long lines of miners waiting outside the houses of prostitution in Alaska during gold rush days. Were there ever lines of waiting men outside The Bluebird House?

In my dreams of the brothel, I'm always on the outside looking in, and I hear piano music and singing. I'd like to think men came to The Bluebird House for reasons other than the obvious ones. Did the girls also play cards with the men? If so, what kind? Poker? Double solitaire? Did the madam serve drinks? Would she have needed a liquor license? Did the downstairs have a carrying capacity, like restaurants and bars have today? There are only the three rooms upstairs—one each for the madam and two other girls, and their guests or customers or whatever they were called. Or did the madam live in the cabin? Did she work as a prostitute or just manage the business and play hostess?

I realize now that I've been a prostitute most of my adult life—living Bradley's life all those years, giving him the place of honor at the center of my activities. Now I realize what a good way that was to devalue my own life. Of course, by staying in a stale marriage, pretending everything was all right the way I did for so long with Bradley, I didn't have to find out what I wanted to do with myself. But then if Bradley and I were still together, I wouldn't have suffered that humiliation with Dewey.

And I think about Mom and Dwight, both such serious, righteous people, and how I always had to watch what I said around them. They did *save* people, after all. But there's that Technicolor picture, prominently displayed on the walls of my memory, of Dwight in their trailer with his bare butt up in the air, my mom's friend underneath him. When I saw them like that, I slammed the door shut and ran to a friend's house, confused and scared. It wasn't a pretty sight. Later, Dwight made me promise, with my hand on the Bible, that I'd never tell my mom or anyone else. And I didn't. If I recall, the day I caught Dwight in this compromising position was one of those warm spring Montana days where anything can happen, not that it excuses his behavior. Afterwards, he acted so ingratiating toward me that my high school years were far more comfortable and enjoyable than they would have been otherwise.

Yet I suppose this skeleton in the cupboard, this one quiet understanding between Dwight and me, could have been considered yet another form of prostitution.

CHAPTER 13

I'm holding my breath to better hear the faraway sound of flute music—the song of a thrush, tumbling from loud, high notes to softer, lower notes that sound even farther away. "Harmony in suspension," one of my bird books describes the song of this particular bird, and then: "of all the thrushes, this one's song most closely resembles Beethoven's *Moonlight Sonata.*" How magnificent it is out here inside the pungent aroma of resin from the lodgepole pines, listening to music, Darwin's music, while basking in the quiet.

Chug's red flannel tongue drips like a faucet this hot afternoon as we stand on a rutted old road up an unfamiliar gulch.

When I remove my baseball cap to fan my face, a movement up ahead in the trees catches my attention.

Zing! A gunshot. I throw my hat down, grab Chug's collar and dive behind a car-sized boulder. Bark chips rain down on my hair from the pine tree a few feet above us.

"Hello! Hello!" I shout. No reply. I peek around the boulder. From my view near the ground, I can now see part of a log wall, ninety to a hundred feet ahead, through the trunks of several lodgepole pines.

Another shot cracks the air. Shit. This is national forest land, public land. Why would someone shoot at us? Be my luck to run into another crazy Unabomber hiding out in the woods. If I had a white flag I'd raise it. My heart pounds. Chug hunkers against me, panting. A trickle of sweat rolls down between my breasts.

"Hello!" I yell again.

A small hunched figure emerges from the trees carrying a

rifle, the barrel pointing skyward.

"Gumboot! It's me."

I stand up and step around the boulder with my hands up. It's a joke, but soon I realize Gum doesn't know who I am. He brings his rifle down to aim it at me then abruptly drops the barrel. The old coot must be blind.

"Well, I'll be," he says. "It's you."

"Who'd you think I was, Calamity Jane? Good grief. You might have killed me."

Gumboot fiddles with his hearing aid.

"What?" he says, cupping his hand behind his ear.

"I said you might have killed me." I'm sweating even more profusely than when I huffed and panted my way up the steep trail.

"If I'd a wanted to kill you I sure as hell wouldn't have shot the treetops. I always aim high."

"Who'd you think I was?"

"Claim jumper."

"You have a claim up here?"

"Yup. Had it for years." His gravelly voice sounds like mine tailings rolling downhill. He amazes me. He can hardly see, hear, or walk, yet he works a claim up on the side of a mountain.

"Long as you're here, come on up for a beer."

Chug and I follow Gumboot up the rocky route through the trees. Chug walks next to Gum, who pats her head. I follow along on legs still shaky from fright. Off to the side of the cabin a black maw, an adit, opens into the heart of Cinnamon Peak. An ore cart, spilled over on its side not far from the adit entrance, lies with its axles and tiny wheels rusted and silent. Old ore cart tracks lead into the adit. Rusted buckets, coiled cables, shovels and pick axes litter the ground.

Gumboot stops to rest and sees me looking at the mining

relics. "All this old mining crap's gonna rust 'til it's gone. Hell, my bones is rusty."

The floor inside the cabin slants several degrees off level, almost as much as my porch roof. A cot lines one wall, on the downhill side. A table and two chairs occupy the other side of the room, and a lantern hangs from a nail overhead on a log rafter. A crude plank countertop holds one-gallon plastic jugs of water and coffee cans filled with rocks. Shelves underneath the counter offer cans of sardines and Western Family brand creamed corn, peas, and tomato soup. That's Gumboot, all right, a one-man Western family. I'm glad to see he eats vegetables. The window by the table looks out at the adit.

"Have a chair. Be right back," Gum says. He ambles out the open door in his slow motion gait, listing like a car with a flat tire, and disappears into the dark adit. I'm still staring at the hole in the mountain where he disappeared, when he steps back out into the sunlight holding two bottles of Coors. Dewey's favorite beer.

A minute later, sipping a tall cool one, I say, "Not a bad refrigerator."

"Yup."

"Gum, what are you digging for up here, if I may ask?"

"Aw, a little of everything: gold, silver, lead, zinc. I work up here ever summer, prove up on my claim to keep it going. Just a matter of time, 'fore I find a good vein." He pauses to fasten his rheumy eyes on me. "People don't usually come up here."

"Chug and I were just out for a Sunday hike and . . ."

"Only Dewey knows where I'm at. After I drive the jeep up, I drag logs and branches onto the road. When I leave I move 'em aside, drive through, stop and put 'em back across the road. Dewey comes up to help me work the claim every now and then."

"Who feeds your chickens while you're staying up here?" I ask.

"Them's scratch chickens, but you can toss 'em some grain once in a while. Lay bigger eggs that way." Gum studies me. He must know his chickens keep me in eggs.

"Sure. I can do that," I reply. "You know, I came out onto my porch earlier today and Chug was licking the head of one of your chickens. The chicken just sat there on her nest by the woodpile, shaking her head every now and then like she couldn't figure out what was getting it wet."

Gumboot laughs and slaps the table. When he catches his breath, he says, "You're all right, Molly."

My throat tightens, like a small hand grabbing me around the neck, the small hand in charge of my emotions. I hadn't realized how much I wanted old Gumboot to like me, and I'm not even sure why. Or maybe I'm still feeling weak and vulnerable from being shot at.

"Haven't seen you at the bar since the party," Gum says, now very serious. "It's Dewey, ain't it? That boy's like a son to me, but he never wins big with the ladies. He's always in trouble with 'em, or one of their husbands."

I don't say anything, just look out the window at the hole in the side of the mountain. What a fool. Dewey didn't seem like a ladies' man. What would I say to Gumboot, anyway, that Dewey said my tits are okay for someone so incredibly old?

"I thought so," he says, tilting his Jimmy Stewart hat.

I choke on my beer. Somehow the old geezer read my mind.

"That really rots my socks," he says. "You were a damn good audience. Hell, everyone else has heard my stories a dozen times, maybe more. Now who am I supposed to B.S.?"

I sigh, relieved that Gum isn't psychic after all. "Tell me a story now. I'm in no hurry."

Gumboot sips his beer, tunes his hearing aid, and sits up a little taller in his chair. I rearrange myself so I can sit with my right ankle on top of my left knee to brace my body against gravity and the slant of the chair, the same slant as the floor—downhill and to the north. Chug sprawls just outside the door, her tail and legs draped over the edges of the plank step, holding her in place.

"Well, there was lots of hardrock mining going on in all these adits, long before I arrived. A few men always worked placer claims in the creeks, too. Dewey's grandpa, Hermann, done it. I know from doing it myself that it was like having two jobs, one of them gambling. You just never could tell when you might strike it rich. Well, one day old Herm come down out of the hills off Try Again Creek a grinnin' like an idiot. He know'd he found something good, just didn't know what the hell it was. Odd shaped piece of rock, heavy, about as big as a bird's egg. Took it into town. Turned out to be a goddamn diamond. Pure diamond. 'Course it wasn't all polished and fauceted to catch the shine, like the ones you see on rings, but the thing was worth tens of thousands. Hell, a banker in Helena offered him fifty grand for it. Lots of money, them days. He wouldn't sell it, no sir. Thought it was worth way more 'n that. What a fool. Didn't have the thing two weeks before he got drunk and lost it gambling at the 'Shadow. And you know who to?"

Gum waits for me to speak, as if I might have been there.

"No, who?" I say.

"Ben's grandpa. They never got along, and there was hell to pay after that. What I heard is their fathers, that's Ben and Dewey's great grandfathers, come out here after the Civil War. Herm's dad was one of them Confederates, the other one was a Yankee. It was like that war followed them out West."

"What happened to the diamond?"

"Nobody knows," Gumboot says, looking sideways at me like he sometimes does, his eyelids half closed. I wonder now if this is because he spends summers on a slant. But his lips are also clamped shut in a way I've never seen before.

"What about Ben's grandpa?"

"Long story, Molly. And it's time for my afternoon nap."

"Now Gumboot, if I come back some time to see you, how will you know it's me coming up the hill?"

"We'll do it the same way as before," he says. "I'll shoot high."

CHAPTER 14

"Ben?"

"Up here," he yells. "I'm on my way down."

A big work boot, then another, descends the ladder, followed by legs as big around as my waist. A sweat-stained, red plaid shirt materializes and then Ben stands in front of me straddling two floor joists.

"Hi," he says.

"Ben, how did you get the trusses up to the roof all by yourself?" From the main road, I had noticed the trusses on top of my warped gray building—new lumber as shiny and out of place as someone wearing a white tuxedo to the Snowshadow Bar.

"Here, I'll show you."

I follow him outside.

"See this fixture on the front of my truck?" he asks. "It's called a block. A wire cable wraps around it and runs up over a temporary ridgepole on the roof. On the other end of the cable is a tackle, something like a pulley. When I was ready to hoist a truss, I just brought down the tackle, cinched a truss onto it, cranked her up, set the brake on the block, climbed the ladder, and released the truss onto the upstairs floor."

"But the old flooring won't support me," I say, "let alone a truss."

"Well, first I had to replace the floor beams and lay the subfloor up there. That's what took so long."

I shake my head, amazed at the feats he has pulled off alone in less than two weeks.

"I know what you're thinking, and you're right," he says. "Be easier with a helper. But I enjoy figuring out how to do these things alone, using a little physics."

"What's the next step?" I ask, hoping the garish new trusses will be covered right away.

"Two-inch thick tongue and groove decking, scheduled to arrive Monday. That'll take a few days to screw down, then I can cover the roof with building felt and install the insulation panels, then the roofing. Won't look so new and out of place after that."

"Sounds good," I say. "By the way, a friend from work is coming out tomorrow to help us. We'll work at whatever you give us to do. I thought you could use an extra pair of hands."

"Sure," Ben says, looking away.

"Come for breakfast with us, why don't you? He'll be here about eight."

"Thanks, anyway. I'll just eat at home."

Is it my imagination, or did I say something wrong? He seemed so pleased when I first arrived, now he's quiet and distant.

In the morning I cook an enormous veggie-cheese omelette in a cast-iron skillet on my wood stove while Gary drinks coffee and tells me about a blind date he had the night before that didn't turn out so hot.

"The guy wanted to get fresh on the first date, and kinky stuff, too. Wait 'til I get my hands on the friend who lined me up with this one."

"Well, you don't look easy to me," I say.

"Thanks," Gary says, "I knew I could count on you to say the right thing."

Chug and Big Al sit watching me cook. When they smell eggs cooking, they know I'll cook extra for them. Before Gary and I begin to eat, Al and Chug are eating their omelette snack out of their dishes on the floor. As I raise my fork to take my first bite, Chug finishes her omelette and approaches Al's dish.

Al spits in her face and raises a paw, claws ready. Chug sighs, circles around and around in front of the open door, sinks down with a deep sigh and watches the rest of us eat.

"Your carpenter's sure a big dude," Gary says, watching Ben out the window as he walks from his truck to the brothel.

"Don't you think he looks like Paul Bunyan?"

"Yeah," Gary says, still watching Ben.

"Gary, I'm quite sure he's straight."

"He made a pass at you yet?" Gary says, taking a bite.

"Of course not, but he did leave me an intriguing note one evening that said, 'Where there is ruin, there is hope for a treasure.' Anyway, Gary, I'm not interested. Besides, he's younger than I am. And I got my haircut so I can just be a person, not a gender." I haven't told Gary what happened with Dewey. That's my own little secret.

"Okay, okay," Gary says, patting the air in his *calm down* signal. "And I think you're doing a darn good job of not flaunting your gender. You haven't flirted with me once."

We laugh. We always laugh together. He's like the younger brother I never had, or maybe a little sister.

"And I think it was a good idea to start wearing that sports bra," he says. "Now it looks like you don't even have breasts under those tailored shirts. This alone should promote your gender-free agenda."

"Well, I certainly hope so." Nothing Gary says ever surprises me. If it did, I'd never let it show. But I do wonder how he knows so much about sports bras.

"Ben?" I call from inside the back door of the brothel.

"Up here," he yells back, as he usually does when he's "up there."

"What would you like us to do?"

Ben does not come down the ladder like he always does

when we talk. Instead he kneels by the stairwell on the second floor and I look up at him from the foot of the ladder. Gary stands nearby.

"Ben, this is my friend, Gary."

"Hello," Ben says, his voice a little chilly on this warm summer morning.

"Happy to meet you," Gary replies.

"If you want to remove the old boards from the walls downstairs," he says in a boss-like manner, "that would be a big help. You'll find some assorted crowbars in the back of my truck, and some hammers to remove the nails before you stack them out back. You'll both need leather gloves."

It would be so much easier to communicate if Ben would come downstairs, but he doesn't seem willing to do that. His behavior is different from normal, for some reason, not that I know him so well.

"I think we'll need a ladder to reach the tops of the boards," I say.

"In the back of the truck. It'll be easier if you bring in a sheet of plywood to lay over the floor joists so you have something to stand on. Just do what you can."

So, Gary and I do what we can, each with our own crowbar. After we dislodge a few boards from the inside walls, we carry them outdoors to remove their square nails.

"Aren't we the little worker bees?" Gary asks. "Six boards down, only about a hundred to go. At least they're one-by-eights, not narrower."

"Don't you just love this old brothel?"

"Umm, well." Gary stops removing nails to study the back of the two-story building. "I'd say it has potential."

"Good choice of words."

"Thanks," he says. "And the creek makes such nice background music. You can leave the windows open at night and be lulled to sleep. Of course, you'll have to watch out for non-paying customers trying to sneak in."

"Gary, you're a hopeless tease. I don't know why I have a thing to do with you."

"You know why, Molly. It's because I'm safe."

"Let's get back to work."

"I'll tell you what would improve the quality of the workplace for me," Gary says, "and that's if these old boards could talk."

"I've thought the same thing."

As I climb the six-foot ladder to wrench the top of a board away from the wall, we hear Ben overhead using a power tool on the trusses. Power tool noise, then a pause. Power tool noise, then a pause.

"The man is like a machine," Gary says. "What's he doing up there?"

"You know, he got those trusses up there all by himself. I don't know much about his personal life, or even where he lives, really, but he's an amazing carpenter."

By one o'clock Gary and I have muscled about half the boards off the walls, removed their rusty nails, and stacked the boards in a neat pile behind the building.

"I'm hungry, how about you, Gary?"

"Thought you'd never ask."

"Ben?" I yell up the stairwell.

"Up here."

"I'm going to fix some sandwiches. You want a couple?"

"Brought my lunch, thanks."

"Will you take a break and join us for lunch by the creek?"

"Sure, thanks," Ben says. I hear him place tools on the floor and then the tromp of his heavy footsteps. We both watch him climb down the aluminum ladder, and we watch as he steps onto the floor joists and turns toward us. It's the first time he's come near us today, and I think I smell bacon on his clothing.

"I'll meet you at the creek," Ben says, walking toward his truck. He reaches into the cab of his old gray pickup and grabs a black lunch pail, the kind that houses a thermos in the rounded lid, and heads toward the shade under the cottonwood tree. Inside her fence, Chug makes no move toward Ben. Maybe she's finally adjusting to his presence.

Gary and I walk over to the cabin, where we wash our hands in the wash pan, and I start to make tuna salad sandwiches.

"Smells like Ben had bacon and eggs for breakfast," Gary says, wielding the screwdriver to open the Kelvinator for a can of frozen lemonade.

"Grab the mayo while you're in there," I say. I do not want to talk about bacon right now.

As we approach Ben he does not look at us. He sits leaning against the cottonwood tree, sipping water from a jug and watching the creek. As soon as we drop to the ground to eat, Ben reaches into his lunch pail and grabs a sandwich.

"You from around here?" Gary asks.

"Never been more than a hundred miles any direction from Snowshoe. Got everything I need, right here." He makes a sweeping gesture with an arm that looks too heavy to sweep.

"Nice day for a picnic," I say.

"Weather's been real good for working outdoors, too," Ben replies. "Dry though. Now that the danger of a flood is behind us, we can worry about forest fires. We've had a few of them up here. All the shacks and businesses burned down in the early 1880s. By then the trees were mostly cut off the mountainsides for firewood and for building cabins, sheds and adits, but they piled the slash pretty high. I suspect your cabin was built right after that fire, the brothel 'long about the turn of the century."

"I just stopped worrying about flooding," I say. "I'm going to try not to worry about forest fires just yet."

Except for our chewing, we sit without making a sound as the creek murmurs past, now well below bank level. Sitting out here near a mining camp brothel with my gay friend and a carpenter who looks like Paul Bunyan, I'm overtaken with happy tiredness and contentment.

"What?" Gary says to me, noticing my expression.

Just then, a small dark bird flies along the creek and lands on a rock not far from us. The bird bobs up and down for a few seconds, then disappears into the water and stays there. We all watch the water where the bird went in.

"Did it drown?" Gary asks.

"Dipper bird, also called a water ouzel," I say. "It's walking around on the bottom, eating crustaceans and stuff."

"The ouzel is very special," Ben adds. "The Japanese Ainu people believed that if a man ate the still-warm heart of a water ouzel, he would become wise and fluent in speech."

"I didn't know that," I say. Ben is so full of surprises, so mysterious.

"Guess I'll head back up top," Ben says, not getting up. "Might finish fitting in the trusses today."

"And Gary and I should be able to remove all the boards from the walls downstairs. I can finish taking the nails out of them later. After sitting in the office all day it's real pleasant to work out here in the evenings."

"I could come out and help," Gary says.

Ben rises, walks to his truck, drops his lunch pail in the back, enters the brothel and heads up the ladder without another word. Gary looks at me. I shrug and shake my head at Ben's lack of social skills.

Back inside the brothel, Gary and I don our dust masks. We each pick up a crowbar and I climb onto the ladder to wrench the top of each board away from the two-by-fours. The boards come away, groaning and screeching as the nails pull out. Gary gains leverage behind the board from below, prying it away from the wall. Then he lifts the board aside, walks it out to the back yard, lays it on the ground and returns to remove another board. Every time we get six or eight boards off the wall we both go out back to our small stack of lumber to remove nails, tossing them into a coffee can. When we resume work indoors, Gary takes a turn on the ladder. The work goes faster near the windows, where the boards are shorter. Above us, Ben works his power tool magic.

As Gary and I work, we chat about the people at the lab.

Gary says, "Did you hear old Floyd at our team meeting about reinventing the way we do business?"

"No," I say. "I missed that meeting."

"You won't believe this, Molly, but he said, 'If anyone has any more visceral to get out, let's hear it.' "

"Sounds like something he'd say. What a character."

In this way, the afternoon passes and by the time the sun drops behind the mountain across the creek behind the brothel, we have just a few more long boards to remove on the north wall near the old stairwell.

Gary wrenches the last board away. "There's something here, Molly."

"Like what?"

"Don't know yet. Looks like an old newspaper. It's leaning against the wall on one of the horizontal two-by-fours."

I pry away the lower half of the board and we lift it away from the wall. Gary grabs the package and hands it down to me. I carefully untie a faded blue ribbon, then unfold the brittle wrapping of yellowed newspaper.

"It's a book without a title," I say. The stained leather cover is smooth and cool to my touch. Opening the book, I see handwriting. "I'm not sure," I say, "but the handwriting looks like German. I see dates here, and the first one is 1893." I leaf through the artifact in my hands until I come to a drawing. "And here's an old map of Snowshoe," I whisper. "Gary, this is someone's diary."

CHAPTER 15

I shift down as I approach a curve, hanging my jaw slack to keep my teeth from clattering against each other, while trying not to drool. A full-sized red pickup truck swerves toward me and shoots past, an arm waving out the window amidst the explosion of dust and gravel. The driver honks and waves, a driver with long pale hair, sitting short in the saddle. Could have been Laine. I wave back, too late. Maybe it was convenient for her to visit Dewey. It's been over two weeks since the grading of the road and Gumboot's party. That's way too long for this road to go without a grader, and too long for me to go without a soak in the hot springs.

The fact that the repugnant event with Dewey happened right after the most fun party I'd ever been to makes it worse by contradiction. Truth is, before I went with him up to his tepee, I had found him unpretentious and charming. Sure, we had our differences, but I felt comfortable with him, too comfortable. I'm disappointed in him. Mostly I'm disappointed in myself for being so weak, so naive. I almost wish I could believe that his remark had been a compliment. But I cannot.

At least I have other things to think about. Like the diary or journal. Too bad it's in German. I have yet to verify the name of the madam, but I want to believe the journal belonged to her. I was able to make out the name, Lempi Shunk, unmelodious as the name sounds. Part of me believes the contents of her journal are still private, but my curiosity is too great to honor that notion. What was her life like? If her life wasn't pretty, certainly it was at least interesting, unlike my own life before I moved to Snowshoe. The first journal entry is in 1893, the last in 1918, with almost every page of the journal filled, like a book. Certainly she spoke English, but she may have felt more comfortable writing in her native language. Of course, by writing her thoughts in German, she also may have felt she'd have more privacy. It's not exactly a message in a bottle, this diary hidden in the wall. And now *we* find it. When I think about the newspaper and magazine articles I found in the walls earlier in summer, about Darwin and music, about turning a hotel into a brothel and breaking all ten commandments in one night, I don't end up with much of a personality profile. Then, too, the madam may not have been the one who collected those articles and placed them in the walls. Maybe one of her *girls* did. Maybe they each had a hiding place of their own. Maybe one of the girls was planning to start her own brothel someday. Yes, if only the old boards could talk.

When I drive past the Snowshadow on my way home after work, I always look into the parking lot. I usually see Dewey's pickup. The German shepherd is often chewing on a bone, and I regret that Chug only got to gnaw steak bones from the Snowshadow for a short time. The week after the incident in Dewey's tepee, when I first stopped going to the resort, Chug looked so hopeful when I'd come home, so disappointed when I showed up empty-handed. That week Ben built her the little fence under one side of the cottonwood tree, and she still waited for those steak bones.

This evening after work, when I drive past the Snowshadow and look into the parking lot, Dewey is unloading cases of beer from the back of his truck onto a dolly, the kind you use to move home appliances. He stands up, looks my direction, and waves, looking at me as hopefully as a dog expecting a steak bone. But I look away from him toward the road ahead and Cinnamon Peak. He has nerve.

When I turn onto the lane that leads back along the creek to my place, I stop my truck, for I am met with a new insult. One entire side of the brothel's roof sports bleached blond decking. My aging old Hemingway character, with its elegant, sun scorched patina, now wears a hat like a contrary and contentious old busybody. At least the original roof, in its weather-beaten condition, looked like it belonged on the building, like it fit in, here in this town. Now I'm embarrassed for my brothel.

I pull in next to Ben's truck. The sound of the power tool, drilling in screws, buzzes and stops, buzzes and stops, as I climb out of my pickup.

Inside the back door of the brothel, I wait for a break in the power tool sound before I yell, "Ben?"

"Up here."

He lays down the drill and hovers over the opening where the ladder goes up to the second floor.

"You covered a lot of roof today. Wow."

"Sticks out like a sore thumb, doesn't it? Saw you stop out by the main road to look at it."

"The new wood looks so rude next to all the other old boards. Can I come up?"

"Absolutely. I'll hold the ladder."

I climb up the ladder and step onto the new upstairs subfloor. With all the partitions removed, the space is entirely open and seems much larger.

"Everything looks so different. I love it, from the inside."

"I think you'll like the look of the new lumber on the ceiling, after we stain it. Tomorrow I'll frame in the two skylights, then heap some more insult onto the old girl. The sooner I lay all the decking, the sooner I can cover it up with the metal roofing. Then she can resume her historic look."

The man's amazing. He can do improbable feats of carpentry yet talk like a prose artist. I say, "I can't wait to see the new roof."

"Is Gary your boyfriend?" Ben asks abruptly, looking at me intently.

"Oh my goodness, no," I say. "We work together and we're friends." I think I won't tell Ben that Gary is gay, or that Gary was making eyes at him. But now when I look at Ben, I blush. I wonder if he's jealous. The thought had not occurred to me until this second.

I clear my throat. "Do you know if the diary we found yesterday might have belonged to the madam who ran this brothel? Did you ever hear her name?"

"You know," Ben says, "I never heard any of the girls' names, or the madam's either. Prostitution was never discussed in our house. Sure heard a lot about mining and miners, though. Gumboot might know. And Dewey would have heard the names." Ben says this with slight sarcasm.

"Well, I don't stop at the Snowshadow any more so I can't ask Dewey."

Now it's Ben's turn to shake his head, only he adds a sigh to his gesture. Even though he never goes anywhere near the Snowshadow, I'm sure he knew I'd been stopping there to soak and shower. Apparently, he didn't realize I no longer frequented the place. This is good. The birds don't tell him *everything* after all. I suppose he can guess that I had some kind of run-in with his old enemy, Dewey.

"In the summer I use a solar shower, two of them: one to wash, one to rinse," Ben says. "I can rig you up a shower stall out back next to the old blacksmith shop, if you want. If you don't mind primitive, it works great."

"Thanks. I'd like that very much. I can shower at work, but that's not always convenient. And a shower on the weekends would be lovely."

The next evening after work I drive up to my cabin and park, all the while trying not to look at the gaudy decking on the roof for fear of becoming blinded by the glare. Ben is gone, but I can see that he's built a shower stall over near the creek. I walk to Chug's fence to greet her and let her out, and we inspect the newest structure in Snowshoe. The stall is about the size and configuration of an outhouse, except it has no roof. Ben has built the four walls, or rather, the three walls and the door, using some of the old boards Gary and I removed from the interior of the brothel. The panels start about a foot above the ground and reach to the top of my shoulders. On the ground, a panel to stand on with sanded boards spaced about a quarter of an inch apart for water to drain away. Two coat hooks just outside the door will allow me to hang my towel and clothes where they'll stay dry. He's built a small shelf for shampoo and soap. And suspended from the limb of the cottonwood tree overhead is a black solar shower bag, filled with warm water. A miracle. A thoughtful miracle.

After eating my evening salad and going for a walk with Chug on the old railroad bed, I shower under a ceiling of cottonwood leaves fluttering in the canyon breezes.

CHAPTER 16

This time I wave a stick with a white handkerchief tied onto the end of it as I wait for the shooting to start. I'm quite sure Gum wouldn't shoot to kill me or anyone on purpose, but in his infirmity, he might do it accidentally. Dead is dead.

"Gumboot!" I yell from the safety of the huge boulder by the road. He probably doesn't even have his hearing aid turned on.

"Gum!" I yell again, waving my white flag. And then I wonder, does anyone ever call him just Charlie any more, or Charles?

Crack! One shot, high into the tree above us, causes a small branch wearing a pinecone to drop on the ground near me.

"That you, Molly?" his raspy voice croaks.

I stand up then, waving the stick with the white flag.

"Yes, Gum. It's me."

"Good to see you, girl. Come on up."

At least he's calling me *girl* now, not *boy*. I follow along as Gumboot takes a few steps up the trail to his cabin, then pauses. Chug moves into position beside him, and Gum leans against Chug, his hand on his head, as they make their way up the hill together. I've never seen Chug act like that, like a Saint Bernard on a lifesaving mission. Gum looks tired, a little unsteady. A person would expect this behavior of someone as old as ninety-two, except he's usually so full of spirit. Maybe I woke him from his nap.

I enter the cabin and sit at the table to watch Gum on his somnambulant trek to the adit for our beers. The cabin looks the same inside as it did last time, its contents slanting downhill, the place dusty but otherwise tidy. Flies buzz against the inside of the windows and overhead, around and around the kerosene lantern, even though it isn't lit. Another hot, dry July day. I don't make a habit of drinking beer in the middle of the day, but this social lubricant seems to be an important part of Gumboot's repertoire.

"Whew," Gum says, setting the beers on the table and lowering himself onto his chair. "Heat takes it outta me, that and being as old as some of these rocks up here."

"Finding anything good?" I ask, twisting the cap off my non-lite beer.

"Molly, I see no one has taken the time to tell you the rules about mining. Never, never ask a miner if he's found what he's looking for. He usually hasn't, and it makes him cranky. If he has, he sure as hell ain't telling nobody. If he did tell, he'd have to spend all his time shooting, none finding."

"Sorry I asked. It's none of my business, I . . ."

"Answer is, no I haven't, and I realize if I don't find it pretty damn soon I never will. And the whole sorry empty possibility of that really pisses me off."

"You must have a good reason to believe there's something up here to find."

"Oh, it's here. Millions of years ago, right here in these mountains, a big bulge of granite pushed itself up, and all around the edge of it the heat made gems and minerals. Least that's what some geologist at the bar told me. Called it the Boulder Batholith, some damn thing like that. Something caused it all. Hell, even diamonds like old Herm found."

"What do you dig with to find a vein, or is this another trade secret?"

"That there's the problem. Me and my pickaxe just ain't enough. Need some bigger thunder. Thought you might be Dewey, when you showed up. He promised to come up today with some dynamite, help me out."

Oh, God. Now I have to worry about running into Dewey up here, too. I say, "I hope you find something good soon, I really do."

We each nurse on our bottles. Gum is quiet, so I take my chances.

"Gumboot, do you know if the madam who ran the brothel on my place was German?"

Gum clears his throat and sits up a little taller, as he always does when he begins a story.

"I weren't exactly of age to find out first hand who or what was in that brothel, when I moved to Snowshoe in '16, but I did hear she was German. Had two, sometimes three girls there. Heard she had one of the nicer places, for what it was. Kept to herself, kinda off to the side of town back there along the creek. Even had the groceries and booze delivered. Cut down on the insults, I suppose, from folks in town who didn't think much of her and the girls, but then Snowshoe had every brand of service, them days. The madam had one of them early cars and went into Helena pretty often, 'cept in winter. By the time I was thinking I'd go over to The Bluebird House for a visit myself, the madam up and died and the brothel closed down for good. Last place of its kind in town, too."

Of course, I can't tell Gumboot I'm curious about what went on at the brothel, and I'll bet he'd know. He probably visited more than one brothel in Helena after the Bluebird House shut down.

"Heard tell she wasn't all that good looking," he continues, "but she was honest and generous."

Of course, I'd have to buy a brothel once run by that Old West cliche, the good-hearted madam. What a place Snowshoe must have been. When I think about it, the faded old town still packs quite a wallop. I taste my beer, trying to think what to ask him next. Gum takes another drink, too, and then I hear a sound, different from the flies buzzing against the windowpanes.

"Do you hear that?" I ask, walking to the cabin door to listen, away from the flies and Gum's wheezing breaths.

"Don't hear a thing," Gum says, fussing with his hearing aid.

I finally make out the noise. "It's a vehicle, coming up the hill toward us."

"Must be Dewey with the dynamite," Gum says, leaping up from his chair, suddenly chipper.

"Gumboot, I have to be going."

Chug and I don't wait for a proper goodbye but tear off down the mountain in the opposite direction of the engine grinding its way uphill toward Gum's cabin. I will avoid Dewey at any cost. If I lose my way, I'll just find a creek and follow it downhill to the main road. What I've discovered since the night of Gumboot's party is that if you're mad at someone in a town of only thirty-some residents, it can feel as if you're being stalked.

CHAPTER 17

Only two people answer my ad in the *Independent Record.* I decide against one prospective translator of the journal, a nun at one of the Catholic churches. The other person, a retired schoolteacher who had lived and taught in Germany for many years, sounded like a more promising candidate. I meet her after work one day at her home. She has both a proper, kindly manner and blue hair in tight little pincurls. In the end, I determine that the little blue-haired lady will not be the one to translate the madam's journal. I don't know what's in the journal, but I don't want Lempi Shunk's life to be judged and I don't want anyone to go into shock from reading whatever she wrote.

But I'm obsessed with finding someone to translate the journal. What was my brothel's former tenant like? What is the history of my building? Two weeks after the ad starts I receive a call at work. A scientist who had done cancer research for twenty years in Berlin before retiring to Montana calls from his small ranch south of Helena. He agrees to drive into town to meet me at a coffee shop after work.

When we meet he seems down to earth and friendly, and I'm comfortable enough with him after a half-hour to show him the journal. He reaches for it and opens the first pages, his movements deliberate.

"Mmmm, this journal was begun when the writer still lived in Germany. Looks like Essen, not far from the Rhine."

"Mr. Everett, I bought an old building in Snowshoe that I'm having renovated. We found this in the wall."

He continues to leaf through the old journal, then stops,

absorbed in a passage. I wait for his reply, but he seems to have forgotten all about me.

"Mr. Everett?"

"Uh . . . Yes. I've been looking for a project to use my German. I haven't met anyone else here yet who speaks the language, and this does look interesting. I would like to do the translation."

Maybe I should introduce him to the nun and the little blue-haired lady. "How long do you think it will take?" I ask.

"My ranch keeps me fairly busy in the summer, but I can set aside time in the evenings. Realistically, it could take me a month or two, maybe longer. German is constructed quite differently from English, as you probably know, so each sentence takes a little thought and time to translate. And I want to capture the spirit of the diarist. I don't want to change any nuance of feeling she might have meant by her words. Also, since she wrote this in German, she probably never learned to speak English with all its idioms, although I can't be sure of that. I would try to keep the writing as authentically hers as possible. My point is, the process can take a bit of time."

"I want you to do the translation," I say. "If you like, I can give you an advance for doing the work."

"Oh, that won't be necessary. The money isn't important. I miss many things about Germany, and this gives me an opportunity to use the language. I can see that this journal is valuable to you, so I'd recommend you have it copied. I'd be more comfortable working with a good copy than with the original."

"I can have it made tomorrow. If you tell me where you live I'll deliver it."

"That won't be necessary. I drive into town most days anyway. I can meet you here again at 4:15, if that works for you."

"Four-thirty would be better. That will give me time to pick up the copy. Mr. Everett, there's something you should know."

"Yes?"

"I have reason to believe the writer was a madam. You see, my old building was once a brothel. I don't know what you'll find in the journal. In fact, if you think you might be offended by the contents, I would prefer you not translate it."

"My dear, I think the madam and I will get along quite well. And I'll consider the material confidential."

As I turn off the highway onto The Snowshoe Trail, I see Laine out near the road at the edge of her fenceline, standing next to an old horse. She flags me down.

"Hello," I holler out my window as I pull over and park. I cross the road to the fence.

In the slanting August sunshine, the horse's coat shines so black it looks dark blue, on a frame as swayback and sprung as one of Snowshoe's junkyard cars. Her drooping eyes stare up at me, or past me, from a head sagging close to the weeds in the pasture.

Laine watches me approach. "I'm afraid old Pepper's days of showing and winning are a dim blur," she says. "I keep her around for decoration and for kids when they come for a ride. She's real gentle."

I do not tell Laine about the madam's journal. The only thing we have in common is Dewey, and I'm not about to talk to her about that S.O.B.

"Nice, shiny coat," I say. "Looks like she's had a good life."

"We've spent a lot of time together the last twenty-some years. Riding in rings, showing off. I used to take her to ride with a group of women friends . . . we call ourselves the

Saddle Bags. One year we met in New Mexico. And Pepper traveled with me on the Centennial Cattle Drive in '89. She loved it as much as I did—the other people and their horses, the wagons, the dust, the miles, the scenery. Felt like we were making history, not just celebrating it." Laine sighs and hugs Pepper's neck. "It was incredible being part of Montana's twelfth largest community, and every day we packed up and moved. Felt like I was inside a Charlie Russell painting."

"It sounds wonderful. I realize this is an odd confession, being from Montana, but I've never ridden a horse before. Not that many opportunities came along, and for some reason my grandparents had a few cows but didn't keep any horses."

"Why don't you come with me on a short ride? I'll trailer a couple horses up the canyon. There's a special place close to the divide I think you'd like. I try to ride up there every fall when the aspens turn. How about Sunday? You can ride Pepper. She'd enjoy it."

Boy, Laine really bolts when an idea hits her. She's a little too fast for me. "Can I let you know? I might have to do some work around my place. You know Ben is working on the two-story, trying to put it all together so I can move in by winter. There's a lot to do yet."

"You and Ben managing okay?" Laine asks, studying me.

"He's been pleasant enough, and he's an amazing carpenter."

"Quiet one in school," Laine says. "He did put a tack on my chair once in the sixth grade and I kicked him in the shins for it. The boys were such brats that year. Not sure he ever spoke to me again. Guess I scared him."

"Do you think he could have killed someone?"

"You know, I really don't think so. But, hell, I'm a better judge of horses than men." Laine spits a dark streak onto the dry stubble near our feet. "Speaking of men—haven't seen you at the 'Shadow for weeks. Place needs more women. Don't tell me Dewey got to you. There's something almost irresistible about him, but sometimes I swear, he has his head up his butt. Come on. Tell me what he did."

Maybe it's that she cusses and speaks her mind so freely and I've had so much trouble doing that myself. Maybe it's because she chews tobacco and spits, but whatever the reason, before I know what I'm doing I'm blurting it out.

"Said my tits were okay for a woman my age."

I look away, embarrassed that I told anyone. Laine begins her shrieking hyena laugh. She doubles over. Pepper's ears prick up. She turns her drooping head toward Laine and stares up at her in what looks like disbelief. Pepper must be accustomed to Laine's Hitchcock movie laugh by now, after twenty-some years.

"Honey," Laine blurts out, laughing and choking, "that's no reason to get your tits in a wringer!"

I hate her for laughing at me. But the thing is, it's funny, now that I think about it, and Laine and Pepper are even funnier. Next thing you know I'm laughing, too—laughing hysterically, loudly, convulsively, from the pit of my stomach. In the unhurried way of a tired old horse, Pepper turns her head and stares at me. Laine and I look at each other. Some dark bits of chew are clinging to her chin and all her teeth are revealed to me as we laugh and shriek together so hard I struggle to keep from falling to the ground.

"I've got some advice . . ." she says between convulsive bleats, ". . . and I'd encourage you to follow it. Just pretend nothing fuckin' happened. Stop in at the Snowshadow. If you don't, you'll hate yourself, 'cuz the hot springs this winter might be the only thing that saves you. Pretending nothing happened? It's a way of life. Hell, it's worked since Lewis and

Clark wandered across the state. Try it. You'll see."

"I'll think about it," I say, wiping away my tears.

"Sunday for a ride?" Laine asks.

"I'll have to let you know."

Pepper and Laine watch me wander back across the road to my truck and, with one last wave at Laine, I climb in. I can't stop grinning as I head out on The Snowshoe Trail toward home, to my little log cabin on the creek.

CHAPTER 18

"Well, what do you think about your new roof?" Ben asks, meeting me at my truck as soon as I pull into the yard after work.

"I love it. That's the way a roof should look—a color that's only one step ahead of the rust. What are we doing next?" I'm in the habit of saying *we* now, too, even though I know Ben works alone.

"Concrete truck's scheduled for Monday morning. We'll pour a perimeter foundation to give the building a firm standing. While the concrete dries, I'll cut the beams to length. Should only take a few days to put down the new floor beams, insulate between them and lay the subfloor."

"Just imagine," I say. "Something solid to stand on."

"Then we'll put the ladder aside and build a stairway to the second floor. And on the walls, instead of two-by-fours every four feet we'll add in rough-cut timbers to bring them two foot on center. After that I'll insulate." Ben looks up toward Cinnamon Peak. "Could start snowing any minute."

"I can help you tomorrow."

"Good. I got the truss plates the other day. Designed them to strengthen the trusses and give your ceiling a finished look. Trouble is, right now they're raw steel. If you want, you can sand the edges, spray them with primer and then paint them black. We have everything you'll need."

"You show me how and I'll do it."

"Come on inside. You'll want to see where the foundation's going to be."

Inside, I'm faced with bare boards that now serve as the thin wall between the inside and outside, held together by the widely spaced two-by-fours. The ground is about a foot below the level of the old floor. The rotten wood is gone. Ben has built plywood forms inside the trench he's dug in the sandy soil underneath the four walls. I can't believe what a different place I'm standing in, after only six weeks. Ben has done so much in so little time, that it does seem as if he works with an invisible partner. Already the old brothel is more substantial, appears to stand a little taller.

"I sawed up the old floorboards into firewood for you. It's out back if you want to stack it some time."

"Why, thank you, Ben," I say, feeling guilty. He probably did all this while I drank tea on my coffee break this morning, joking with Gary and Myra.

"It's nothing. Couldn't see wasting it, and you'll need it this winter."

"How will you move the wet concrete from the truck to the trench?"

"Wheelbarrow," he says. "It'll all happen pretty fast."

"I'd like to help," I say.

"Won't happen for a few days, but we can arrange that."

The next morning Ben arrives and says to me, "Do you know what's in the log building behind your cabin?"

"Actually, I've always thought it was empty. And I don't have a key to the lock."

Ben grabs a large screwdriver out of his toolbox on the front porch. "Let's go take a look."

A rusty hinge on one side, a rusty hasp and lock on the other side are all that hold the double wood doors together, doors wide enough for a vehicle to drive into the building. Ben unscrews the hasp and swings one door aside to the darkness inside.

"I'll get a flashlight," I offer, heading for the cabin.

When I return to the open door of the log building, Ben is

nowhere in sight. I shine the light around. Cobwebs drape from the items visible during my quick survey of the space: an old Monarch wood cookstove, a wooden ladder, a kitchen chair with three legs, gunnysacks filled with something lumpy. But no Ben.

"Ben?"

"Up here!" he answers in a low bogeyman voice.

I scream and run outside.

"I'm sorry," he yells. "I thought you'd know it was me."

I can't tell him that's the problem, that I'm none too sure he didn't stuff bacon in a guy's shirt and leave him for wild animals to eat. And anyway, I'm still a little jumpy since the moose incident, and the event with Dewey. Probably being shot at hasn't helped either. Strangely enough, though, I'm not so startled when Gumboot shoots his gun as I am by the sudden sound of a grouse flying up from the ground when I'm hiking, or even sometimes the start-up of mice chewing and scratching at night.

"No problem," I say. "I didn't notice this place had a loft. What's up there besides you?"

"Old wooden water pipes, used before the town got a water system. More old boards, too. Look. An old bicycle," Ben says, pointing to a corner on the ground floor, then leaping like a cat from the loft and landing on the floorboards near me with a heavy *thunk!* This, too, startles me.

The Model A of bicycles leans against the wall. It's rusty, like almost every other metal object in town. Next to it, folded to the floor and frosted with cobwebs, is a large collapsible baby buggy. The buggy's bassinet and hood material is cracked. The wheels, of course, are rusty.

Anything I might say would be obvious, like, "What an odd thing to find in a shed behind a brothel." We stand in silence, the flashlight illuminating the baby buggy, until I highlight the gunnysacks, four of them leaning against the wall in the corner.

"What do you suppose is in those?" I ask. "I'm sure not going to open them."

While I imagine the bones of old miners, Ben unties a cord at the top of one of the gunnysacks and holds it open. Pieces of coal. He says, "They must have used this sometimes instead of firewood."

Other treasures we come across include an old metal wheelbarrow. Ben grips the handles. Even with a bent wheel, he can still push the old relic.

"You can use this with the concrete," I say. I hope he knows I'm teasing.

"Don't think so." Ben seems preoccupied, says nothing. I guess Paul Bunyan doesn't have a sense of humor today.

Pickaxes and shovels lean against one wall, and a can of square nails sits on a single shelf.

"Over here," Ben says.

I flash the light in the general direction of his looming, shadowy form. He has found something good—two old sawhorses. "Now we can set you up properly," he says, grinning, like this is the highlight of the morning.

Soon I am standing in front of the sawhorses in the yard between the brothel and the cabin. I'm facing the alley and Gumboot's junky back yard. Gumboot can't be seen, but his chickens wander around scratching and pecking and leaving droppings. Right now, my guess is that one is laying an egg by the woodpile on my cabin porch.

The truss plates, three for each truss, are lined up on some boards resting on the two old sawhorses. Using a square steel wool pad, I'm sanding the edges of each plate smooth. This takes a lot of time. Ben is inside the brothel, building additional forms and placing them in the trench. Robins sing not far away, their songs sounding close, then farther away. I can tell they are flitting from the big cottonwood to the fir trees across the creek and back again. And I hear ravens—never any shortage of these black flapping characters—gossiping, scrapping, and cleaning up the neighborhood.

Now, at midday, the sun shines into the canyon, shedding light on my task. Doesn't look like it could snow any minute. What a perfect day to be working in long sleeves at a mindless and repetitive job outdoors—it's downright relaxing.

"Close your eyes," Ben commands, suddenly behind me. "Do exactly as I say, and you won't get hurt."

I freeze. Here it comes. I'm unable to speak or move. I should have known not to turn my back on him.

"Are your eyes closed?"

"Yes," I squeak.

"Don't be alarmed. You'll be all right."

Sure. I'm about to die, smelling of bacon. I don't even eat bacon.

"Now, I'm going to take hold of your arms and move you backwards. Just relax."

I do not relax. His big hands grab both my arms, just above my elbows, and pull me backwards until something cold and hard bumps the back of my legs, just at my knees. He sits me down in the rough palm of the old wheelbarrow.

"Okay. Lift up your legs and open your eyes," Ben says. "We're going for a ride."

Ben pushes the wheelbarrow at a fast walk, laughing as we head out to the alley. When we pass Gumboot's old truck filled with garbage, ravens protest and flap off up the canyon. I hold on as we turn the corner and roll past the rusted car bodies, their doors wide open. Ben picks up speed. No longer afraid, I begin to giggle like I did the time grandpa pushed me in a wheelbarrow on the ranch all those decades ago, when he pushed me faster and faster all the way to the mailbox. How can someone as big as Ben run so fast? The bent wheel and the sandy soil are all that keep us from flying, and when Ben stops running my upper body keeps going and I almost lose my grip. We've reached The Snowshoe Trail.

"Do that some more," I say, kicking my legs, embarrassed at my childish glee, yet unable to pretend any longer that I'm a grownup.

Ben turns our buggy around. With a low rumbling giggle welling up from deep in his chest, he trots me back to the singing birds, the truss plates, and the old brothel that sits waiting by the creek.

CHAPTER 19

"Just relax and move with the horse," Laine instructs.

Pepper and I plod along behind Laine on her young, prancing horse, past aspen leaves, some still lime green, others a golden yellow. Chug follows behind me. We zigzag uphill, often within spitting distance of a tiny trickle of stream. Otherwise, the woods are silent.

"Laine, what creek is this?"

"Lost Fork of Try Again. Joins the main Try Again, then flows into Cinnamon Creek and on past your buildings."

"In beautiful downtown Snowshoe," I add.

This is one of the creeks that gave miners a reason to be in Snowshoe and, after they had endured the long, cold winters, this is one of the creeks they feared would swell and flood their cabins in the spring.

Laine stops and dismounts. "Let's walk the rest of the way," she says. "From here on the ground is fragile."

I'm stiff from riding, and stand bow-legged, or is it bowl-legged, waiting for my joints to straighten out so I can stand upright.

"I'm not used to this."

"Stick with me. I'll have you barrel racing at the rodeo," Laine says as she drapes the horses' reins over the limb of a small aspen tree.

Once we start walking, my legs work fine, and although we're no longer following a trail, Laine seems to have a destination in mind. As usual, Chug and I walk around flattened places in the grass where animals have slept. Each time we do this Chug glances at the grass nest, then up at me, and I like to think she understands why we're making the detour. I'm glad to see that Laine also performs this small act of reverence.

We reach a clearing, a sloped grassy area no bigger than my back yard in Helena, the one I no longer maintain. Clumps of aspen trees skirt the perimeter of the ground in front of us, not like the lodgepole pine and fir forest we've been riding through the past hour. I stand mesmerized by the beauty of this lush, green glade, until icy water seeps into my boots. When I try to back up, my boots pull free with a loud sucking noise. I lurch forward, then back again, trying to regain my balance.

"Molly. Over here," Laine says, grabbing my arm and steering me toward higher ground. "We'll sit on these rocks."

"Must be the headwaters of the Lost Fork," I say, removing my boots and wringing out my socks. Chug licks my cold feet with her warm tongue before I can pull my socks back on.

"I love it here," Laine says. "The place is like a shrine to me. Every fall I make a pilgrimage up here to spend time with the aspens and honor the passage of time."

Sitting in the quiet, I think about collecting and storing peacefulness. The aspen leaves rustle their soft, soothing sound in the clear chill. Mixed with the divine, complex smell of decomposing leaves and their ancestors is the scent of licorice. I reach down to pick a few leaves from several tall, spindly plants.

"Wild licorice," Laine says. "I named my first horse after the plant."

We are quiet again. There's no need to speak but I am curious about other, more interesting, things and ask, "Were you ever married?"

"About twenty years ago," Laine says, "but only long enough to decide it wasn't for me. Found myself acting all passive, waiting for contentment to strike. Got to be a habit. I'd probably still be waiting, except one morning I woke up early and stood out on the porch, just staring at nothing, staring at everything. A red-tailed hawk circled above the rim of the hill, catching updrafts, swooping down. Right then I decided to cut the fence and leave. Moved back home to the family ranch and I've been there ever since. Don't misunderstand. I do love men—but on my own terms."

The aspen leaves continue their timid gestures. I know the petioles attached to the leaves are flat, and because of this special design, they catch the slightest air movement. "I don't know why I waited so long to leave my marriage," I say, more to myself and the aspen leaves than to Laine. "It's almost like it didn't occur to me."

"Maybe it wasn't time yet."

"Maybe. But when I think back to all those years, it's like seeing an old black and white movie. I'm living a prismacolor life now, in comparison."

"You're like this headwaters," Laine says. "You're just starting out."

"I guess so."

I listen now, listen for the sound of water seeping downhill under the ground, even though I know this isn't something a person can hear. At this place, this accident of geology, if it is an accident, water collects until it feels the pull of gravity and is released, constantly and generously. I'm none too sure about religion these days, but if there is a God, I'm feeling such a presence here in this glade.

A sighing, swaying of branches and treetops begins downhill and advances in our direction, gaining momentum, and moving uphill from one tree to the next. The aspen leaves begin to rattle as the burst of wind lifts Laine's long hair and flattens my short hair against my head. Yellow leaves shower down on us. Then it is tranquil again.

A gentle *thud* just downhill, the palest grunt, startles me. Out of the corner of my eye, in the trees at the edge of the clearing, I see a brown ear, an eye, then hear a sudden bounding away. Of course, deer would gather here to drink the water that pools in their tracks.

Tiny bits of snow begin to fall, like salt from a shaker.

Laine rises and we walk the short distance to our horses. We untie their reins and Laine mounts, and then, with some straining of muscles unaccustomed to such a stretch, I pull myself up into Pepper's saddle and turn toward the trail that leads downhill along the tiny creek.

Laine pauses, pulls up on her reins, and says, "There's something you should know, Molly." Her horse dances sideways and then makes a complete turn. "The man I married was Dewey."

CHAPTER 20

Ben looks up at me from the new plywood subfloor he's kneeling on in the far corner of the brothel.

"Must be nice to have a job where you can see so much progress at the end of the day," I say. "My job isn't like that, at least not lately."

"Wish I could see even more progress," he replies, rising. "Need to get you moved over here. Tomorrow we'll start building the stairs. Next week I'll install your storm windows downstairs, then clean up the old wood cookstove and move it over from the shed. And I'll find you an airtight wood stove, one with a fan. Your six cords of wood will be here by Saturday. That should keep you warm."

"Thanks. That's a lot to do. How can I help?"

"I hate to say this, Molly, but we're going to have to cut down that old cottonwood before winter."

"Ben, you know I don't want to lose that tree."

"Come with me. I want to show you something." Ben steps from one floor joist to the next and I follow him out the back door.

We stand at the edge of the creek and look at the old cottonwood tree, towering sixty feet or so in the air in its lean away from the creek, over the top of my building.

"The tree's old and hollow," he says. "And see where the creek has undermined the roots? If it survives the winter standing, it'll blow over in the spring for certain."

"It means giving up one more reason I bought the place," I say, resigning myself to this new loss. But any fool can see it. The tree has to come down. What can I do but shrug and nod my head to reality?

"I wouldn't ask you to help, but it's a matter of safety. And we'll need a third person. We could do it this Saturday."

"I'll ask Gary to come out again to help."

It's Ben's turn to shrug and nod his head.

First one of the lowest branches drops, then another—branches that robins, even mountain bluebirds, flew into and out of. This cottonwood is not only the tree in my dreams, but all those other cottonwoods along the Big Hole River, lined up like leafy green giants.

Next Ben ties ropes, like nooses, around the trunk of the tree. Gary and I stand across the creek, about twenty feet apart, each pulling on a rope to keep the leaning trunk from falling onto the brothel. Ben makes a final cut with the chain saw and his use of physics proves successful again. The tree falls clear of us onto the bank of the creek, severed and sweating like a defeated tyrannosaurus. In one final gasp, the tree gives off its pungent smell and I taste raw, wild mushrooms.

While Ben saws limbs off near the top of the tree, and Gary drags them over to our trucks, I kneel next to the fallen cottonwood. Touching its corrugated trunk, I peer over the edge of a deep crevice in the bark, my eyes following its dark gray walls, steep and rough, to the bottom of a canyon. I close my eyes and see smoke curling up from a stovepipe on an old two-story building next to a creek and a towering cottonwood tree.

"Shoo!" Ben yells.

From my position near the cottonwood corpse, I open my eyes to see Ben running toward the porch. A few seconds later Chug trots toward me from behind the brothel, looking over her shoulder as she slinks in my direction. Stopping in front of me, she watches me, her tongue waving like a red flag.

"Chug?"

Ben strides with great purpose in our direction. “Damn dog just straddled my toolbox and took a great big Saint Bernard leak!”

“Ben, that’s awful. I’m sorry,” I say. Chug lowers her head and stares at the ground. “I’ll wash the tools and your toolbox right away, and I’ll make sure I dry everything thoroughly.”

“Good,” Ben says. “If there’s one thing we don’t need any more of around here, it’s rust.”

When Ben extends his hand to help me to my feet and I reach back up toward him, Chug watches but doesn’t growl or charge toward Ben. She circles in place, lies down next to the fallen tree, and puts her head on her paws with an enormous sigh.

CHAPTER 21

The days are diminishing in length, now that it's mid-September. No more plaid patterns of shade and shadow on the winding Snowshoe Trail when I drive home from work. Only shade. I shift down and pass the spot where Dewey picked me up the day of the moose incident. Odd to see it now, with the divorce final as of today and the settlement check in my purse. The bronze-colored leaves on the red-osier dogwood bushes distinguish themselves from the fading yellow leaves on the aspens. The county hasn't graded the washboard road for weeks so, as usual, I relax my jaw as I drive. This should save on future dental work.

Nearing Snowshoe, I catch the fading light on top of Cinnamon Peak, and it occurs to me that it looks ordinary, even forlorn, until the sun rises or sets on it. A solid cover of white stuff now clings to all the mountaintops around town, yet Cinnamon Peak is the one peak that glows pastel. As I turn off the main road onto the lane that leads to my place, the lights beam yellow and warm from the brothel's downstairs front windows. Ben stands on the porch, watching me drive up. Now I can pay him the total amount of his last statement. At the end of each month he dutifully provides me with a handwritten invoice listing the work he's done and the cumulative amount I owe him.

I park, grab my bag and climb out of my truck.

"Moving day tomorrow," he says. "And just in time. Big snow predicted."

"Well, let's see what kind of place I'm moving into." Every evening I am surprised at the progress Ben has made during the day. Sometimes he's still here, sometimes not.

The yellow door stays open while Ben works, but this evening it is closed. He turns the black doorknob. “After you, madam.”

“Very funny, Ben.”

When I look around the room, I see that he has performed new miracles. “Hey, the sink cupboard and countertop look great.”

“The cupboard isn’t attached to the wall yet. That’ll have to wait until I hang the sheetrock. Shouldn’t collapse on you, unless you climb up on it.”

“I think I can handle that.”

“Found some good faucets at the building recycling place. You’re all hooked up to the town water system, just like at the cabin.”

“And how did you move the old wood cookstove over here alone?”

“Used a dolly. Oh, and meet your new airtight heater. It’s a good one. Should see you through the winter, that and your electric baseboard heat. Electric’s expensive, though, so I’d suggest you only use it for backup, when it’s forty below.”

“Forty below?”

“You didn’t know it got that cold up here? No one told you?”

I shake my head. It already feels forty below out, but it’s warm in my new old house with both the cook stove and the heater burning full blast.

Because fluorescent lighting sheds so much light, I had requested it, and Ben had recommended full-spectrum lights for Snowshoe’s dark winters. Now the reflection from the overhead lights bounce off the tin-foil-covered insulation on the walls and ceiling, and flashes back and forth around the room.

"Still some finish work left to do inside, but I can do that while you're at work."

We climb the new stairs, not exactly the stairs in *Gone With the Wind* but wide and generous, with a smooth, honey-colored two-by-six for a banister.

"Sure looks different in here without all the tools and lumber and sawdust around," I say.

Upstairs, what's left of the evening light slants down through the two skylights onto the floor where I plan to put my bed, then reflects off the insulation on the walls. Even without the finishing touches, like real walls, I love the room. The truss plates I painted black do add a nice touch to the ceiling timbers, just like Ben said they would. The narrow, vertical windows remain bare. I long to tell Ben about the twig shutters I want to build, but I'll wait until we finish more important work.

"I'll put my bed against this wall so I can lie and watch the stars at night."

"Well, I guess I'd better head on up the hill, Molly." Ben's large male voice echoes in the rustic, elegant open space of my upstairs, the same space used by ladies of the night to entertain male customers. "I'll be back in the morning about nine o'clock to help you move."

Late Saturday morning, Ben and I start to carry my belongings, mostly loose items placed in cardboard boxes, from the cabin across the yard to my new home: clothes; back issues of *Sierra Magazine*; my field guides; my hiking boots, now with their mouse-chewed tops; and lots of miscellaneous items too numerous to mention. Together we transport my small couch. The only other large items I have are a simple wooden table and chairs, and one pine dresser. With each trip across my yard, I feel a growing apprehension or anticipation;

an uncertainty tinged with hope that my life will become something very different from what it's been until now.

Ben tells me, "Molly, I can carry this over myself, you know." His words come out in great puffs of breath in the cold air. It's true. His gait is awkward as we walk sideways together toward the brothel, Ben holding one side of my dresser, me gripping the other side.

"I know you can," I say, not letting loose of the dresser. Can't he see how important it is for me to help carry the few things I still own over to my new home?

At first, the low clouds spit tiny bits of snow on us. With every trip between the cabin and the brothel, the flakes grow fatter and just before lunch they begin to swirl. We stop for cheese sandwiches and vegetable soup, heated on the Monarch cookstove, and we eat at the table we placed in the center of the downstairs room.

"Did you ever get that journal translated?" Ben says, taking a bite of sandwich.

"A man is working on it. Used to live in Germany. When he called me at work the other day to give me an update, he said it was taking longer than expected. Promised to have it done by Christmas."

"That'll be a nice Christmas present, then."

"I really can't wait, but I have to." I chew for a while, then say, "Tell me about your childhood here in Snowshoe, Ben."

He wipes his mouth on a paper towel, then looks out the window at the snow. "On a day like today we'd already have our sleds on the mine tailings. Their angle of repose was just right for fast sledding. Even before there'd be enough snow, we'd be pulling our sleds and old inner tubes up and down the slopes." He pauses and smiles. "Sure went through a lot of inner tubes before the snow got deep enough to cover the rocks."

"Who did you play with? Who were the others?"

"Well, there was Shawn," he says, taking a small bite. "A fat Irish kid. Still in Snowshoe, I think. You might have seen him at the Snowshadow. Probably still round and short. We always called him 'the furnace man's kid,' because his father worked in the heating business."

"Who else?"

"Dewey and I were best friends for a long time. We combed the gulches together, found old claims and used a metal detector to dig up jars of silver dollars buried next to old miners' shacks. Nearly got buried ourselves a couple times, in some old adits." He looks at me, grins and adds, "More than once. And one time we found a cave, quite a ways west of Cinnamon Peak. Found a two-pound tooth in it, and a battle-axe and some stone tools. Carried most of the stuff out of there. Took turns carrying the tooth. Must have been from a dinosaur or a mastodon. Then my mom took it all into the historical society. Never saw it again. Should go ask to see it. Best stuff we ever found—even better than the silver dollars."

I listen for further information, hoping he'll continue.

"Haven't talked to Dewey in years." He drinks soup from his bowl.

"Isn't that difficult, in a place as small as Snowshoe?" I know the answer, especially when it comes to Dewey. He seems to be everywhere.

"He took something of mine once, and it wasn't the two-pound tooth. Now we don't like each other. Simple as that."

With this he pushes back his chair, places his plate and bowl in the sink and says, "Let's move the rest of your things over here."

By mid-afternoon the snow is about six inches deep, except where we've tromped a path back and forth between buildings. We stop often to stand near the stoves in the brothel, but finally move the last few loose items, including the mattress and foam pad. We carry my makeshift bed to the upstairs floor of the brothel, where I'll sleep until the furniture store delivers my new bed next week. What will it be like to sleep in a real bed again? Will it feel too uptown, compared to my cozy nest in the loft of the cabin?

"To celebrate your first night here I have a surprise," Ben says. "I'll be back with dinner about 6:00."

"Thanks, Ben. But you've done so much already."

"That's okay. I'll send you a bill," he says, smiling.

"Oh, speaking of your bill. I can write you a check when you come back."

"All the more reason to celebrate."

After Ben leaves, I'm exhausted. Big Al and I rest on the mattress upstairs. Chug still refuses to enter the brothel. After spending the day in her fenced area, she's staying over in the cabin tonight.

The creek, low this time of year, splashes and gurgles among the boulders in the stream bed. The sound of the creek is muffled by the closed window, and is barely audible over Big Al's purring. Still, I listen. The sounds relax me, and I drift into a deep sleep.

> *I am sitting in my dressing gown at my vanity table near the window, brushing my long hair. I stop brushing and pull aside the sheer curtains so I can look out at the night. The creek water catches light from the stars and reflects it back to me. The moon illuminates the side of the log building, the ground, the cottonwood tree, and the creek, in a dim half-light. I open the window to help ease the pain in my heart, to hear the rustle of the*

cottonwood leaves and the murmur of the creek, soothing me as when I stroke my lover's back, my lover whose compassion is soft and gentle like fine fur. But my darling Wilbur has just left with our baby crying softly in his arms. "I'm sorry, liebchen. Don't be sad. I'll bring him back to you," he had whispered to me from the shadows before he closed the back door. And I know he means what he tells me. Wilbur is true and wise and strong, like the best cloth. Yet I am sad.

Suddenly a movement, a shadow, catches my eye on the ground below. Another shadow appears from around the side of the old blacksmith shop. I hear shouting, mean words, angry voices. "I'll kill you, you son-of-a-bitch," one of the men yells, and then I know who it is. "Wait! Where is my baby?" I call out. I can see that Wilbur is no longer carrying him. "Wilbur . . . what is . . ." I try to yell, but I cannot, and it is too late. Two shots rip through the night at the same time, and the two forms fall to the ground, completely still. Only the low murmur of the creek now. I drop my brush and run down the steep, narrow steps, "Wilbur . . . my baby!"

At the bottom of the stairs, I run into a large, solid form.

"Molly, what's the matter?" Ben says, setting down the two grocery sacks he's carrying. He grabs both my arms to hold me still.

"I must open the back door." I am panting, trembling, frantic. "A shooting. A shooting just happened, next to the creek. Two men. And a baby is out there somewhere."

Ben opens the back door and we run out into the cold darkness, the swirling snow. We hear nothing, see no sign of a baby or two men dead on the ground.

Back inside the warm brothel, I slump onto the couch.

"Tell me exactly what you saw," Ben says, sitting down next to me. "Are you sure you weren't dreaming?"

"I could swear it happened. I . . . the window had a sheer curtain, and I was wearing a long dressing gown. Wilbur had just left with the baby, our baby, and I felt so sad. I sat near the window brushing my long hair, listening to the creek, then heard angry voices below the window followed by two gunshots, almost at the same time."

Ben stares at me, eyes big, disbelief on his face. "Molly, what you just described actually happened here in Snowshoe shortly after the turn of the century. My grandfather, Wilbur, and Dewey's grandfather, Hermann, shot each other behind this brothel."

"Why didn't you tell me that? And what about the baby?"

"I'm not real proud that my grandpa got himself shot behind a brothel. And the shooting kept me from ever knowing him. But I've never heard a thing about a baby. No one even knows for sure why they shot each other. Some claimed it was over a gambling bet." He pauses, shakes his head. "Nope, no mention of a baby."

CHAPTER 22

On Sunday night our time zone fell back an hour, and now it's dusk by the time I arrive home from work. The location I call home wears dusk in strange, uncommon ways. Living in Snowshoe inspires me to examine this concept of daylight saving time, of time zones in general. What does it mean, really, to leave work, travel for thirty minutes, and arrive home nearly a century earlier? And to a place where bizarre dreams turn out to be true stories. Maybe the time zone of a place like that, a place like my old brothel in Snowshoe, is the twilight zone—a place of unsolicited dreams, where one relives unfortunate and reckless events of the past.

As I turn off The Snowshoe Trail onto my lane I see smoke rising from the new chimney, lifting and looping into the sky, promising warmth. It's been cold, in the teens and twenties, but it hasn't snowed again since I moved into the brothel a couple weeks ago. Ben says not to hold my breath, that the weather gods are saving it up to dump on us all at once.

At the end of the road, I also see that a light has been left on for me. I park the truck and step onto the porch. The black doorknob turns easily in my mitten and the door, only locked at night, swings open into a warm room and a furry greeting from Chug, who announced one evening last week that she would now be staying with me in the brothel. Ben rebuilt the back entrance to include a sizeable doggie door. Now both Chug and Big Al can come and go whenever they wish.

A spicy, unfamiliar aroma welcomes me. Salivating, I realize that I'm hungrier than I usually am after work. The table in the center of the room is set: plate, utensils, a single unlit candle, salt and pepper shakers, a small jar of some condiment. Maybe Ben, too, attended the White Gloves and Party Manners class. A bottle of wine, already uncorked, sits in front of the place setting, and a wine glass reflects the dim lamplight. A piece of paper peeks out from under the wine glass.

Molly—Your dinner is in the oven. New recipe I'm trying. The wine is an Elderberry I made last year. It should go well with the dish. Remember, all things in moderation. Ben. P.S. I hope you like your new floor upstairs.

Ben is the only man who has ever cooked a meal for me. On my first night in the brothel, the night of the sinister dream that seemed so real, Ben had brought an eggplant casserole, precooked, that he reheated in the oven. The meal was delicious that night, but I remember nothing more about it thanks to my rattled condition. I had thought of the meal as a fluke, an isolated event, a bachelor's attempt at thoughtfulness. Maybe this time he's playing a joke, except Ben's only been silly around me that one time with the wheelbarrow. He's been friendly and businesslike, considerate but never solicitous. Maybe he just had some leftovers to share. But if he cooked the meal here, where are the dirty dishes? One thing for sure, the man is secretive.

I feed Chug and Al their own food in their own dishes, then run upstairs to look around. Random lengths of eight-inch sanded pine boards cover the plywood subfloor. The holes where Ben screwed the boards down are filled with wood plugs, sanded smooth. This gives the floor a finished look even though he hasn't stained and sealed the wood.

The smell of food draws me back downstairs. Using a potholder, I carry my dinner from the oven to the table. Chug follows me so closely that I nearly trip on her. She must think the food on my plate will taste better than her own food. I set the dish on the table and peel off the foil. A hint of cinnamon?

Chili powder? Chug sniffs the air and whimpers. It looks like beef strips in thick gravy, along with new potatoes graced with slivers of greens, and whole steamed carrots. He must not know that I rarely eat meat. My protein is in the form of fish or tofu or organically grown chicken. If I eat all this, I'll be too stuffed to walk. I sit down and stare at the steaming plate. I should give the meat to Chug. I really should. But I think of the effort and care Ben went to. The preparation. The presentation. And I'm hungry, starving. It won't hurt me this once to eat some red meat, to eat food that I cut with a knife. A few more fat grams than usual, but what can it hurt? I pour a glass of wine and take a sip—dreamy, mellow, a wine to make me smile. Exquisite, with or without meat. I look at the condiment jar. Where would he buy something called *Edna's Honey Fire Mustard*?

First I take a bite of the potatoes, done perfectly with chives, I think, and some parsley. They shine like they've been braised. It's been a long time since I ate bacon, but I detect a hint of that gloriously smokey taste. Then a carrot. Tastes like he used butter and what is that, brown sugar? I clean my palate with another gulp of wine and prepare to taste the meat. I apply a spot of the curious mustard near the edge of my plate, cut a piece of meat, dip it into the condiment, and take a bite. Cinnamon, but not too much, garlic, a little heat—cayenne pepper? The meat does not require excessive chewing—just enough to taste the spices and sauce with the mustard. I take another bite and close my eyes. *A man cooked this for me.* What an amazing thing. I wish I didn't like the meal so much, especially the meat. If this is to be my last supper of this style of protein, in this quantity, I will truly be distressed.

Chug sits watching me, whimpering. I open my eyes. I have never eaten a better meal, and I do not want to share any of it with Chug. If I don't give her some, though, I know I won't be able to live with myself and she'll be surprised and hurt. She stares at me with her big watery brown eyes.

"Okay, Chug. You win."

I scrape one last piece of meat and some sauce into her bowl, along with the remaining chunk of potato. Instead of savoring the food, she wolfs it down with one gulp, snuffles, looks up at me hopefully, and smacks her big doggie lips.

"Sorry, Chuggie."

My boots crunch snow. The cold night air reminds me that I have nose hairs. Chug and I are walking through town past former bars and mercantiles, some of the buildings vacant, some of them occupied. Except for the smell of wood smoke rising from a few chimneys and the faint light behind thickly-curtained windows, I might think we were alone in this particular time zone. When we head home and turn the corner onto our lane, I see a light on at Gum's, although he's probably at the Snowshadow. Or maybe that's the chicken coop and he left a light bulb burning to keep the hens from freezing. For all I know, he may have butchered the chickens. It's been weeks since I had a fresh egg.

When we reach my truck, I stop and grab a special gift I bought for myself earlier. This winter I had hoped to hold title to a place with indoor plumbing—the kind you flush—but the county sanitation engineer Ben invited out the other day had dashed this particular dream. He said that since my building was so close to the creek I needed a specially designed system. "Your outhouse is grandfathered in," he had said, "so you're welcome to keep using it." Like he was handing me a gift of some kind. Does this make sense? I do understand the need to keep raw sewage out of streams, to keep water clean. After all, I do spend my days studying slides of water samples. But I had never put it in the context of going to the outhouse in the middle of the night when it's forty below zero. I carry my prize, my antique chamber pot, into the warmth of my new home.

Every evening, about a half-hour before bedtime, I turn on the lamp over my bed, switch on the electric blanket, and put on a tape of Beethoven, Vivaldi or Haydn. This time I also carry my chamber pot and slide it under the bed. No more nighttime forays. No more worry that my flesh will stick to the frosty toilet seat like a tongue to the cold metal of an old sled. Still, as wonderful as my new purchase is, the meal Ben cooked for me takes first place this day.

I sit near the stove for a while with Big Al and Chug, listening to the music. I tell them about my day, and sometimes, when we feel particularly smug in our spartan lifestyle, we talk about the survival of the fittest and discuss what Darwin said about music. Without the sound of a voice, even my own, the silence is too loud, too lonely. My animal companions are a fine family, although I'm looking forward to seeing Scott and Jeremy at Thanksgiving. The last time they saw me I was flat on my back in the hospital. Seeing them alone, without their father, will be different for us all. I hope they've adjusted to the divorce. Each time I talk to them on the phone, it seems as if they've grown more accustomed to my decision.

When Chug and Big Al and I finish with our evening ritual near the stove, I lock the front and back doors and set the wood stove to burn on low all night. I say goodnight to Chug, who settles down by the front door as Al and I climb the stairs to our boudoir. After I'm in my silk pajamas, I reset the cassette in the clock radio, Beethoven again, then slip into bed.

At two o'clock in the morning I awaken suddenly, caught in a spotlight. Half asleep and groggy, I wonder what is wrong, what I've done, what crazy dream is overtaking me.

But this event is real. The full moon, shining down on me through the skylights, holds me in place in bright focus. But I am not alone. There is something else in the room—a presence, a kindly, sympathetic presence. Moonlight streams down through the skylights, reflects off the snowy ground below, and bounces back into the room through the windows. The presence in the room is luminous, an incandescent feeling, yes, a feeling.

"Is that you, Lempi Shunk?" I ask.

The glow diminishes as I wait and watch, as the moon continues on its path beyond the skylights. At last I close my eyes and settle into my usual position under the down comforter—on my side, with one knee up. I'm curious about the sensation of not being alone, and I don't know how much time goes by, but before I am fully asleep I feel a bump against my bed. I hold my breath and open my eyes. Just as I do this, something, or someone, embraces my back and the side of my head, warmly, lovingly, as if I'm a small child and this is my mother, a mother tucking her child in for the night. For a brief second, I am that child. Then the presence leaves the room and I drift off to sleep, smiling and hearing, through a distance of walls and decades, old-time player piano music.

CHAPTER 23

When I step onto the porch, I hear the phone ringing. Must be Jeremy. No one else even knows I had a phone installed today except Ben, and he doesn't have one himself. I fling open the door, slam it shut, and run for the phone.

"Hello?"

"Molly, now don't hang up on me. Just hear me out."

"You've got a nerve, calling me."

"Well, I'll admit I might not act real polished all the time."

"I don't need to ask how you know about my phone. The lineman probably stopped by on his way out. You gave the guy a free beer and he blabbed my phone number."

"Molly, I'm sorry about what I said that night. It was a clumsy, stupid thing to say. You're a beautiful person. I admire your spirit for living out here all by yourself. And I miss you. We all miss you. Come back to the 'Shadow. Let bygones be forgotten."

"I might and I might not. And Dewey, so help me God, if I hear that anyone else knows what happened that night, Snowshoe will have one more unsolved murder."

I slam down the receiver. Ben had talked me into putting in a phone, said I might need to call my office some mornings when I'm snowed in. And now Dewey, of all people, is the first person to call me.

Still fuming, I look around to see what changes have happened to the brothel interior today besides the new phone. Ben has finished laying the new wood flooring downstairs. This floor looks so much nicer than plywood. The shine from my fluorescent lights overhead and the lamps still bounce off the tinfoil surface of the insulation on the walls, but I know he'll be installing sheetrock yet this winter. With insulation beneath the flooring and on the walls, and the wood stove going twenty-four hours a day, I'm not the least bit cold inside the brothel. Of course, I do leave the faucet dribbling at all times and the cupboard doors open under the sink so the pipes won't freeze.

I can think of at least two reasons why miners visited brothels in the winter, and one is this: he could count on at least one small part of his anatomy being warm for just a little while.

The weather in Snowshoe is living up to its reputation. I swear it's like living in Siberia. Snow's been falling for days, big polar bear snowflakes at first, and now we have about two feet of white stuff. At work, our hydrologist, Bo Knows Water, told me that winter storms move in from the west, stall out over the Continental Divide and drop tons of snow. Most of the time, all the snow drops on the mountains before it can reach Helena. He must be right, because at the moment there's not an ounce of snow on the ground there, yet the mountains all around the Prickly Pear Valley are white. Besides the difference in snow cover, it's at least twenty degrees warmer in Helena than it is in Snowshoe.

The other morning when I shoveled the path to the outhouse so I could empty my new chamber pot, the cold made the bags under my eyes ache. How does old Gumboot manage? I'm not complaining, just speaking the truth. With all this snow and the town's history of strange murders, Snowshoe seems to me like a wolf wearing sheep's clothing.

It's a good thing Ben comes to work on the place, because he plows his way in every day and plows his way out when he leaves. That way I can drive all the way into my yard when I get home from work. Otherwise, I'd have to park out on the road and walk in, and if I had to do that I couldn't plug in the engine block heater in my truck, which means I might not be able to start the engine the next morning. I was so insulated from winter when I lived in town, where I not only had a garage but a heated one with a garage-door opener. Now if it weren't for Ben plowing my lane and leaving hot meals, I could start to feel like a member of the Donner Party.

Chug snuffles to draw my attention to her food dish. Looks like she'll have to eat straight dog food tonight, since Ben has not left us a hot meal. He often leaves something for me on Friday evenings, but the night varies with the way he prepares the meat; he has a stunning array of delicious recipes. But tonight I'll warm up some curried lentil and rice stew.

This time when the phone rings, I know it must be Jeremy.

"Hi, Mom," he says.

"Hi, honey. I was hoping to hear your voice."

"So, Mom, are you coming to Seattle for some culture along with your turkey?"

"Culture *shock,* that's probably what I'll suffer, Jer. I can't wait to see you and Scott, but I'm not looking forward to the big city. My plane arrives at 3:45 p.m. on Tuesday. I'm catching the early afternoon flight out after I drop Chug and Al off at Myra's."

"Great, Mom. And can you cook the turkey?"

"I can't believe it. You went to chef school, you work in a French restaurant, and now you want me to cook the turkey?"

"Sure, I could do it, but you do it so well. Please?"

"Of course. If you'll order me a fresh turkey, not one of those birds raised on steroids or whatever, we can pick it up on the way home from the airport."

"Great. Patty's coming for dinner. Scott and Jessica will be here, too. It'll be almost like old times. Except, of course, you and Dad aren't together."

"Please, don't start on that. The holidays can be difficult for families when things change, but we'll just have to make the best of it. You can still see us both, just one at a time."

"I know. I love you, Mom. See you Tuesday at the airport."

"Bye, Jeremy. I love you, too."

At 10:00 p.m., after my busy evening on the phone and a brisk stroll down Snowshoe's Main Street with Chug, I crawl into bed under my comforter. Big Al leaps into place next to me and begins to purr as I pet him and think about my day at work—writing reports on the computer summarizing the data I entered last month. Then I think about Thanksgiving with my sons. The last thing on my mind before sleep is how Dewey can call and bother me any time he wants to, now that he has my number.

I hold my long skirt as I walk around barrels of potatoes and gunnysacks bulging with coal. A longhaired gray and black striped cat lies, purring loudly, next to several sacks of flour and rice sitting on the wood plank flooring. Bolts of cloth and spools of ribbons and lace line the walls of shelves in the mercantile, and the store has many of the items I need. Now the clerk is helping me buy some eggs. Suddenly I glimpse a familiar figure out of the corner of my eye as he enters the store. It's him, no doubt about it, dressed in a brown coat and leggings, with his limping gait, wearing his ridiculous oversized mustache. I excuse myself and duck behind some display shelving filled with hardware, then realize this is not a good place to hide, for he has surely come into the store for hardware. I circle around to the end of the shelves, near the front door.

"Ma'am, you forgot your eggs," the shopkeeper yells. Ignoring him, I dash out the door and across the street, into the path of a horse and wagon. The horse is Pepper. Laine is driving the wagon, and she yells Whoa! The wagon stops just in time, before Pepper and I collide. "Molly, what's your hurry? Here, let me give you a ride."

"I'd like that," I say, out of breath as I lift my petticoats and climb into the wagon. But the wagon does not move. "Dewey is buying a few things for his tepee. I'll be giving him a ride, too," she says, then laughs her hysterical shrieking laugh, and I feel trapped, like this is a set-up, a joke. "I've changed my mind," I say, gathering my skirts in preparation to climb back down out of the wagon. "I think I'll walk." But here comes Dewey out of the mercantile. He climbs up onto the wagon before I can get off, and while he sits slowly down next to me, he looks over the top of his walrus mustache at my breasts, and leers.

CHAPTER 24

"So, Gary, how was your Thanksgiving?" I ask, sitting down for lunch with him and Myra at the table in the break room. It's my first day back to work after my trip to Seattle.

"Spent the day with a girl I dated in college."

"You're kidding," I say, digging into my salad. "You dated a girl?"

"Well, kind of. Mostly we were good friends, that was until she started pressuring me for a more intimate relationship." Gary lowers his voice and continues. "Then I had to confess that it was her brother who appealed to me, not her. Since her brother's girlfriend was pregnant at the time, I knew he wasn't interested in me. Anyway, she got the point."

"It gets even better, Molly," Myra says.

Gary continues. "Angie still lives in Missoula and she's married to a guy named Stan. He's an engineer and he'd make a nice end-table lamp if you wired him. I don't know what she sees in a guy like that. He has zero sense of humor."

Gary takes a bite of his sandwich and chews a while. We keep eating, knowing he'll continue when he's ready.

"Angie invited quite an assortment of people. We had a middle-aged Russian couple she tutors in basic English; a lesbian couple; and Angie's brother and wife and the kid they had—now a teenager with a ring in her nose. Turns out the Russians are both scientists, and most of the talk at the dinner table consisted of Stan trying to discuss the ins and outs of fractals with them."

"That must have been fascinating," I say. "Fractals are quite the deal. From what I gathered in an article I read a few months ago, scientists can use them to explain nature.

They're almost always irregular, and the shape of each part of any object in nature is the same shape as the whole object, like a snowflake or a piece of tree bark."

"Sounded brainy, all right, that is what I could understand of their talk back and forth over the turkey carcass. While I chewed a mouthful of stuffing with cranberry sauce, Stan said something about fractal simulations being used to plot the distribution of galaxy clusters throughout the universe. No one said much after that, and as soon as I recovered from overeating and hearing so much about fractals, I left for Helena."

"How about your Thanksgiving, Myra?" I ask. When I picked up Chug and Big Al the evening before we didn't have time to visit.

"Jim and I decided to have dinner at home. You'll be happy to know that both Big Al and Chug ate some turkey and yams. We asked another couple to join us but they had to go to her parents' house for dinner, so they came over later for dessert. They're the ones who have the llamas out at the foot of the Big Belts. A few days before Thanksgiving one of their llamas disappeared from the pasture, so they reported it to the Sheriff's office. Well, a butcher here in town who cuts up deer and elk for hunters called after that to tell them a man had brought his first elk in to be cut up and packaged. The proud hunter had drawn a cow elk permit and thought he'd shot himself a 'slow woman elk.' Except it wasn't an elk, it was their missing llama. The guy moved here last summer from out of state. I thought they'd made it up, but it really happened."

"There's so many crazies out there," Gary says. "I have a cousin in Idaho who refuses to wear an orange vest when she hunts because they'll shoot at anything they catch sight of. She wears a gray jacket to blend with the woods. If you ask me, it's suicide to be out during hunting season, no matter what you're wearing."

Myra and I nod our agreement.

We overhear part of the conversation at the next table. "So, when I heard those shots I ran down the face of the mountain," Floyd says. "Thought I'd hit the road and head back to help the others with their kill. I was running along pretty good, jumping logs and brush. But when I got near the road I could see a big bear running like hell up the road, and we were on a collision course. So I kept on running. Leaped over that bear and just kept going. Scared him half to death."

"That bear's probably still talking about it," one of the other men says. They all laugh. "Yeah, he probably ran all the way to Canada, you scared him so bad."

Aside from the llama incident, it's one of the better hunting stories I've ever heard. Gary and Myra and I look at each other, smile and shake our heads. I don't believe the boss has run anywhere in years, least of all down a steep mountainside. Some days, the stories I hear in the lunchroom are like being awarded a bonus just for coming to work.

"Molly, what about your Thanksgiving?" Myra asks.

"First of all, one of the best parts was arriving home to see that Ben had covered all my walls with sheetrock, even taped the seams smooth as glass. You'll have to come out one of these days to see how different the place looks. And we can go skiing."

"Sounds good to me," Gary says. "Now, how about your Thanksgiving?"

"Well, it rained from the time I arrived in Seattle 'til I left. I didn't mind it too much, but then I was only there a few days. Anyway, Jeremy met me at the airport, and the first night Scott and Jessica came over. We had a lovely visit. The next day Jeremy and I took in Pike Place Market, and on

Thursday we got up early to start dinner. I cooked the turkey and Jeremy took charge of everything else. He acted all excited and anxious. I thought it was because he'd invited his new girlfriend to dinner. About an hour before the others were scheduled to arrive, we began to set the table with a tablecloth, candles, and lots of shiny serving dishes. Then he hands me six plates, and as I set them out I start counting: Jeremy, his girlfriend, me, Scott, and Jessica. That's five. I said, 'Jeremy, you gave me an extra plate.' 'Mom,' he said, 'Dad flew in yesterday. He'll be coming to dinner with Scott and Jessica.' " I pause to finish my salad.

"Well, then what happened?" Gary asks.

"All during dinner I could hardly speak, or eat. Bradley kept looking at me, studying me. Scott asked me at one point, 'Mom, how's your renovation project coming along?' 'Fine,' I said. Then he said, 'Mom, how do you like living out there in the woods in that little old town?' I longed to say how free I feel, how interesting my new life is compared to my old life, but I didn't want to hurt anyone's feelings. All I said was, 'It's all right.' My Thanksgiving Day was just awful."

By now the others have left the break room for their desks, and we gather our things to head back to our cubicles.

For a while I just sit at my computer, staring at the screen, thinking about Thanksgiving Day. When Bradley had arrived for dinner, I reverted to my old ways of trying to please everybody. I practically rolled over on my back like a cowering pup with my feet up in the air. I hated myself for that. At the same time, I was furious at Jeremy and Scott for not telling me Bradley would be there. But, Scott had said later, "You might not have come if we had told you, and we thought that if all of us got together again, you and Dad would somehow make up. You know, Mom, Dad wants to, Jeremy had told me." I felt bad for Jeremy and Scott, even a little sad for Bradley. He isn't an ogre; he just isn't for me. Living with him made me feel subdued. I suppose it was because his worldview was so conservative, while I longed to break free and explore. I guess, for me, the run-in with the moose was a kind of awakening.

Another thing that bothers me now is that I'm not able to tell my sons very much about my new life. If I told them about the severe weather or about Ben being a suspected murderer, or even about how Gum shoots my way when I visit him at his mining claim, they'd worry about my safety. If I were to tell them about my strange dreams or ghostly visits, they'd wonder about my mental health.

And all during Thanksgiving dinner I had thought about Ben's surprise meals, how every dinner he had left in the oven for me was more delicious than my turkey—even if I didn't know exactly what he was feeding me. In fact, I had thought about Ben several times a day while I was gone. What was he doing? With whom? And I had hoped with all my heart that he hadn't spent Thanksgiving in his cabin up in the cold, snowy mountains all alone.

CHAPTER 25

The large red numbers on the clock radio say 9:30. Oh, great. I'm an hour and a half late for work. Then I remember hearing music earlier. The music had soothed me, lifted me, given me hope. I felt so much hope, in fact, that I failed to crawl out of bed. Hope about what? Maybe nothing more than the wish that everyone's life could grow in new directions, as mine has in so many important ways.

Bewildered and dazed as I am I must leap up, dress myself, gulp a little coffee and breakfast, brush snow off the truck, start the engine, unplug the engine block heater, scrape the windows and then drive all that way in to work while watching for deer on the road. From my warm bed, I reconsider the situation. If I hurry I can call in sick, but if I wait too long, I may have to call in well. I do not like to tell a lie.

The rumbling sounds of a snowplow moving toward the brothel jolt me into action. Ben! Throwing my jeans and a flannel shirt on over my pajamas, I dash downstairs. Before I stoke the fire, I turn the damper on the stovepipe so smoke won't pour into the room when I open the door. Only a few red coals remain, and I throw in a couple small pieces of wood, hoping they'll catch fire.

Now, to actually sound *sick,* when I call in sick. The department secretary answers the phone. She hopes I'll feel better soon, and tells me she'll pass along the message to Floyd. Good. No sign that she doesn't believe me.

I haven't seen Ben since before Thanksgiving. Maybe I should do something to prepare for his arrival. Why am I so nervous? Now that it's winter, everything feels different. When I'm home and Ben's working here, I'll be trapped indoors with him. He's so big, such a strong presence, that sometimes I have trouble catching my breath when we're in a room together, as if there isn't enough air. And right now I have to pee, which means I must hurry to the outhouse. It's too late to use the chamber pot upstairs because Ben will be coming through the front door any minute. His truck stops out front. Tromp, tromp, tromp on the porch. I open the door and hand Ben the broom to sweep snow off his boots.

"Molly. Didn't expect you to be here. Is something wrong?"

"Well, no, I couldn't seem to . . . I didn't feel all that well, and now I have to . . ." My words trail behind me as I dash for the outhouse, knowing what lies in store for me when I sit down on the ice cold toilet seat. But I'm in a hurry, and my fears are realized all too soon as I drop my jeans and pajama bottoms and concentrate on what I must do so it will happen quickly. By the time Big Al has realized where I went and reached the door of the outhouse to join me, I'm on my way back into the house. Late at night and early in the morning, I find I'm quite fond of my chamber pot, that fine piece of Old West indoor plumbing.

When I step into the brothel, Ben is loading up the wood stove. In my brief absence, he has filled the woodbox from the covered woodpile out back.

"Ben, could I make you some coffee?"

"If you're sick, I should be waiting on you."

"Well, actually, I'm better. I'm fine, really."

As the coffee maker finishes gurgling, the sun begins to shine on the tops of the mountains. Soon it will throw light onto the brothel, and remain a couple hours in my narrow corner of the canyon before it sets behind the mountains. Most days I'm not home to witness this and I open the curtains above the sink so I won't miss the phenomenon.

Ben sits at the table, his coat over the back of the chair.

"Thanks," he says as I hand him a mug of coffee. Unless it's my imagination, I detect warmth radiating outward from him through his wool shirt.

"The walls look wonderful, Ben. You accomplished so much. I hope you didn't work here every day over Thanksgiving."

"Well, I rented some equipment for the project and I wanted to finish. Worked every day and a few hours on Thanksgiving morning before driving into town to have dinner with my mom. I cooked dinner for her and her friend, Kurt."

"Did you cook a turkey?"

"No. Mother likes sweet and sour dishes, so I made one of those."

"What meat did you cook?"

"Chef's secret." Ben smiles at me and holds his coffee mug to his lips, and I wonder if I will ever know what he's been feeding me. "I'll have to cook you pheasant with trail sometime," he says.

"What in the world is that?" Sunlight begins to stream through the frosty windows onto Ben's back.

"First you have to catch a pheasant and wring its neck. Then you pull off all the feathers and set the whole bird in a roaster on a big piece of toast and put it in the oven. Cook it until you see a trail on the toast behind the bird, and then serve dinner."

"That is perfectly gross. Now I'm really worried about what you've been cooking for me."

"I think that recipe's a joke. Must be. But I did run across it in an old recipe book. Of course, I also found some other recipes I'm never going to cook—one for elephant stew and another for stone soup."

"Stone soup? Sounds like something the miners around here used to eat."

"That and crow," he says, getting up from his chair to set his mug near the sink. "Today I thought I'd start paneling the gable ends upstairs, but if you'd rather have some peace and quiet, I'll do it next week."

I'm still thinking about pheasant with trail and eating crow, so his sudden change of subject catches me off guard. After thinking about it I say, "Could you use some help?"

"Can you cut boards with a hand saw? That way we won't make much sawdust."

"You measure twice and I'll cut once," I say, repeating a wisdom he shared with me early in the summer.

The knotty pine boards fit together perfectly, side by side, one after the other, over the foil-covered insulation. Using finishing nails and a hammer, Ben nails each board in place vertically, moving up and down the ladder as he goes. While he's putting up one board, I'm cutting the next one on pencil lines he has drawn for the exact angle and length. By four o'clock, we have one gable end done and I have a blister on my thumb from sawing the boards.

After Ben removes the saw horses, ladder, tools and the canvas he had spread on the floor to catch the small amount of sawdust, we stand together in front of the two windows overlooking the snowy landscape outdoors, and study the finished gable end.

"Soon as we panel the other end I can put the trim around the windows and replace the window sills."

"For once I can see that I actually accomplished something for all my efforts," I say.

"You did. I wouldn't have been able to finish this end alone in one day. You saved me dozens of trips up and down that ladder."

"I want to build some shutters for these windows," I say, my voice suddenly husky. Determined to talk about this now, I ignore the pressure in my chest that always signals big feelings. "I'd like to make shutters for these windows overlooking the creek first. I don't really need curtains on this side, since no one can see in. It's more for decoration." I say it all in words breaking up like those of a young boy whose voice is changing. From my small desk near the window overlooking the creek, I take out my magazine picture. "I want them to look like this."

"Those will certainly dress up the room, and you'll see a nice pattern when the light peeks through between the stems."

"They'll have to wait until spring when I can gather some red-osier dogwood branches," I say.

"I can help if you want," Ben offers. "We can cut some perfect red-osiers up at Try Again Meadows, if you don't mind going part of the way on snowshoes. The snow freezes in spring, so Chug should be able to walk on the top of the snow."

I stare at the window nearest me, overwhelmed with gratitude toward this huge, generous person, this suspected murderer who is becoming so important in my life. The lump in my throat grows bigger. I'm not used to a man being so capable, so helpful and considerate. No man has ever been that way with me.

"I'd like that very much," I manage to say, caught and mesmerized now by the frost patterns on the lower corners of the window panes where the intricate, exquisite arrangement of pure white flowers shows the random dignity of natural objects.

CHAPTER 26

On the shortest day of the year in Snowshoe, Montana, it was dark when I left for work and dark when I got home. That was a couple days ago. Now it's dark again, or still, and it's minus fifteen degrees Fahrenheit at 6:00 on Christmas Eve morning. I climb into my warmest long underwear, use the lint remover to lift the cat hair off my best corduroy slacks before pulling them on, add wool socks, then a turtleneck and wool sweater. My felt-lined Sorel boots are warming by the wood stoves.

We work until noon today. Even better, I'll be meeting Mr. Everett this afternoon to receive the best Christmas present I could imagine: the translation of the madam's journal. My Christmas will be quiet this year. No Christmas tree in the brothel, since Al would soon shred all the ornaments. The tree at work is enough for me. And I'm having Christmas dinner tomorrow with Myra and Jim. Otherwise, I'll spend my Christmas vacation reading the journal and maybe doing a little skiing in the woods.

On Christmas Eve, after feeding the animals and myself and after Chug and I take a brisk, snowy walk on The Snowshoe Trail, I sit on my bed under the reading lamp, listening to Haydn's Symphony No. 6 in D, and I begin to read the journal of Lempi Shunk.

28 August 1893

Why was I born the homely one? I am so skinny and my nose is so big. Papa tells me no one will ever marry me. Maybe I will change. I am only fourteen. I do my best to make up for it, and today I dug more potatoes than anyone. At supper, I take little food, so to leave most for the others. Hattie is the pretty one, and she will find a husband in the village. The boys already whistle and holler sometimes when they see her.

2 September 1893

Today Hattie and I put a harness on the goat and she pulled us one at a time in the cart. Hattie would lead the goat with me in the cart. Then we would switch. Mama would not ride in the cart, but she laughed, and this is something she almost never does. When she is happy her face is so beautiful to me, but happiness is something I do not see on her very often. Papa was working in the village at the rug factory. If he had been home, he would not have let us take time to play. When he is here we must always be working.

11 September 1893

Papa is still at the factory in the village. Last night when he came home he had been drinking and he was angry. He heard that soldiers were in the countryside. Until now, they were always somewhere else, in someone else's countryside.

13 September 1893

Mama is sad, very sad. Hattie is upstairs in her bed, crying. They hurt her, the soldiers who came on the track yesterday, five of them. I wish they had hurt me, not our beautiful Hattie, but they did not take me or Mama upstairs, just Hattie. Mama yelled, No! You can't have her, but one of them hit Mama, and after that we stayed in the corner of the kitchen holding onto each other while Hattie screamed and screamed. When the soldiers came back downstairs some time later, they were laughing and joking. They took our flour and sugar and the bread I had baked in the morning and walked off down the track. Mama made me stay downstairs in the kitchen when she ran upstairs, yelling Hattie, Hattie, my poor baby, my little cabbage.

17 September 1893

Papa has been drunk for four days. He does not work on our little farm or in the village. He just sits in his chair with his head hung down. Mama cooks potatoes and turnips for us, and takes food upstairs to Hattie, who stays in bed. Papa won't eat. I think it is not just this terrible thing that happened when the soldiers came through. Papa has always been in charge and that is the way of it, but now something has happened that he couldn't control. I think he wishes it had been me and not Hattie.

19 September 1893

Mama is usually quiet and does everything Papa wants, but I have heard her pleading with him to let Hattie go to America. Mama's brother lives on a farm in a state called Indiana, where they grow corn. He had written earlier in the summer to say that he knew a couple on a neighboring farm who needed a house girl, and if Hattie wanted to come to America they would send a steamship ticket. Papa had said No, we need her here to work on our own farm. Now Mama begs, We could not protect her here, but we can do this one thing for her. She can still get there before winter. I am afraid Papa will beat Mama, but finally Papa yells, I can't stand it no more. She can go to America. Lempi will have to do Hattie's work, too, then, he said. I will miss Hattie very much, but I do not mind working hard in her place. She looks dull now, not pretty. Maybe she will have some hope in her new life. Maybe she will recover from the soldiers when she goes to America.

16 October 1893

I am lonely without Hattie. Mama misses her terribly. Now I am the last one still at home, and I cannot take Hattie's place for Mama and Papa. We do not know when she will arrive in America. She promised to write, but it will take months to hear from her.

CHAPTER 27

The ears and legs of dead deer stick up at all angles from the snowbanks. Along with fresh snow, the snowplow shoves dead deer off the road—deer hit by cars and pickups since the last time they plowed the road. Especially at night, it's a grotesque and spooky sight. Driving The Snowshoe Trail in the best of conditions is a bit like running a gauntlet, and now, after enjoying Christmas dinner with Myra and Jim, I'm anxious to reach home to see my animals, and to crawl under my down comforter and read Lempi's journal.

So familiar is the route that my truck knows the way. My thoughts wander back to the journal. The way Lempi felt she had to work extra hard because she was the ugly duckling in the family makes me sad for her, and then the horrid scene with the soldiers and Hattie. What a tragic childhood. At least her mother loved her. After Lempi's older sister went to America she wrote letters home saying she was working hard and eating well on the farm, that the cost of her passage would be repaid within a year and her English was improving every day. But Lempi said in her journal that Hattie wrote she was lonely. Could Lempi please join her? She could work on a farm, too, and her own American family would help arrange it. Lempi wanted to go to America, but her father had said he needed her help on the farm. He relented, finally, just as he had done with Hattie, after her mother kept pleading with him to let her go. She wanted a better life for her girls, a life with some hope and opportunity. Lempi had carried a bundle containing a small handmade quilt and her best clothes, onto which her mother had embroidered her favorite pattern so they wouldn't look so plain. She took some cheese and dried bread, and a little money in a pouch she wore like a pendant close to her chest. Lempi saw a falling star the night before she left in a cart with her father for the train station. She had wished upon the star for a happy life with her new family in America. Wearing a note pinned to the side of her dress with her name and destination on it, she boarded a huge ship at the port of Bremerhaven. She spoke no English, but her American family wrote that they would send someone to meet her at the dock in New York.

That's all I know so far. So many unanswered questions, like how did she get from a farm in Germany to a brothel in Montana? Somewhere along the line she became a prostitute. The thought of all those strange men lunging on top of her, huffing and grunting their foul, snoose-filled breath until they fell in a heap on top of her. I can't imagine . . . what's that?

I don't see the deer standing in the middle of the road until I'm almost on top of it. I pump the brakes too hard, too fast. The tail end of the truck whips to the left, then to the right, and I catch a glimpse of the deer, its eyes like miniature headlights, and then the truck swerves past the side of the beast. The deer leaps out of the way. But I'm still pumping the brakes. That's what I'm supposed to do, if I remember correctly. Will I never come to a stop? One bank looms in my headlights, a few feet in front of me, and then a second later I'm skidding toward the opposite bank. The truck jerks as a wheel catches an edge in the snow floor, and in an instant I'm spinning around. My right fender catches a snowbank and abruptly stops all time, stops all sound. In the silence I sit, shaking and panting, facing back toward the highway, thinking, oddly enough, about what Jim had said to me earlier at dinner. "Lives can take odd turns. Take yours, Molly. Did you have a clue this time last year that you'd be making so many big changes in your life?" Sitting here on The Snowshoe Trail at night facing the wrong direction in a state of mild shock, I would have to say, No, I didn't. None whatsoever. I owe it all to an irate moose. It's like I needed some disaster to wake me up. At this moment I can honestly say, however, that in the last year I've had about all the *interesting* I can take.

After pulling forward and back, cranking the steering wheel, pulling forward and backing up, again and again, I start for home, this time at a crawl. When I arrive at Snowshoe, I turn into the Snowshadow parking lot before I realize what I'm doing. Dewey's pickup is there, of course, and Laine's, and several other familiar cars and trucks in various stages of dent and disrepair. Many of them have hit a deer or a snowbank in recent history. Uncertain why I stopped, I turn off my engine and wait. I'll just sit here for a minute in the glow of the Christmas lights decorating the entrance and listen. The German shepherd chews half-heartedly on something, oblivious to the cold. When I roll down my window, muffled voices drift out into the parking lot from inside the Snowshadow, and then I hear Laine's shrieking laugh. I open my door, walk past the German shepherd and grab the antler door handle. Maybe I'll turn back and go home. But then I hear Gum's gravelly voice and pull open the second door, without removing my coat. If I'm still wearing my coat, I can make a fast getaway.

When I step into the bar, every person on every bar stool sets his drinks down in unison and turns to stare at me, just like they did last June the first time I came into the bar. Old fashioned Christmas tree lights, the kind that bubble, decorate the antlers of the moose head, and a string of tiny colored lights runs along the top of the mirror behind the bar. A few of the other residents of Snowshoe are here—the dark, bearded man with the hawk nose and the Fuller Brush eyebrows, and the round, red-faced man wearing black suspenders to hold up his frayed black pants, cut off just above his boot tops. Must be Shawn, Ben's childhood friend, the furnace man's kid.

Laine climbs off her stool and walks over to me. "Molly, I'm so glad you came." She hugs me in front of everyone and escorts me, in my dazed state, over toward the bar. Most everyone resumes their drinking and talking. I still can't believe I came in here.

"Molly! Come on over. Grab a stool," Dewey hollers, holding a mug up for me. "Here's a chamomile lite draft for you, on the house."

"How the hell are you, girl?" Gum says, all bleary eyed. He's aged since I saw him late in the summer, if that's possible for someone ninety-two years old. He's all dressed up with red suspenders over a denim shirt with pearl snap buttons. Holding out his arm toward me, he says, "Come over here by me."

But Laine walks me over toward Dewey so I can take the beer he's offering. I will ignore him. I will pretend nothing ever happened between us, and I will not make eye contact with the son-of-a-bitch. No sir. When I take hold of the mug, though, Dewey doesn't let go if it and we stand at an impasse, his hand on the mug, my hand on the mug, and me looking at the moose's head. The others at the bar become quiet again, and I imagine they are watching our strange little showdown. I look past Dewey to the mirror behind the bar and see the bald spot on the back of his head, but he still won't let go of the glass. I am forced to look right at him, and when I do this, I try to project my disdain, all my feelings that say: okay-you-win, but-you-really-don't. And in his expression I see that he is both relieved and pleased, and when he smiles at me with contriteness written all over his face, one side of his walrus mustache moves up about an inch, and for some reason I am reminded of a teeter-totter. In spite of myself, I smile, too, and shake my head at the hopelessness of trying to dislike Dewey. In this small, unspoken way, we agree that the war is off, that we will be something again, the two of us, even if it's just acquaintances with an indiscreet past.

"Thanks, Dewey," I say, taking the beer from his hand. Laine is watching us, smiling. The others have resumed their talking and drinking. Hopefully, she's the only one who knows what happened that night in Dewey's tepee. And if he's her ex-husband and she can be on friendly terms with him, well, then so can I.

Next Laine ushers me over to Gumboot, whose arm is still extended toward me. It's like he forgot he was holding it out there. This must be tiring, but when I approach him he grips my arm and pulls me next to him in a sideways hug. A tear forms, which I quickly suppress. My emotions are out of control lately, or maybe it's the feeling of being comforted after my near death experience with the deer.

"Hello, you old coot," I say. We're friends enough that I think I can say this, and besides, he's too drunk to defend himself. "Life's been dull. Haven't even been shot at since the last time I saw you."

Gumboot's in worse shape than I thought. His head rolls under his Jimmy Stewart hat as he leans in toward me and clinks his glass against mine and doesn't miss. His thin arm, wiry and strong like a steel cable, pulls me in a little tighter.

"I've been thinking," he croaks out. "I was wrong about something, and you know that hardly ever happens." This takes him a minute to say, a word or two at a time, like a record winding down. That's what I like about bar talk. The exchanges that take place don't require much from a person, and I don't mind it at all. My coat is now too warm. I should either take it off and stay, or leave, but Gum has a pretty good grip on me.

To give him time to rest up from his efforts, I ask him the obvious next question.

"What were you wrong about? Let me hear it."

He adjusts his hearing aid and continues. "I said once your place was an eyesore." He pauses. "But you know what?" Another pause. "Now I'm downright proud to have you as my neighbor." Gum continues to pin me against him, forcing me to hold my beer with my left hand.

"Thanks for saying that, Gumboot."

Dewey has maneuvered himself over in front of the Fuller Brush eyebrows sitting next to Gumboot, who turns loose of me in order to give Dewey his full attention.

"Yep," Dewey says, "I've lived in Montana for forty-eight years, most of them right up here in Snowshoe, and at least once every winter I drag my orange fifty-foot extension cord all the way into town, the one I use to plug in my engine block heater. Did it again yesterday on a beer run."

"What a fool thing to do," Gumboot says, perking up. "Never happens to me."

"That's because you don't have one to plug in, Gum. You still set a pan of hot coals under your engine to thaw it out."

"By God, it works," Gum says.

"Yeah, but only 'til you catch your car on fire and burn the whole shitteree to the ground."

Gumboot turns to me. "Now Molly, have you ever seen snow catch fire?"

"Molly hasn't even been on a luge ride yet," Laine pipes in. No one except me seems the least surprised at this shift in topic matter. "Come with me some time, why don't you?" she says, putting her arm around my shoulder. "You won't see snow burning, but when you're flying down that hill on an inner tube, believe you me, you'll swear you're making smoke."

"Maybe," I say, and I think, Why not? Feels like I've been on a luge ride ever since I moved to Snowshoe. "I'll think about it, Laine. But right now Chug is waiting for me."

"How is ole Thug doing?" Dewey says.

"She's fine. Thanks to a good-sized doggie door, she can come and go when she wants to, right through the back door."

"Oh, like shy customers used to do?" Gumboot says.

"You're probably right," I say, setting my mug on the bar.

Gum grips my arm again and pulls me close to whisper something in a hoarse voice everyone can hear, "I hope you'll come back and see us again real soon."

"Me too," I say, holding my face against his whiskery, bony cheek. "Merry Christmas, Gum."

As I head out into the silent, starry night toward my truck, I wonder about what just happened to me in the Snowshadow. Was I really even in there? I must still be in shock. After only one beer my head spins, as if I've nearly hit another deer on The Trail. Only now I'm thinking about engine block heaters and dragging orange electrical cords, about snow catching on fire, and running the luge course with smoke trailing behind me, and somehow that thought hooks up to Ben's joke of a recipe, Pheasant with Trail. Then I recall Dewey's teeter-totter mustache when he smiled at me. And I can still feel the tenderness of Gumboot's strong arm around my shoulders.

I reach up and touch my face where it rested against Gum's whiskery old cheek. Either what happened to me in the Snowshadow meant everything, or it meant nothing at all.

CHAPTER 28

"Chug, want to go for a ride?" I toss my skis and poles into the back of the truck, and my date today, the day before the new year, jumps onto the passenger seat. Even though her breath fogs up the windows immediately and I have to keep the heater fan on defrost, it's wonderful to have her great big Saint Bernard company.

We drive past cabins and shacks with smoke coming straight up out of their chimneys to about fifty feet, where it takes a ninety-degree turn—all the smoke columns in unison—turned at right angles, heading south above my truck. What a strange canyon. Even the air defies normal activity.

We park at the end of the plowed road south of town, where I click into my ski bindings, slip on my daypack, and Chug and I take off into the white afternoon. The sun shines longer here than where Snowshoe proper warms its feet near wood stoves in the narrow shaded canyon. Here the canyon opens up and divides into two separate gulches, one on either side of the base of Cinnamon Peak.

It seems that only snowshoe hares, rehearsing their chameleon shifts, could live in this ivory landscape. But what about the owls, coyotes and mountain lions that feed on the snowshoe hares, or would, if they could see one in all this snow? All the trees look like all the other trees; their branches drooping under clumps of snowflakes everyone agrees are not identical. I'll have to follow our tracks home to find my way back. If I don't, I'll have to consider the tangents of sunlight and the math of the sky to find my course, on this last day of the year. And math is not my strong suit.

Gary had planned to come out to ski with me, but decided instead to drive to Missoula for New Year's Eve. It's probably best not to ski alone, but after reading in Lempi's journal again most of the morning, I need some fresh air.

Chug dogs along behind my skis, an occasional snuffle reminding me of her presence, as we follow the route to the southwest on a path packed down by a snowmobile a few snowfalls ago. Bright sunlight reflecting off the snow sends tiny flashes of light dancing all around me before bouncing back up into the deep cobalt sky.

What a surprising turn Lempi's life took when she reached New York in 1895. It had never occurred to me that when young, innocent girls arrived in America they might have been picked up by scoundrels pretending to represent their American sponsors. I don't know how often it happened, but Lempi, unaware of her fate, was whisked away by train to serve as a prostitute. Angry and sad for Lempi, I ski faster and faster through the snowy brightness.

The blue wax I used on my skis, along with a purple kicker, turns out to be the right choice today, and I step forward and glide without slipping backwards. I'm almost glad Gary couldn't come out today. Myra and Jim skied with him last weekend and said he got so mad when his waxless skis kept slipping on the snow that he took off his skis and threw one like a spear about thirty yards. He then had to wade in snow up to his crotch to retrieve it while Myra and Jim waited for him in the cold. Still, he's my friend and most of the time he's good company.

My nose begins to run and I stop to remove my fat mittens, dig a tissue out of my coat pocket, and blow my nose. It's about twenty degrees Fahrenheit, not all that cold for Snowshoe, and there's no wind. Even so, my hands like it when I put them back in the mittens. Chug's favorite weather. She trots along behind me, the thick warm fur under her belly gathering balls of snow.

My thoughts return to Lempi's journal. With almost no knowledge of English, she'd been unable to protest her kidnapping and be understood by the train conductor. When the man took her off the train, he led her to a large building with many small rooms in a busy logging camp, where young women who spoke little or no English served the sexual needs of the loggers. Another German girl told Lempi she was in northern Wisconsin. Lost as she was, Lempi did not know how far she was from Indiana and her sister, and even if she knew how to get there, she had no money. A prisoner in the huge building, she was forced to let the men have their way with her. Sick at heart, she could not eat and she grew ill.

For months, Lempi wrote nothing in her journal. The next entry describes days of monotonous routine and nights filled with misery and pain and disgust, except for one of the loggers named Einar who always asked to be with her, none of the other girls. He treated her better than the other men did, teaching her a few words of English each time he visited. Knowing she had to give most of her earnings to the manager, he gave her a little extra money each time. She wrote about how the girls were forbidden to go outdoors, and how during the day she watched out a window at the streets below and saw the men riding horses and horses pulling wagons. She wanted to climb on a horse and ride away. Maybe Einar could tell her where the trains went from northern Wisconsin. She would ask him how far it was to Indiana, and how much the American coins and paper money were worth. If only she could survive until she saved enough money. Einar was good enough to her, but could he be trusted? She'd have to be careful with her questions.

I'm obsessed with the writings in the journal and can think

of little else. I stop again to blow my nose. Chug and I are climbing steadily uphill, curving right, then left along a narrow old mining road on the snowmobile path, but I'm not familiar with the route from my hikes last summer. With all this snow, everywhere looks like everywhere else.

The sun, along with the temperature, just dropped behind the ridge. It's as if someone switched off a floodlight. I'm far enough from Snowshoe now that I can no longer smell the smoke snaking from the tops of chimneys. Dusk can mean trouble, and if the curtain of dusk turns to night, it'll already be too late.

"Come on, Chug. We'd better head down as fast as we can."

I tie my scarf around my face, remove my clip-on sunglasses and put them away in their case in my daypack. Soon I'm gliding down the slope, on the dent in the snowy surface made by the snowmobile. My eyes begin to tear from the cold, and I blink to clear them. I gather speed, dipping and swooping through the surreal blur of white silence, faster and faster, running along with my big dog.

No sense losing control. Time to step off the snowmobile path onto the unpacked snow to slow my speed. There, I'm skiing more in control now, although Chug has stayed on the packed trail. Smart dog. Curve coming up, slight drop off down to the left, no problem, just a little snowplow turn, a little inside edge on the outside ski to slow and take the curve. I blink more tears away so I can see better. Exhilarating. I don't need any more intoxication than this on the last day of the craziest year of my life.

Without warning my outer ski catches something hidden just beneath the snow cover, and suddenly I'm skiing over the edge, out of control, heading toward a giant fir tree, its branches, drooping, laden with snow to the ground. Holding my ski poles to my sides and back, I duck down, bringing my left mitten up to cover my face.

Crashing branches, snow dumping all around me. Sudden stillness. I'm lying, twisted on my side in a tree well at the foot of a huge fir tree. The tip of my right ski is embedded in a wall of snow, my left leg is doubled back underneath me, with the heel of my ski jammed in the snow of the opposite bank. The ski binding holds the toe of my left boot captive. My right arm is twisted behind me. The strap of the ski pole is pulled tightly over my wrist and the basket of my pole is hung up in a tree branch. My glasses, still in place but wet with snow, must have been held in place by my hat. My left forearm and hand are free. I can move no other part of my body. If I could push the point of a ski pole down hard in a hole in my binding, I'd be able to free my boots. But one ski pole is missing, and anyway it would be impossible to release the bindings, jammed as I am into this frozen dark hole.

"Chug," I groan. "Help!"

Chug barks. She hasn't left the road. Can she even make it down to me in the deep snow? "Chug, come here, girl."

She whines and whimpers and makes the snuffling sound she cannot help but make. Snow and silence surrounds me for a moment, until I hear a muffled plowing aside of snow as Chug lunges downhill toward me, jarring loose another pile of freezing cold snow all over me. I wipe snow off my face. God, my nose and cheeks are cold. My feet are freezing. Wet snow has frozen on my glasses. Chug's whimpers draw closer, now near the edge of the drooping tree branches, buried in snow except for those I broke loose during my crashing fall into the tree well. Certainly she can find her way under the branches into this shallow cavern. Here she comes, slithering, clawing her way through the branches, bringing another pile of snow in with her.

"Good girl." I pet her head with my left hand. "Chug, please, you've got to go for help."

Chug whines a few times and gives one low bark, as if clearing her throat. She sits down on my leg, for there isn't much room. Does this mean she won't leave me? I push on her with my left hand. "Go on, Chug. Go! Get help now." Instead she licks my face with her hot mop of a tongue. When she stops, the veneer of wet saliva freezes on my face. "Chug, leave. Go now." I push on her face as hard as I can. I've never pushed her away; how can she not know what I mean? She nuzzles under my arm that is twisted behind my back, then grips my left mitten in her teeth and tugs on my other arm. This pulls my upper body enough to cause shooting pains in my right shoulder. When Chug lets go of my mitten I slap her head and yell, hoarsely, "Go. Get help. Sniff your way to some smoke and bring help!" She sits down again and looks at me. I stare back at her with my most serious, earnest look. She rises, turns to look back at me with one last whimper, then claws and scrambles her way out of the hole. I listen as she lunges and digs her way up the slope to the road.

But she does not leave. She stays on the road above me and barks over and over. *Hurrumph, hurrumph.* Like a giant bullfrog, she throws her entire weight into each bark.

My arm, wrenched behind me, is now numb. I wiggle my toes. Nothing. My face feels frozen. All the transitions, the shifting around I've done this year—all for nothing. I imagine I'm seeing the moose, just before it charged me; then I picture my beautiful sons and their errant hopefulness that their father and I might reconcile. I think of all the unanswered questions about the madam, and the work I've done, Ben has done, to save the brothel. All of it, everything, ends here with me in a hole under a tree on the side of a mountain—a frozen corpse.

Hurrumph, hurrumph. Chug continues to bark. I know she will bark until she cannot bark any longer, until she, too, freezes in place, in the middle of a *hurrumph.* No more. I cannot move. I cannot think. I'm too cold. Sleep. Put aside the cold, now, and sleep.

CHAPTER 29

Through a numb, frozen fog I hear Chug growl her deep, throaty warning, then whine, as someone tromps toward us above on the road, huffing, out of breath. A deep familiar voice, the most welcome music I have ever heard, says, "Chug, it's okay girl. Where is she?"

"Here," I groan up out of my bad dream, this one all too real. I'm not sure I actually made a sound. If so, did it leave my frozen lips?

"Here." I think I made a sound this time.

Chug plunges down the slope, plowing snow, and charges into the hole bringing with her more loose snow. She licks my frozen face, and my tears.

"Come on, Chug," Ben says, with gentleness. "Out now, so I can get in there." Chug seems to understand, and crawls back out of the hole.

"Oh, Molly . . . Molly," Ben whispers. "Darling, are you hurt?"

"Arm." What I mean and cannot say is that my arm *would* hurt, if it had any feeling.

Ben maneuvers over my extended leg and reaches up to unhook the basket of my ski pole. He gently brings the ski pole down, lowering my useless arm with it. Removing my mitten and the ski pole strap, he replaces my mitten then pokes the tip of the pole into the dimple on my ski binding, releasing my boot. After unbending my left leg, he releases the binding on my other boot. I am free now and all in one piece, but so cold, so cold and numb I cannot speak.

Ben removes his parka and folds it around my feet and legs before he unbuttons his thick shirt, lifts me onto his lap and holds me against his chest, wrapping his shirt over me and covering my face. He bows his head and I feel his warm breath on my face and the furnace warmth from his huge chest.

"Molly, Molly," he says, rocking me like a baby. "Started out as soon as I heard Chug barking. Ran as fast as I could. You'll be all right. As soon as you're warm enough, I'll take you home to my cabin."

I do not know how long I am held and comforted and warmed before Ben sets me off his lap and puts his parka back on. He crawls out of the tree well and reaches down to grip me under my arms to pull me out of my icy grave. I am aware of being lifted and carried, and hearing the slow shoving aside of snow, and being set onto the road in the shadows of trees now merging into the darkness. I curl up on the road, and Chug licks my face again while Ben fastens his snowshoes.

I am picked up, and then wrapped again, this time in each side of Ben's open parka. I rest against the warmth. As he steps forward on each snowshoe, I move with his warm body—a rhythmic, swimming motion. My legs dangle, lifeless and numb, off to the side like loose ropes. At one point, he walks so fast that the motion is jerky. I groan, and he slows down again. And then I remember—when Ben first arrived, he called me darling.

The creak of a door stirs me. The sudden warmth of a room flows over me and I feel myself being laid out onto a bed. My ski boots are being unlaced, my ski pants unzipped and pulled off. As if I'm a small helpless child, I feel Ben's large hands fumble as he removes my jacket, my sweater, and my pullover. The clothes are worthless, anyway, in my shivering, frozen state. Warm hands hold my feet, still in wool socks. Wearing only my long underwear, I am rolled to one side and covered, head to toe, with blankets and quilts. My teeth are chattering. Ben lies down beside me. What is happening? But I am too cold, too weak, to resist. Wrapped in his arms, as if in a cocoon, Ben holds my body against his, against the warm thin wool of his long underwear. He caresses my hair as he speaks. "I'm so glad I found you. You're safe now. You'll be all right."

I lose track of time as we lay like this, but finally my teeth stop chattering and my shivering subsides.

"Turn around," he says.

With his help, I do as I am instructed and lie with my back to him, and when I snuggle up to him he moves away, so his body does not touch mine. Still I am gloriously warm. With all my heart, I know what is most true—that when you are cold, nothing in the world feels better than finding warmth.

When I awake sometime in the night, Ben is sitting in an armchair near the wood stove. The small glass in the door of the stove emits a soft golden glow around the small room. Chug is asleep near the door. I try wiggling my toes. A few of them don't respond, although they hurt, and my shoulder is a little sore. But overall I feel warm and grateful. I wish he would come back to bed with me. Maybe in the morning.

I awake to a Bach concerto and light streaming in the windows. I open my eyes and seek the source of the music—a radio sitting in the window above the sink. I cannot see Ben anywhere in the cabin. When I pull myself upright and then stand, Chug trots over to me and nuzzles my leg. I sit back down, a little dizzy, to pet her head and hug her.

"Chuggie. You did bring help. I love you, girl."

As I make my way toward my clothes, draped on a chair near the stove, Chug follows, leaning against my legs. The two smallest toes on my left foot hurt when I step down. My muscles are stiff and sore, and my shoulder continues to hurt, but nothing about any of this surprises me. I dress slowly.

Each button requires my full attention. Groaning, I bend over to tie my ski boots.

Shiny stainless steel pots and pans dress up the rough-sawn boards on the wall near a small wood cookstove. Each pan reflects a different scene in the room, and I am drawn to them, thinking about the meals Ben has left for me. On the counter below them, near the sink, I see a notebook and pick it up. I know Ben's handwriting from the renovation sketches he did last summer, and I read a poem he has written.

Mountain Feelings

Rumblings
disturb the silence,
remind me of my past,
when freeze-thaw
broke me loose,
split me into fragments.
Now thin air like silk
caresses my flanks.
But what will I be tomorrow,
or in a million years?
Will clouds that veil my face
spill water to wash me flat?
Will the rain
ease my pain?

Tears form and spill down my cheeks for this huge, misunderstood mountain man. How gentle, tender, caring, capable, and strong. On top of all that, he's a gourmet cook and writes poetry.

Reaching for my jacket hanging from a large nail in the wall near the door, I step outside to look for the outhouse. In mid-morning, the trees are covered with snow and frost, and I see an antenna jutting into the sky from a tall tree. This must be how he's able to get NPR on his radio. As I walk past the woodshed, I spot a tiny structure that could only be my destination. As usual, I make my visit a quick one. From the outhouse I see another shed with an assortment of animal traps in many sizes and shapes decorating the exterior wall. Next, I wander over toward the building. After inspecting the traps more closely I continue around the shed and lift the latch, swinging open the double doors to a scene both grotesque and grisly.

Suspended from the rafters by hind legs bound together with a rope is a frozen, horse-sized carcass. Only bone remains on one hind quarter and part of a shoulder has been hacked away. A bloody axe is chopped into a nearby round of wood, ready for use. On the wall to my right hang saws, hammers, levels, and squares. More carpentry tools line shelves and benches, and in the darkened corner I see a brown lump leaning against the wall. The object could be an old overcoat, thrown over something. Mesmerized, I walk closer, careful not to touch the form dangling from the rafters, until I am close enough to make out ears, a face, long like a shoe box, and huge bulbous eyes staring at its own carcass. Screaming in recognition, I turn and run toward the opening, smack into the figure blocking the open doorway.

"Molly!" Ben says, grabbing me.

"Jesus, Ben. That's what you've been feeding me? Moose?"

CHAPTER 30

It's easy to sit here now, safe and warm near my wood stove, and think about what Darwin said about music, about adaptation, about the survival of the fittest. Snowshoe is like an island, not an island set out in the ocean, but one set back in time—where people did things differently, and where they still do. The residents in this edge habitat aren't transients. They're tenants, hunkered down to stay, staying on even when the conditions and events become downright harsh.

At 11:00 in the morning, on this second day of January, the sun shoots a beam of light down into our narrow slit of canyon, reminding me of the moon beaming down through my skylights on full moon nights. But now the snow catches fire, illuminating the negative spaces between rounded, snowy forms. Even the north sides of objects and structures are dimly lit with new insights. Mounds like whipped cream conceal junk cars, old mining equipment, rusted debris and secrets.

Within minutes, old Gumboot turns out the light in his shack, opens his door, and slams it shut. Up and down the lone Main Street, other doors open and close, the sounds echoing off the canyon walls. Then other winter sounds begin: the chopping of wood, snow being shoveled, car engines turning over, or not. Gumboot leans on his axe and looks up. Shielding his eyes from the glare, he yells, his raspy old crow's voice insulting anyone within earshot. His verbal offenses reverberate in the frozen crystalline air, doubling and tripling the population, intensifying every ancient grudge.

And I am reminded of the grudge everyone in town seems to hold against Ben.

Yesterday, Ben confirmed that he'd been cooking moose meat for me, and that yes, he had heard about my run-in with the moose. But he said he hadn't only fed me moose meat, that he'd also cooked me some elk. Could I tell the difference? There goes my good standing as a member of The Society for the Prevention of Cruelty to Animals. In a confusion of feelings, I had asked him to take me home. The next thing you know I was zooming downhill on a toboggan holding on tight behind Ben, with Chug loping along behind us. White trees blurred past on both sides, until we came to a complete stop against a snowbank near his truck. We didn't talk during the short drive to my place, and when we arrived at the brothel, I did not invite him in.

"Let's not work on the place for a week or two," I said. "I need some time alone." Ben had nodded his understanding. But as his old gray truck pulled away, I remembered something important and ran after him. When he stopped I opened the truck door and said, "Ben, thank you for coming to my rescue yesterday. I appreciate everything you did, more than I can tell you."

Now, as sunlight floods the canyon, I try to sort through recent events. First, there's my near-death experience in the woods. Resting here by the wood stove will help with that. Then there's the shock of seeing a dead moose hanging in Ben's shed. But my thoughts keep returning to Ben's tender warmth, the gentle strength of this man I know so little about. What I do know, I like. What woman wouldn't? It's what I don't know about him that worries me. Could this mountain man, who probably reads *Martha Stewart Living* in his spare time, have murdered someone? Could a loner who listens to Bach and writes poetry be the one who stuffed bacon in a man's shirt and left him tied up for wild animals to chew on?

And what does it mean to move from the city, out of mainstream society, to a collection of weathered, ramshackle buildings in an old mining camp in the woods, to a place where people have adapted to change with one foot in the past using old survival techniques that either work, or never worked at all. A hundred years ago, Snowshoe's residents probably considered their town the center of the universe surrounding it, especially the miners who searched the hills for riches. They came into town to spend what little they found on supplies, and many of them came to The Bluebird House to buy a little extra warmth and sustenance.

Now I've rescued the old brothel and its colorful past from the brink of extinction. I made it my home, then discovered the old building is still alive with events that happened long ago to a woman who worked at home. She earned a living the only way she knew how, in the economy of the day—gold and silver, ore and flesh. And what does it mean to be the intermediary between the madam and the mysteries she left behind: the identity of the child she bore, the whereabouts of a raw diamond as big as a bluebird's egg, and the secrets in her journal?

With Big Al purring on my lap and Chug guarding the front door of my quiet day, I read excerpts in the madam's journal.

7 ***August 1898***

My dear Hattie: The loggers leave behind only stumps and hills of branches that look nothing like our home in Germany. From the windows I can see a few trees still standing. The German men like to talk to me in our own language, and they say the slash is tinder dry. They are afraid lightning will start a wildfire, and if that happens it will run for many kilo-

meters. The fire could even wipe out our camp.

18 August 1898

Einar came last night, Hattie. He said a fire has started a few miles from here. If the wind blows in this direction, it will be very bad for everyone. We would have to lay in the river until it was over, and then we might not be safe. I said I wanted to get on a horse and leave here. He said, That wouldn't be wise, little Lempi.

20 August 1898

Dearest Hattie: I see horses tied up to hitching racks down on the street. I watch how the men get on and off the horses. I remember how our goat pulled us in the cart, and I wonder if I could ride a horse, too. If only I could escape. But Henry watches us all the time. My things are tied in a bundle, including my money. I tell Einar that if I get a chance, I will run away.

23 August 1898

Hattie, the fire is coming closer. Everywhere is chaos. Einar came again, and when Henry was nowhere to be seen we sneaked down the back stairs to the street. Einar had a horse for himself and borrowed one for me, and we rode in the moonlight a couple hours away from the fire to a town where I could catch a train. We didn't know if Henry would find us and stop me from leaving. Are you going on the train, too, I asked Einar, for I know he likes me. No, he said. I must go home to my family. When the train arrives in Milwaukee, you ask for the train to Montana territory.

And that is where I am now, Hattie. In Milwaukee waiting for a train to the west. I am too ashamed to send letters to you or Mama. I write my journal to you because otherwise I'm so alone. But I will write when I find a good job at this place called Last Chance Gulch.

25 August 1898

Dearest Hattie: I am on a train again. At one station, I saw waitresses called Harvey Girls. One girl told me she loved her job and was paid well. I asked how I could get a job, too. She began to stutter and then said to me that Mr. Harvey only hires girls who look a certain way. I said, And what way is that? She said, Well, I'm sure your nose is too big. And you aren't allowed to have a wart on your face.

26 August 1898

Yesterday I arrived in Helena at Last Chance Gulch. Hattie, this is a very busy place and everyone seems quite excited. I walked from one mercantile to another and from diner to diner, looking for work. I was without success. I used a little of my money to stay in a hotel, and then looked for work again today. One store-keeper, they are all men here, told me, You might try Little Rita's down the street. Tired but still hopeful, I asked directions. But as soon as I reached the doorway, I knew what Little Rita did to earn money. I needed a job. I will do this work again only for a little while.

A door had opened for Lempi, too, an escape from the sordid

world she'd been kidnapped into, a brief time of hope as she walked from door to door on Last Chance Gulch. Poor Lempi. America had not been a land of opportunity for her. Instead, she'd become lost on the northern frontier in a sea of missing persons, in a situation where rescue seemed impossible. Risking danger and uncertainty, she had sought a new life, without realizing how difficult it was for a young woman alone to earn a living, without knowing that she would be denied the ordinary life she would have preferred. Compared to Lempi Shunk's life, I could have taken many different chances, made many different choices. Instead, I had married Bradley.

I skip ahead in the journal, anxious to find out how Lempi ended up in Snowshoe.

17 July 1900

My dear Hattie: I must leave this place. It is dangerous. One of the girls, who often stole things from the pockets of men's clothing, was choked half to death last night. I do not steal from the men, as I do not want any trouble. They can be rough enough without making it worse.

19 July 1900

Hattie: A businessman I will call Mr. X was here last night. He does not want anyone to ever know he visits Little Rita's. Because he usually sees the girl who was choked and she is recovering from her wounds, he was with me. Do you steal, too? he asked me. I say, I never steal. I never have stolen. I take only what is given to me and I save what I can. He is not a bad man.

25 July 1900

Mr. X was here again last night. He gave me a tip. Thank you, I tell him. I save money so I can be independent someday, and have my own place. Mr. X says to me he has claims in a camp in the mountains, maybe I would like it there. Anywhere but here, I tell him. He says the buildings are on the creek, on a back street. Lots of men. Business should be good there, he says. If you have a down payment I will write an agreement for a lease-to-own deal, and transfer the property to you after you pay for it. I think, If I can't escape this work, at least I will be a manager. It is a step in the right direction. Some day I can sell it and find you, dearest Hattie.

13 August 1900

I am moving out to Snowshoe, the camp Mr. X told me about. I took the spur train out there today. Eugenia, another girl who wants to leave Rita's, went with me. She said she would work for me, and she knows another girl who will work too. I tell her she can if she does not steal or lie. There are a few buildings on the plot. A blacksmith shop that is no longer used, a little log cabin I can rent out, and a shop building. The newest building is made of boards, and is two stories high. This was a mercantile for a while, but the location was not good, as the store on Main Street took all the business. For me, the location is good. We will move in two days. I must manage my money with care so I can make regular payments to Mr. X. My girls

> *will receive honest wages for their work, and when they have saved enough money I will try to help them start a new life.*

After lighting the canyon floor for only a couple hours, the sun drops behind the western ridge. I stop reading and listen as the echoes of opening and closing doors bounce off canyon walls again, and when I rise to turn on my lights I see Gumboot withdraw into his shack carrying one last armload of firewood. While the top of Cinnamon Peak glows red like a bed of coals, everyone pulls their curtains shut against the icy darkness on the canyon floor. Shadow and wood smoke bridge the silence that fills the rest of today. Soon the evening migration to the Snowshadow Bar will begin and there my neighbors will put aside old grudges for a little while, or pretend to, as if they're at a church. While they won't be listening to a preacher, they'll tell their own truths while avoiding their own realities, painting pictures of their world in a way that softens the edges. We're all in this together, after all. Let's have a drink to celebrate the end of another winter Sunday in Snowshoe.

CHAPTER 31

Swimming up out of a deep sleep, I am filled with symphonic sounds, beautiful and warm, and I am overcome with sadness for Lempi. It's as if we've bonded, as if the pain she suffered in her lifetime is now my pain, as if we're sisters. I turn onto my other side, and thoughts of Ben take over. I recall his warmth, his thick strong arms holding me, willing me to thaw, exciting my blood to flow freely again.

But I must wake up now. I must not think so much about Ben, about this perplexing man. His *differentness* drives me crazy. Why didn't he *tell* me he was serving me moose meat, when he knew all along about my near-death encounter with a moose? Was he practicing some odd form of wilderness vigilante justice using food? If I knew more about him, if he'd let me close enough to know more, maybe I'd really be afraid of him.

I wiggle the toes on my left foot. While feeling may never fully return to my toes, at least they didn't fall off. And, surprisingly, my shoulder hurts only a little when I lift it over my head. At this moment, I'm grateful to be alive and comfortable. I wish I could stay in bed. I wish I didn't have to leave my warm bed, find clothes to wear, start my truck in the subzero darkness, scrape the windows, and drive to work. If only I didn't have to do all those things, I would be even more grateful.

Myra and Gary are all ears. While my lunch is cooking, that is the hot water and my instant soup are getting acquainted, I bring my two friends up to date on the contents of the madam's journal. I'm noticing, though, that there's more and more going on in my own life that I do not tell anyone—just like the madam, who told the details of her life to her sister, but only in her journal. In the past I talked openly about my life, but of course until I moved to Snowshoe there wasn't much to tell. Why not tell someone, if they ask, where you bought your fleece jacket? What does it matter if you brag about learning to change the oil in your car when your husband doesn't want grease on your hands? And what can it hurt to share your favorite muffin recipe? I've decided not to tell Gary or Myra about my skiing accident, because then I'd have to tell them about being in bed with Ben and seeing the moose carcass in his shed. Telling them would lead to dozens of questions, questions I cannot answer. It would take every lunch break the rest of my life to even try, so for now I'll offer small talk or share pieces of the madam's journal. And anyway, Gary keeps asking about the journal, reminding me that he's the one who found it.

We sit at the same small table in the corner, the edge habitat of the break room. We always sit at this table. It's as if it has a reserved sign on it. There's a fourth chair, but while we're on good terms with most everyone in the office, no one else sits down with us. The same four guys, including our boss, Floyd, sit at the table next to ours and talk about what's in the newspaper or they tell those tall hunting and fishing stories.

I summarize the journal contents. "Lempi named her establishment *The Bluebird House* because when she was in that brothel prison in northern Wisconsin, she saw the flash of bluebird wings out the windows and that gave her hope. She also said her new building reminded her of a birdhouse. I have to agree that it does, with that false front."

"So, after she got all moved in at Snowshoe," Myra says. "How hard was it for her to set up the business?"

"Sounds like that businessman in Helena she called Mr. X, the guy who helped arrange the deal for her, gave her some valuable support. The place had been a mercantile that didn't make it financially, and Mr. X had a carpenter come out to remove the shelves and counters and to spruce up the interior. She wrote that Mr. X had stopped by the Snowshadow to announce the opening of this new 'boarding house' and told everyone they could find entertainment there. He also paved the way with the local authorities, although she didn't say what that meant."

Gary listens intently, chewing his sandwich. As I open my soup container and stir the contents, the aroma of lentil soup with curry joins the lunchroom smells of leftover lasagna and tuna fish.

"Snowshoe must have been a rip snorting little town back then," Gary says, "with all the mining going on and the train coming and going."

"I guess so, but it's hard to imagine much happening up there in the middle of winter except hibernation. That's all I want to do these days, stay in my nice warm bed until spring."

"Alone?" Gary says. He cannot resist making these not-so-sly remarks.

"You're incorrigible."

"Speaking of which," Gary says, "how much detail does the madam go into about her actual work?"

"Gary, honestly!" Myra says, nudging his arm.

"Not as much as you'd think," I say. Actually, she wrote quite a lot about her life and I've been preparing for this question. I continue. "It's like she lived through it once and didn't want to write about it, too. At least that's what I think. She does say she rented out the cabin next to her house to a miner and his beautiful wife, and that the couple did some work for her. Lempi never learned to cook much besides bread, potatoes and turnips, so the wife cooked supper and delivered it, and the man took care of wood for the stoves and did maintenance. They did these things in exchange for rent. She wrote that the husband sometimes looked longingly at the girls."

We're interrupted by loud guffawing from the next table. "Yeah, that fish had so many lures dangling from his mouth we called him *Jingle Bells,*" my boss says.

"They like to talk about the one that got away," Gary whispers.

"What about her girls?" Myra asks. "Did she talk about them at all?"

"Speaking of getting away, one girl, named Eugenia, played the piano and the other girl, Stella, sang. Lempi had two girls at first. When Eugenia left, a black girl nicknamed Canary came to work for her." Anticipating Gary's question, I continue, "Lempi wrote that she had wondered how this would work out, but that Canary was very busy and quite popular."

"Canary?" Gary says. "Like a canary in a gold mine? Or did she like to wear yellow dresses?"

"The madam didn't say."

Shifting the subject, Gary says, "Myra, whatever happened about the llama that guy mistook for an elk during hunting season?"

"My friends made a deal with the man to buy them two champion llama calves in the spring. And, in addition to paying a big fine of some kind to the state he has to take a class on hunting—you know, the kind kids have to take before they can get a conservation license. Can't hunt again until he does it. Wouldn't that be embarrassing?"

The same Beethoven symphony awakens me this

morning. The only other sound is silence—eerie, detached and far away. After flipping on the lamp, I lift the mountain of flannel and down comforters off me, slip on my polar fleece robe and tiptoe to the window overlooking the creek. Through the fractal frost patterns I see only darkness. I hurry downstairs to stoke the fire. Chug rises, yawns and lets me know she wants out, even though she can come and go out her doggie door. When I open the front door I see why. Snow has fallen all night, filling and leveling every empty space. Snow is still falling. Chug saunters on the porch along the front of the brothel, where the snow has not yet stacked up. I stand in the doorway. Fat fluffs of snow drift to the ground. The temperature is warm, about thirty degrees, and then I realize. Darn, I'll have to call work. I'll say, *Hi, this is Molly. I'm snowed in up to my armpits. Can't possibly make it to work today. Don't know if they even assemble snowplows big enough to move all the snow between here and Helena. Might be days before I can get there. Hell, I might have to wait 'til spring.* Snowbound. What a heavenly word. Close the door, fool.

Coffee drips. Both the wood cookstove and the airtight heater purr. Big Al scratches in the kitty litter box under the sink. It's out of the way there, and anyway, I have to keep the cupboard doors under the sink open all the time so the pipes won't freeze. Soon as it's light enough, I'll shovel the path to the outhouse and dump the kitty litter. All this time on my hands today. Makes me want to play a Strauss waltz and dance around the table with the snow shovel.

Chug pads along the porch. I open the door to let her in, but she sits stolidly on her haunches, watching the snow.

After calling work to leave a voice mail message for the receptionist about being snowed in, I sit in my rocking chair near the stove drinking my second cup of coffee. The silence is soon broken by engine noise and the rumbling sound of snowplow on roadbed. You're kidding. It's barely light outside and someone's already wrecking my isolation and solitude by plowing the road. The sound comes closer. Chug lets out a giant *hurrumph.* Wearing my robe, I open the door and look toward The Trail. Above the ocean of snow, I can make out the top of a pickup truck, pushing, backing up, pushing forward again. Once again, it looks like Ben is coming to my rescue. As much as I don't want to be rescued this time, a sudden fullness in my chest informs me that my heart has decided, on its own, to pump my blood a little faster. I find my lack of discrimination in men both entertaining and amazing. First, I decide to be a neuter and maintain a short hairstyle. Then I get half drunk and allow a lewd barbarian to paw me in his tepee. Now I'm drawn to a kindly, hulking Neanderthal who can build things and cook, and, incidentally, may have committed a gruesome murder in his younger days. Ben's snowplow moves closer.

From my upstairs window, I can now see that the snow on top of the dilapidated blacksmith shop is stacked as tall as a man. Without a new roof, the brothel would not have made it through this snowfall, and I doubt the blacksmith shop will still be standing in the spring. By the time I descend the stairs fully dressed, Ben's truck has reached the front of my building and pushed snow away from the front porch over toward Gumboot's yard. The truck stops.

"Hi girl. How're you doing, Chug?" I hear Ben say.

I hear him tromp, tromp, tromp to rid snow from his boots and I open the door just as he starts to knock. He looks like a giant snowman, and he's holding my cross-country skis and poles.

"Thought you'd be needing these so I went back to get them."

"Thank you. Yes, I will be wanting to ski again." I take the skis and hand him a broom so he can sweep off his boots.

"Molly," he says, handing me back the broom, looking at me, saying nothing else.

"Ben. Please come in."

"Well, uh, you see, Molly. I need to talk to you, or at least I need to try."

"Let me take your coat. Coffee?"

He nods, removes his parka, and hangs it from one of the coat hooks behind the wood stove. His wool shirt gives off a warm, moist heat that threatens to steam up my glasses. He sits down at the table, and I hand him a mug of coffee and pull up a chair.

"I'm not going to say this right, so I'm just going to say it. Molly, maybe because I'm alone so much, I guess it's not easy for me . . . it doesn't even occur to me to say things."

"When I asked what you were feeding me," I say, "you wouldn't tell me. Didn't you wonder how I'd feel, eating moose meat?"

"Moose and elk, deer and muskrat, a fish now and then, that's about all the meat I've ever cooked or eaten. And beyond that, things get real complicated. There's liking to cook, there's a hungry woman I want to feed, and there's my recipes. Killing the moose—that was the simple part."

"The question that keeps running through my mind is where did you shoot the moose?"

"Try Again Meadows. Had a permit. Plenty of moose up there."

"What about smaller animals, then?"

Ben rises, talking as he opens the damper on the cookstove, "You know I trap in the winter. I have permits." He grabs a couple pieces of chopped wood, opens the lid of the cookstove, and tosses in the wood. "It's all regulated for conservation and I'm real careful. My dad taught me how to do it so the animals don't suffer any more than necessary. I sell the furs but don't like to waste the meat, so I learned to cook. At first I just roasted everything and ate it with my mom's special mustard. Then I bought some cookbooks and about went crazy buying pots and pans and kitchen gear. Even got a garlic press."

"I don't eat much meat, Ben, but I have to say the meals you left me were so delicious I couldn't help myself. And I'm always full of energy the next day."

"Thanks for the compliment. It's good, lean protein. This year for Thanksgiving I cooked moose meat sauerbraten. You would have liked it."

"I know," I say. "I know I would have."

CHAPTER 32

I'm alone in the small hot springs pool this Friday night. As I slip into the pool, the water climbs my body, stewing my goose bumps. When you're my size, you get so many of them in the winter. Thank you, Lord, for hot springs. Laine was right. A person needs a good hot soak in the middle of a Snowshoe winter.

A vaporous cloud wraps around me, then clears. On the other side of the steam-drenched window wall, I decipher the dark, ghostly figures in a row at the bar—Dewey, Laine, many of the town's other thirty-some residents. The shortest of the faceless forms, the one wearing the fedora, is Gumboot. I wonder how many more Snowshoe winters my gnarly old friend has in him—how many more stories, how many more insults? I also think about the ghostly profiles of men who once visited my brothel, and the madam's sister and parents and how she never saw them again after she left Germany.

But mostly I'm in the mood to celebrate. I had always dreamed of being snowed in somewhere, and yesterday it happened. On top of that, after Ben showed up to plow me out he said, "I'm heading back up the canyon now to run my trap line, but if you want I can start work again on Monday. I can bring my tools and we'll finish the inside of the brothel." There's that *we* again. But this time when he said *we,* I think he meant *us.*

What amazes me most about being snowbound is this: by the time Ben left and I had shoveled a path to the outhouse and filled the wood box, darkness had crept back into the canyon. In what seemed like minutes, my big day of being snowed in took leave, and today I resumed the slow drive in the dark to Helena to work and the long drive in the dark to get back home.

Laine's laugh invades the pool area. I close my eyes and imagine her laughter reaching all the way out to the icicles hanging off the log stringers of the Snowshadow. I watch the icicles tremble, the decibel level too high for them, and then drop to the snowy ground and shatter. I have to smile. When I'm around Laine I feel free, because if she can make it through life with that outrageous laugh, I can darn well say whatever comes to mind.

When I'm dry and dressed again, I saunter into the bar. Dewey, already holding a mug under the keg for me, watches as I walk toward Laine.

"We were all talking about you a while ago, Molly," she says.

Dewey reaches across the bar, offering me the mug of beer. He won't let go of it until I look beyond his raffish outlaw's mustache straight into his Big Sky eyes, and smile at him. My secret password. By this act of feigned camaraderie, by giving in, I will score what I want—a beer. And besides, that insulting event in his tepee happened so very long ago, or maybe it never happened at all. There's that song again, the one that seems to most represent Dewey: *some girls don't like boys like me, ahhhhhhhh but some girls doooooo.*

"Oh, really," I say. "So, what were you saying about me?"

"How it's time you went on a luge ride. It's a requirement of anyone crazy enough to live up here. You didn't know that? Even Gum's been on a luge ride. 'Course it's been a while. Gum, tell her about it."

Gumboot cups his hand behind his ear and studies Laine, who points at the hearing aid appliance clipped to his shirt pocket.

"Oh, guess it's time to turn on the manure scoop," he says, fumbling with his hearing aid. "There. Now what was that?"

"I said you went on a luge ride a few years ago with Dewey."

"Oh, hell yeah." He stops, wheezes, then continues. "We was on inner tubes. Dewey went first. Boy, oh Jesus, did I fly. 'Bout had to change my long johns, time I got to the bottom. Still think Dewey greased the run."

"You should have heard him," Dewey says. "Yelled all the way down, something about catching on fire."

"What do you think, Molly?" Laine asks. "I haven't been down the run yet this winter. Let's go tomorrow."

I'm thinking, why not? They aren't going to let me out of it, and besides, living up here has been nothing but one big honkin' luge ride. But then, I've made it this far in one piece, and that includes nearly freezing to death. No sense tampering with that small miracle. "I might," I say. "First I want to know a few particulars, like how long is the run, how many curves, how dangerous is it, and how do we reach the top?"

"We're famous, here at the 'Shadow, for providing white knuckle fun," Dewey brags. "Haven't had an ambulance up here in years, not since we switched to inner tubes. I packed down the new snow so it's fast, but not too fast." Dewey slaps a tattered, beer-stained map of the luge run on the bar. "The run is only eight, maybe nine hundred feet long, and the curves slow you down. The first one here, this little wow, is the Pauper's Dream."

"Pauper?" I ask, looking up from the map.

"You know, real poor. The Dream was a mine up here that never paid out. Anyway, then you pick up speed and bank into the Bucking Mule, right here, and then the Jawbone. After that, you sail on a straight stretch that shoots you right on out this big turn here, the Silver Wave. Dumps you into a clearing above the parking lot."

"Where'd you get the rest of those names?"

"All old mines. Some of 'em sold millions in ore."

"Worked in every one of them hell holes," Gumboot says.

"You'll take us to the top on the snowmobile, right Dewey?" Laine says.

"Sure will."

"What do you say, Molly?" Laine says.

Everyone looks at me expectantly, even Dutch, the moose. Before I realize what I'm doing, I smile and nod my head up and down like one of those idiot toy dogs people put in the backs of their car windows.

Gum grabs my hand in a wiry grip and says, "Be sure to bring an extra pair of drawers."

At twelve noon I'm waiting with Laine in the Snowshadow's parking lot. Dewey's German shepherd is gnawing on the hairy shank of a deer's leg over near a snowbank. A small troop of ravens sits on the Dumpster, croaking, talking strategy, and taking turns hopping down onto the snow to tease the dog.

"You two ready?" Dewey says walking toward us, his frost-covered mustache poking out of the hood of his brown parka. "I've been down the course a couple times this morning. It's perfect." He starts the snowmobile and straddles the beast. "Hop on."

I'm about as ready as I'll ever be. Woke up feeling a little stiff. Probably because I slept all tense worrying about being thrown off the course by the Bucking Mule or chewed to bits by the Jawbone.

Laine climbs on behind Dewey and snuggles close, leaving me just inches of seat, clearly not enough.

"You sure there's room?" I ask.

"Climb on and hang on. I'll go slow."

I should trust this man? But I'm committed now. I've spent time picturing myself doing this new wild thing, watching myself clinking beer glasses later with the regulars in celebration of this initiation rite. Straddling the cold, black vinyl seat, I reach around Laine to grab Dewey's parka sleeves, and raise my Sorel boots up off the snow. Dewey creeps ahead, turns up the hill and even though I hold on with great concentration, gravity causes my hind-end to slide back and sag over the back of the snowmobile seat. This can't possibly work. But Dewey follows a packed pathway uphill across the mountain through the snowy trees on what looks like an old road, then uphill across the other side, then up a steeper area, and I'm still on board. I wish now that I was home by the wood stove, listening to Beethoven. What am I getting myself into?

At the top, Dewey kills the engine and, one by one, we untangle ourselves and disembark. Dewey pulls two inner tubes from a small shed and rolls them toward us. They must be from a large truck. I look downhill at the smooth, bowl-shaped drop off, the start of the course. The sides are three to four feet high, the channel just wide enough for an inner tube. Sunshine flashes off snow crystals. From my bird's-eye view of the canyon, I can make out the top of my roof. *It was nice knowing you, Lempi.* Then I look toward Cinnamon Peak, hoping to spot the smoke from Ben's cabin. No sign of life. The frigid air is freezing the hairs in my nose, and I feel stiff and old and scared. The deep, guttural croaking of ravens echoes in the canyon.

"You go first, Laine." I try not to sound pleading.

Laine sits down on the inner tube, resting her little butt in the center of the giant rubber donut. Grabbing the two handles attached to the top of the inner tube, she bounces over to the starting gate, positions herself with her feet pointing downhill, and pushes off. Her signature laugh echoes all around the canyon walls, carrying, I'm sure, all the way to the Continental Divide. Startled elk and moose are probably jerking their heads up, wondering what species of creature has invaded their territory.

An eerie silence soon takes on new meaning. Did she fly off the course? Is she still alive?

"Come on down," Laine yells in a game show host voice.

Oh God, help me, now it's my turn. I position myself as Laine did. Dewey is here for moral support, or so he can tell the story later in the bar of how I didn't make it down the run and how he had to climb a tree to retrieve me, or the pieces that were left. I do not want to do this. Only a fool would choose to hurl herself off the face of a steep mountain. I'm getting up now. As I lean forward to pull myself upright, I hear the cold squeak of boots on snow and feel hands on my shoulders, followed by a forceful shove. The inner tube and I fly off the top edge into the white chute, drop to a lower elevation and accelerate toward a looming wall of snow and ice. I'm going to smash into it. Banking now, totally out of control, I rush downward, flying inside the icy groove, trees blurring past, sparks bouncing off snow.

"Dewey, you son-of-a-bitch!" I scream. "Shit! I'm going to die!"

I blast toward another curve, the big one, what was it called, the Jawbone, and I'm holding my breath. Tears soak my hat. My body vibrates, humming over the bumpy course. The Jawbone yawns ahead, a new and sudden twist. If I crash now I'll shatter like an icicle. And then I see them—enormous black wings flapping nearby, talons reaching for me. The front of the inner tube begins to lift into the icy blue vault as I flash out of their reach, escape into what I hope is the last curve, the Silver Wave, and suddenly a clearing appears and Laine is leaping up and down, her laughter drawing me onward until I slide to a stop at her feet.

She pulls me up, hugging me, yelling, "Molly, Molly! You did it. You should have heard yourself. Wasn't that great? Wasn't that about the most fun thing you've ever done?"

I'm laughing and shrieking, breathing in rapid gusts, tears and snot running down my face. I can't catch my breath. I'm dizzy, and when my legs sag Laine tries her best to keep me standing, while trying to jump up and down. My teeth bang together above her shoulder, but I'm so relieved to be alive I don't even care. And I'm embarrassed at the awful truth of it, that, *yes,* this *was* the most fun I've ever had in my life.

Then, as if someone else is speaking, I hear myself say, "Laine, come on. Let's do it again!"

After three more runs, Laine and I retire to the hot springs pool.

"Now I have to face life after the luge runs," I say, luxuriating in the hot water. "Everything will probably seem pretty boring after today."

"Yeah. It's all downhill from here," Laine offers.

"You know I'm pleased about my new life. It's interesting. But nothing quite compares to that luge run."

"You're lucky. It's right next door. You find yourself a little bored, just hop on an inner tube and take a spin."

We're both quiet for a minute. I run my hands back and forth in the water, making small, short strokes. "Laine," I say, "I found the madam's journal in the brothel last summer, written in German."

"You're kidding," Laine says. "Tell me more."

"Her name was Lempi. I've had the journal translated and it's quite a story, how she got here. I'll tell you about it some time. The thing that puzzles me most is that in 1904 she had a baby with Ben's grandfather, Wilbur. She called the baby Little Will. Lempi died in 1918 and I don't know what happened to the child."

Laine is silent, staring absently at the indistinct forms in the bar beyond the steamy window.

"I just had a thought," she says, dreamily. "We've all heard that the madam wasn't pretty. It's like her lack of beauty was legendary, or something. Well, in case you haven't noticed, Gumboot's not too pretty, either." Laine chuckles. "I mean aside from the fact that he's ancient. And if he's ninety-two, he would have been born right around 1904, if my math is correct."

"But Gumboot came from Twodot. You remember. He ran away from home after trying to brand gophers and catching the church on fire."

"I know he tells that story. He tells lots of stories, and some of them are true. But I'm not so sure about that one. And there's something else."

"What's that?"

"I happen to know his middle name is Wilbur."

CHAPTER 33

Lempi wrote about the song of the creek behind The Bluebird House and how it varied over the seasons—how the creek roared during spring thaw and everyone's concern about flooding. She wrote about the tinkling, gurgling sounds the stream made when it trickled low in the summer and fall. And then this time of year, there was the frozen silence of the stream.

During the summer months, she wrote in her journal about the sky blue flash of the mountain bluebirds, the music of robins, even the constant background noise of the ravens. She wrote that she felt most like a member of the crow family—common and ordinary, a survivor who dines on life's leftovers but who always makes it through somehow. I'm convinced it was Lempi who found the quote by Darwin and kept it inside a crack in the wall, although she didn't mention this in her journal. There were, in fact, long gaps of time when she wrote nothing at all, and each time she began to write again, she did not explain what happened during the missing times.

As I drive home along snowy, ice-bound Cinnamon Creek in the growing dusk, I continue to think about Lempi and to watch for deer. When I make out several shadowy forms ahead, I shift down to reduce my speed to a crawl. The forms are three mule deer, with their enormous satellite dish ears. Why do I never see a moose on the road, when the men at the 'Shadow say they often see one?

Then I think about how the men in the bar talk almost non-stop, that is except for the man with the Fuller Brush eyebrows. Over the years I've heard so many women complain about how their husbands don't talk much at home.

And I wonder if their husbands would talk non-stop if they went to a bar?

Lempi had written that she preferred to listen to the men talking because she never felt comfortable enough with her English. She had tried to keep up on local events so she could ask questions and keep them talking. The men often came to the brothel for companionship or music, and many times they wouldn't even want to take one of the girls upstairs. Such was the case with Wilbur, the love of Lempi's life. Ben's grandfather was a huge and gentle man, like Ben. Lonely after his wife died, Wilbur had found solace with Lempi at The Bluebird House.

But Hermann, Dewey's grandfather, the man Lempi could not love, was different. Hermann was arrogant, easily angered, and often selfish. Lempi had tried to be as kind and polite to him as she was to the other regulars. He had wanted her, although she had never been close to him; he always took one of the other girls upstairs when he came to The Bluebird House. And Hermann drank too much, and gambled, too, but he worked hard in the mines and searched for treasure in his spare time. When he found the diamond up Try Again Creek he had insisted she take it, saying he loved her. She had told him she did not love him, that she couldn't take the diamond. But he insisted, even though he had his own wife and family at home. So she had kept it for him, hidden in a safe place, with the intention of returning it when he wanted it back. He told her the men in town thought he'd lost the diamond gambling, and that was what he wanted them to believe. Hermann thought Lempi would grow to love him in time, and he was a man who always expected to get his way. But she loved Wilbur. And what Hermann didn't know, what no one else in Snowshoe knew, was that she was pregnant with Wilbur's child.

Eugenia, one of the girls who had worked for Lempi when she first started her business in Snowshoe, had saved enough money to move back to Helena and open a dress shop. Eugenia began to sew all the clothing for Lempi and the other girls. During the last months of her pregnancy, Lempi had stayed in a room behind Eugenia's dress shop, and when Lempi gave birth to the baby boy she left the baby in town with Wilbur's sister. It broke her heart, but she felt it was best for Little Will. Although Wilbur's sister did not approve of Lempi and would rarely allow her to visit the baby in Helena, Wilbur brought Little Will out to Snowshoe sometimes so Lempi could spend time with him. Lempi adored her baby.

When Hermann found out that Lempi and Wilbur were lovers, and saw Wilbur leave the brothel with the baby, that's when he lost his head and challenged Wilbur with the gun. Lempi had written that Wilbur must have laid the baby, swaddled in a blanket, on top of the woodpile behind the brothel. He would have moved away from the baby and grabbed his gun to protect himself. The events in the dream I had right after moving into the brothel actually happened that night in 1904. The two men had fired almost simultaneously, and both had died.

As I pass the Snowshadow's parking lot I try to see what cars and trucks are there, but can't see many because the snowbank between the road and the parking lot is now so high.

When I turn onto my lane, I see that Ben has left a light on for me. I park to the side of the building in the rectangular notch he plows for that purpose. Chug is waiting inside the door with her usual slobbery big dog kisses and nuzzles. Al looks up from the couch. I smell food, good food, chow delivered by snowplow, and see a note on the table.

Molly—Hope your day went well. You'll find a mystery meal in the oven. Hope you like it. Ben.

Instead of heading for the oven, though, I am drawn upstairs. At the top of the stairs, I look out the window down into my back yard, between the brothel and the creek. I try to imagine or remember where the two bodies fell that night in 1904. I search my memory of the dream. No luck. It was dark in my dream, and it's dark now.

I descend the stairs toward the distinctive smell of a gourmet meal, cooked by the grandson of one of the slain men who had, early in the century, lain dead somewhere on the ground behind this brothel, dead from a gunshot wound inflicted by a jealous man.

CHAPTER 34

Floating up the narrow stairwell, I turn and turn again, and when I reach the top of the stairs, I am drawn toward a faintly glowing light. Entering the room, I see her lying on the bed, so pale and thin she appears to be melting into the linens. Even her long brown hair is dull and faded against the white pillowcase.

Lempi turns her head toward me. "You've come."

"Yes, dear Lempi. I'm here with you."

"Please," she whispers, "would you open the window a little so I can hear the creek? The doctor wouldn't do it . . . the draft."

I lift the window a few inches, open now to the silvery shimmer of moonlight on snow crystals. The filmy curtains flow out into the room on the cold night air, poise and hover as if resting on water, then drift back to the window.

"I love the creek, too," I tell her. "The low, splashing murmur among the rocks." I say this even though the stream is now frozen within its banks, its soft sound muffled under layers of ice.

"Are the bluebirds back yet?" Her words, too, are muffled by her illness.

"Yes," I say. "Just yesterday."

"With the girls gone it's so quiet." Each whispered word is weaker than the one before. "And I haven't seen Little Will for so long. I hope he's all right."

I take her limp hand in mine again. "You can see him soon, Lempi, as soon as you are well again."

"I'm so weak. My sickness too big." Her eyes are closed now. "The creek . . ." She breathes the words and is quiet, still as a rock frozen in the stream. I wait. As if in a dream remembered, Lempi's eyelids flutter. I pull the covers up to her chin, against the draft from the open window. "Molly." Her breath, her word itself the merest draft.

"Yes, dear," I say, my face now near hers. I take her hand in mine again.

"The diamond," she whispers, her eyes closed. "Inside . . . hanging on boards . . . Wilbur's."

The tiniest shudder, nearly imperceptible, passes over her frail body, her hand becomes limp, then cooler, and in only moments, ice cold.

"Goodbye, dear Lempi."

I awaken to one of Reichardt's harp and piano sonatas, playing on my clock radio. How long has it been this way? Minutes? Hours? I have no way of knowing, for I cannot open my eyes. I must rise and prepare to go out into the cold, but something heavy and numbing is holding me down under warm, deep water. I must not surrender; I will not be held down. Wild, unearthly animal moans leave my throat as I groan to be released, yet I cannot move any part of my body. Even my hands and fingers do not respond to my commands and with an overwhelming hopelessness, I submit to the unknowable force and return to deep sleep.

CHAPTER 35

I awake to the sound of Al leaping from the bed onto the wood floor, and then it is quiet again. My arms and legs move now, as does my head. Lying still and warm and secure, I think about my dream, about the death of the madam. And then I wonder about the missing diamond and what Lempi's words might have meant, *"inside . . . hanging on boards . . . Wilbur's."* It isn't much to go on. Maybe Ben will have an idea. Where would Lempi have hidden the diamond? A safe place. Where would that be? *We* had not found it in the walls of the brothel. Or had *we?* No. Ben would have said something if he had found the diamond. Poor, dear Lempi.

Other than music, other than my thoughts of Lempi, I hear nothing at all except a lack of sound. Only one other time have I felt this eerie silence. I flip on the lamp and lift the layers of warm bedding off me, slip on my robe and furry slippers, and descend the stairs to stoke the fire. Opening the draft and the stove door, I lay three rounds of firewood onto the still glowing coals, hoping all the while I'm doing this urgent task that my hunch is correct: that I am, once again, snowbound. Lifting aside one of the downstairs curtains I see fat, fleecy snowflakes, loaded with fractals.

The darkness and the falling snow hide the truth until I open the front door to let Chug out. Snow is everywhere—in the air, on the ground, overflowing in the darkness. Must be two and a half feet of new snow, enough to keep me indoors most of the day. I never would have dreamed how much I love to be snowed in, and I wonder if part of the joy of being snowbound is knowing Ben will soon arrive to plow the road to the brothel.

After coffee and breakfast, I call in to work with the sad news that I am, once again, snowed in. I sweep Chug off before letting her come back indoors. I shovel the path to the outhouse to dump the chamber pot and kitty litter box. Back indoors by the wood stove, I hear the rumbling sound of a thunderstorm far off. In a snowstorm, this can mean only one thing.

Ben and his powerful old pickup with its snowplow blade attachment move closer and closer. He's now on the lane this side of The Trail, pushing snow then backing up to gain more drive to push more snow. Now he's in front of the brothel, shoving snow onto Gumboot's side of the alley. And then he turns off the engine and I hear the tromp, tromp, tromp on my porch. I open the door before he can knock and hand him the broom. It's cold outside. Ben closes the door and sweeps snow off his pants and boots while I move back over to the other side of the stove where it is warm and where I will wait for him to open the door and fill the room.

"Hi, Molly," he says, smiling as he opens the door, closing it as quickly as possible and leaning the broom against the wall behind the stove. His words flow into the room past the wood stove, and by the time they reach me they are glowing like an ember.

"Thanks for the wonderful meal last night. Let me guess. Was it bear?"

"Nope. Venison. Bumped into a deer on The Trail the other night, so technically, you were eating roadkill, slow roasted in a sesame-soy marinade with a little molasses and red wine vinegar thrown in. Thought I'd try something a little different."

"Delicious," I say. I'm not cold, but I notice I'm hugging myself and because I've heard that others can read this as a defensive posture, I stop doing it. "Would you like some coffee?" He always wants coffee. I should stop asking and just pour.

"I could use a cup," he says, removing his parka and draping it over a chair. "Think I'll frame in the area under the stairs today, like we talked about before. Make a fine pantry."

"Sounds good. Since I'm snowed in today I can saw boards for you again. But first I'd like to tell you about another dream I had."

"Another one?"

"Yes, and, once again, it seemed completely real. Lempi was dying and I was there with her, I mean upstairs in this building. She wanted the window open so I opened it a few inches. She missed her son and I told her she'd see him as soon as she got well. Then, just before she died, she started to tell me where she hid the diamond."

"What did she say?"

"She said, 'Inside . . . hanging on boards . . . Wilbur's.'"

"Not the clearest indication," Ben says. "I'll have to think about those words. Could be almost anywhere."

"And I have some information on the baby, your uncle."

"He'd be my half-uncle, that is if he's even alive," Ben says. "My grandfather had my dad and two other kids before my grandmother died. After she died, he apparently took up with the madam." Ben removes his next layer of clothing, a wool shirt. He's steaming, as usual, during his transition from outdoors to indoors. "And I'm the youngest in the family. My dad was close to fifty when I was born."

"Ben, I think Gumboot is Lempi's baby. And if he is, I don't believe he knows it. He is the right age, and he could have made up the story about coming here from Twodot."

"Nah," Ben says, shaking his head. "I just don't see it. I think you're chasing rabbits. All the men in our family have been big, like me."

"But wait. The madam was a small woman. And let me tell you what she wrote in her journal toward the end. It's better than fiction. The murder happened the way I dreamed it, details and all. Bizarre, I know. After the shots, Lempi ran downstairs and out the back door to see if Wilbur was still alive. She knelt beside him and called his name over and over, until she realized he was gone. She grabbed the baby from the woodpile where Wilbur had placed him, took him upstairs to his baby buggy, and . . ."

"Might have been the baby buggy we saw out in your log building last summer," Ben says, getting up to put wood on the fire and pour another cup of coffee.

"Yes. And then she ran over to the cabin to tell the neighbors about the shooting, but the man had already heard the shots and left to find the sheriff. Poor Lempi was heartbroken when they took Wilbur's body away. She wrote that your grandfather was the only man she ever loved. But she still had the diamond Hermann had given her. She thought about selling it and leaving by train to find her long lost sister, Hattie, in Indiana. But she didn't know how to explain her past. And anyway, when Lempi tried to claim the baby, Wilbur's sister wouldn't let her have him and, in fact, blamed Lempi for Wilbur's death. Lempi couldn't leave without her baby so she stayed on in Snowshoe.

"One day, when the baby was about ten years old, Wilbur's sister died and Lempi was able to claim the baby. From her journal, it sounded like Little Will thought Wilbur's sister was his mother and that Lempi was an aunt. But Lempi had the birth papers so the courts gave her custody. She brought the baby out to Snowshoe to live with the neighbors across the alley, which, of course, is where Gumboot lives now, where he's probably lived most of his life. By doing so, she could see him once in a while and buy things for him, yet he didn't need to know that she was his mother. Within a year or so the silver prices dropped and lots of mines shut down. The brothels were closed for lack of business and stricter laws. The madam lived alone in The Bluebird House, keeping an eye on Little Will, paying for her own cooked meals as before. Then, when the flu epidemic of 1918 struck Snowshoe, Lempi caught it and died."

I'd been talking so animatedly, I hadn't felt the lump forming in my throat. "And Laine told me Gumboot's middle name is Wilbur." Tears form a pond and begin to spill down my face. Ben looks at me steadily, surprised at first, and then he gives me a handkerchief out of his pocket. As I mop at my face and nose with my right hand, he takes my other hand inside his huge warm hand, big as a paw.

"It's just that Little Will, or Gumboot, if they're one and the same, never knew who his real mother was," I say, crying, sniffling, mourning for Lempi, "and she died without ever seeing her sister again."

"I'm sorry," Ben says.

"It's not your fault."

"I know, but I'm still sorry."

Without saying anything, I rise. My hand is still inside Ben's hand so he rises, too. Chug, napping as usual in front of the door, lifts her head, gazes at us, snuffles once and resumes her nap with a sigh. Ben follows behind me up the stairs. I pause at the window to look down past the frost, past the elaborate fractal patterns to the snowy landscape below, and then I take Ben over to my bed.

I do not know what will happen next. It doesn't matter. All I know is that I want more, more of this man who has become so much a part of my life. I lift my arms up around his neck and hold myself to him. At first he does nothing, and then he puts his arms around me and hugs me strongly, passionately, then holds my head tenderly in both of his big hands and looks into my eyes.

"Darling Molly, I've wanted to hold you for so long." He hugs me again and lifts me, effortlessly, off my feet. "When you were in my bed at the cabin I wanted so badly to caress your skin, your face." His lips are on my closed eyes, my nose, and now my lips as I am lifted onto the bed. He pulls off my boots and socks, and holds my bare feet for a few seconds. Then he removes his boots, outer shirts and pants, until he's down to his long underwear and he's lying beside me in bed. Just like the night at his cabin, I can feel the thin wool of his long underwear. But unlike the night at his cabin, we help each other remove the rest of our clothing, giggling, tugging, kissing, and licking, until Ben wraps me in his arms and holds the full length of me against his hairy male body. Wrapped in his arms I feel both small and large, the size of the universe. As he rocks me, I feel the murmur of water over rounded stones. He caresses my hair and face and kisses me gently, starting at my lips and moving downstream.

I lose track of all that happens, but overhead, sheets of snow break away and calve off the metal roof. The sounds of our mating echo back and forth across the canyon walls. Snow ignites on Cinnamon Peak and flows down avalanche chutes. Wild animals in the woods lift their heads in wonder. And I am delirious with my rediscovery of what is most true—that when you are cold, when you've always been somewhat cold, nothing in the world feels better than to find a warmth you never knew existed.

CHAPTER 36

"You're looking cheerful this morning," Gary says to me during coffee break. "In fact, you're almost glowing. If I didn't know any better, I'd think you were pregnant. Or is it something else? Did you and . . ."

Myra interrupts Gary's line of questioning. "Guess who I saw having dinner at the Windbag Saloon last night?" she asks, then, before we can inquire "who," she says, "Bradley. And he wasn't alone."

"That's kind of a Democrat hangout, for a Republican like Bradley," I say. "Who was he with?"

"Except for her hair color, she might have been you," Myra says. "No kidding. She was about your stature, short brown hair, glasses. Both of them were dressed casually, and she was wearing hiking boots."

"Maybe he was selling her some insurance," Gary offers.

"I don't think so. He looked all relaxed and smiley-faced, not like he was closing a deal," Myra says. "And, I wasn't going to mention it, but Bradley was also wearing hiking boots."

"I don't believe it," I say, shaking my head. "Huh. That is amazing. He always wanted me thinner and, of course, I had to have long hair. It was one of his requirements. And he's never owned a pair of hiking boots in his life; he dismissed the outdoors as *that green stuff out there.*" I shake my head again. "Huh." I can't seem to quit making this stupid sound. "I guess I'm happy for him."

"Well, there went some of her glow," Gary says to Myra.

From the next table in the lunch room, we hear, "Old Floyd called me last night, said he'd had an accident."

Everyone in the room stops talking to listen to this new information. I'm glad for this turnaround in subject matter, but I hope my boss is all right.

"Was he hurt?" two men ask at the same time.

"He said he's okay," he continues. "He was driving home on the highway from town the other night and a black angus bull wandered onto the road. Floyd killed him deader than a doornail and wrecked his truck doing it. Big problem is, he was written up for it. His fault. It's open range. Turns out the bull had the right of way. The rancher is pissed as hell, said it was a prize champion bull and Floyd has to buy it. And old Floyd said, 'Fine, then I'll put him in my freezer.' And the rancher said, 'Like hell.' "

"Floyd wasn't hurt at all?" Myra asks.

"Bunged up his knee a bit so he's seeing a doctor today."

"Sure no loss with that old truck," one of the other men says, rising to go back to work. "The thing was held together with duct tape and bungee cords. Still, no question, this'll put a dent in old Floyd's bank account."

This evening I'm driving home from work with a little more caution than usual. I hadn't thought to watch for livestock before, just deer, and so far I've been lucky. But then I always drive slow like an old lady. I turn off the highway onto The Trail and glance over at Laine's ranch. Not so much snow out here by the highway to see over, and in the dusk, hunkered under a lean-to shed not far from Laine's house, are Pepper and another, younger, horse.

As I drive along in second gear, I stare ahead to look for movement on the road or eyes reflecting my headlights. I'm glad to be on my way home. I hadn't wanted to go to work today. I'd wanted to be lazy, to replay in my head what happened yesterday. That this singular experience with Ben might be renewable is a scary thing to contemplate. I'm not sure I could endure that much pleasure on a regular basis. Oh, I suppose I could try it and see what happens. When I think about the intensity of bliss, the sheer indulgence of being close to Ben, it occurs to me that it felt something like blowing a fuse. This warms me all over, a tropical smile.

Yesterday, after Ben and I were dressed again and sitting back downstairs eating soup, I had the nerve to say, "You know, some people still think you were responsible for that environmentalist's death twenty years ago." And he said, "I couldn't have been more surprised when they questioned me and then put me on trial. What a nightmare. Took years to pay the attorney fees. And I don't know a thing about the murder, except that someone had to be demented to do something like that. For a while after I was acquitted, I worried that whoever did it would come after me."

And now, as I peer through the darkness for shapes of deer, my mind flips to the channel that plays thoughts of Bradley. I think about him with a date and find myself saying "huh" again. It's not like I'm jealous, just altogether dumbfounded. At least the woman he was with seems like someone who'd be nice to Jeremy and Scott, that is if Bradley can fool her into dating him long enough so he can introduce her to them.

Next, my thoughts wander to the dream I had the other night. Lempi on her death bed. Her words, "inside . . . hanging on boards . . . Wilbur's." And then I wonder if Gumboot could be Lempi's baby, Ben's half-uncle? Sometimes I'm sure and other times I think it's my overactive imagination.

Before I know it, I'm turning onto my own lane, and I can see by the light that's been left on that Ben must have worked inside the brothel today. Chug is outdoors on the porch and greets me with passionate whimpers of joy.

"Were you a good dog today, little girl?" I hug her and pet her head. She follows me through the front door and into the aroma of dinner. I see a note on the table.

> *Molly, darling—Dinner is in the warming oven. You will not be eating moose tonight, but you must solve the following riddle to learn what it is you are eating and before you can earn another surprise dinner.*
>
> *My little feets can swim so far,*
> *But I'm not very fast.*
> *My marshy diet is clean and mild.*
> *I'm furry with stripes and really quite wild.*
>
> *Yours, Ben.*

Yours? Huh. Chug dogs along behind me as I follow my nose over toward the stove. "What do you suppose he means, Chuggie? I can only think of muskrat, but I don't think they have stripes. Do you suppose he's feeding us skunk?"

Chug looks up at me expectantly. I feed her and big, furry Al their pet food first, then retrieve my wild gourmet dinner from the warming oven. When I lift the corner of the foil covering the dish, the smell is beyond belief. Wafting upward in the steam is a hint of curry, garlic. Green chili slices? Wild guesses. How does he do it? The meat appears to be small chicken thighs. Chickens have little feets, but they aren't the best swimmers. Braised carrots and whole new potatoes share the plate with the meat. Whole new potatoes? In January? Chug and Al now sit watching me, waiting for their chance. I'm like Dewey's German shepherd, preparing to gnaw on something the ravens want to eat. Curious, I bite into a small piece of meat and, as I carry the plate over to the table, my knees weaken from the taste. Succulent. Delicious. I only wish Ben were here to enjoy the meal with me. And if he were here, for dessert we would go upstairs. My mind wanders to yesterday, but only for a second. I pour some wine. Chokecherry this time. Sipping the wine, I cannot think when I have felt so supremely cared for, so warm and happy.

After sharing the smallest amount of my dinner possible with Chug and Big Al, and after Chug and I take a brisk walk down Snowshoe's Main Street, the three of us sit around the stove shooting the breeze about what we ate for dinner, skunk or what. We agree that even skunk prepared by Ben is better than the nothing-at-all that Bradley cooked for us. And then I tell them about his date. "And Chug, you're not going to believe this, but the man was wearing hiking boots." Chug acts a little startled and snuffles her disbelief. I damper down the stove, say goodnight to Chug, and climb the stairs with Big Al.

In the middle of the night I awaken, caught and held in a bright light. Fully awake now, I remember, and look up through the skylight to a perfect full moon, shining on me, once again, like a spotlight. Light is also reflecting into the room off the snowy ground below. And there is something else near me—a luminous, incandescent presence, glowing like a new candle.

"Is that you, Lempi Shunk?" I ask. I wait, but sense no movement, see no change in the quality of light around me. "If it is you, dear Lempi, I love you like a sister."

As the moon continues on its path beyond the skylights, the magnitude of light in the room diminishes. Lempi's glowing light, soft and pearlescent, fades to the palest rose.

I close my eyes and wait, hoping for some physical sign that Lempi's spirit heard me, that she knows how much I care. And then it happens—the gentle bump against my bed. I hold my breath, not wanting to frighten her away, and soon I feel the gentle pressure of her embrace on my shoulder and on the back of my head, tender and loving. For a brief moment I am the sister of Lempi Shunk, the sister lost to her forever, until now. Then her presence recedes, breathes out as a tide, until it disappears, until I am surrounded with the stillness of feathers, the loneliness of one left behind.

CHAPTER 37

Twisting the black doorknob half off, I swing open my front door and run for the ringing phone.

"Hello?"

"Molly, it's Dewey. Gumboot's in the hospital."

"What happened?"

"Fell off his bar stool late last night." Dewey's voice sounds thin and worried. "He didn't look too good all evening, then he drank even more than usual."

"I'll be right over," I say. I want to talk to Dewey in person, hear the story face to face, learn how such a thing could have happened.

My boots crunch frozen snow as I walk and run through the frigid air to the Snowshadow. This is not good news. When you're ninety-two, you don't need accidents. And I don't want to lose Gumboot. He's so capable, so wiry and strong, so persistent in the way he goes about life here in Snowshoe. But then, I think, his mother did hand down some sturdy genes to him, and so did Wilbur. When I reach the parking lot I see Dewey's truck, and, as usual, the German shepherd chewing on a bone. Good. It's early enough in the evening that Dewey is alone in the bar.

Grabbing the antler handle I pull hard on the outside door and pass through the small room with the coat hooks, without removing my coat. Dewey always keeps the hinges oiled, so the second door swings toward me easily.

"How bad is he?" I ask, flipping back the hood on my coat. Dewey and I are undeniably connected by our fondness for Gumboot.

"Broke a couple ribs, nothing else. Problem is, his lungs

aren't too great thanks to all the mining he did."

"How ever did he manage to fall off his bar stool? That's like a rodeo champion falling off his horse."

"I don't know. Several of us were here. I turned to pour someone a beer and the next thing you know I heard a scraping of bar stool legs and something heavy hitting the floor. Everyone rushed over to him, while he laid there under the bar groaning, one hand on his chest. We all thought he'd had a heart attack. Didn't bother calling 911. Hell, it would'a taken an ambulance forever to get up here, if they could've even found the place, and then they probably would'a hit a deer on the way. So we laid him, limp as a rag doll, on the seat of my truck and covered him with a blanket. I hauled him into town, fast as I could, just like I did with you that day."

"But how's he doing? Is he going to be all right?"

"Oh, yeah. Hell, yeah. No one's tougher than Gumboot." But Dewey's face is lined with worry. I'm not sure I believe him. He continues, " 'Course they X-rayed him and found the broken ribs. Checked his ticker. No problem there. The doc said they could use his heart as a transplant, which I thought was a rude thing to say. Gum flat-out refused to be hooked up to any tubes, although he did allow the IV. I had to run interference, trying to tune his hearing aid, explaining things. He's a tough old fart."

"I'll visit him tomorrow after work," I say. "Is there anything I can take for him?"

"I'll tell you what he's gonna be craving along about tomorrow evening, and that's a few shots of whiskey."

His eyes are closed. If the nurse hadn't given me the room number of Charles Doherty, I would not have recognized my friend without his hat. And I knew he was small, but somehow he'd grown in size over the few months I'd known him, maybe to match the dimension of his stories. Now I see he's skin and bones, a newborn bird.

"Hi Gumboot," I say, putting my hand on his frail arm. He opens his eyes. "You look a little out of place here." It's a lame thing to say, but it's better than revealing my dismay at his appearance or commenting that he doesn't look very tough wearing that nightie. I'm glad to see that the other bed in the room is empty.

His watery red old eyes look at me with some recognition. I think I detect a slight smile. Then I realize he isn't wearing his manure scoop so he can't hear a thing. I pull up a chair, sit by his bed, and take his nearest hand in both of mine. His grip is weak. It's a sad thing to see the likes of Gumboot in such a condition of weakness, in a setting defined by need and helplessness.

Gum lifts his right hand, curved as if he's holding something small, and brings it to his lips. He seems to be pleading with me as he does this. I nod my head in understanding, but then sigh and shake my head to let him know I cannot give him whiskey. The hospital should have a policy that allows a body something so essential. Hospitals are no place at all for those of us with an addiction of one kind or another. Doctors must know what a shock it can be to the system when someone like Gumboot is denied a drink, someone who's probably had a shot or two of whiskey every evening for the last eight decades.

Gum closes his eyes in resignation. I remain by his bed for a few minutes, and when I squeeze his hand to signal that I'm leaving he opens his eyes and looks at me as if he's trying hard to communicate.

I pat his arm and say, "Goodnight, Gum. I'll come back tomorrow evening. You rest easy, now." He cannot hear this, but maybe he can read my lips or feel the vibration and tone of my voice through my hand on his arm. And before I leave, I lay my face against his shrunken, whiskery cheek. "I love you, Gum," I say, hoping he can somehow understand what I'm saying and wondering how many people have ever said "I love you" to Gumboot.

The next evening after work when I stop at the hospital, I'm astonished to see how much better he looks. He's even wearing his manure scoop.

"Gumboot! You look like a peach, compared to yesterday."

"Hello, girl," he says, lifting his hand toward me. His voice is even more hoarse and gravelly than usual.

"Nice dress you're wearing," I say, pulling up a chair and taking his hand in both of mine.

"Trade it for some whiskey," he mutters. "Even trade ole Herm's diamond, if I had it. Goddamn, I want a glass of whiskey. Helps me forget."

"I know," I say. But I don't know how this craving feels, or about needing to forget something so bad that I'd drink to do it. "Anything I can do at your place while you're here, Gum?"

He closes his eyes, frowning to squeeze them together. He shivers, opens his eyes and looks over my head, scared, as if he sees a ghost. He grips my hand as his tired old eyes tear up and begin to flood. "All I ever wanted . . . find a diamond like Herm found." He's babbling, his voice so raspy it's difficult to understand his words. "Them rabbits shutting down all the diggings up and down Try Again, just when I was fixin' to find something good. I know'd it for certain. Bastards ruin't my chances." He's whimpering now, his eyes still squeezed shut, tears streaming.

"It's okay, Gumboot," I say, petting his hand to soothe him. My God, he'll pop a gasket if he keeps going like this.

Maybe I should call a nurse.

"It ain't okay and I gotta tell someone. I'm the one tied that guy to a tree. Hell, I was in my seventies. When the law come around it was easy to play helpless and dumb. Nobody thought a gimped up old miner could'a tied the guy up. Hell, I just pushed him into a hole and made him climb into a rope sling like we used to lower miners into shafts. Had a gun on him. Marched him to a tree, cinched the sling tight and tied him up. I was just trying to scare him, then I was gonna shoo away the animals and send him home in the dark. But I drank too damn much while I waited, and just as he started screaming, I passed out. Woke up too late."

I shake my head, tears streaming down my face. I'm sorry for Gumboot, sorry for Ben, and sick at heart for the innocent man who died such a gruesome death.

"All I ever thought of was finding something, anything, bein' somebody. All my life searching, never finding, scratching in the dirt, breaking up rock. If you're in jail, you can't find no gold, no diamonds, no nothin'. But I'm sorry as hell for what I done."

"Gum, should I call someone to visit you? I mean, do you believe in God?"

"Who?" Gum says. Either he didn't hear me or he isn't religious.

"I said do you want me to call a preacher for you to talk to?"

"Hell, no. Preacher can't help me none. Only whiskey." He's whimpering now, like a worn out motor running down.

I catch a movement near the door and turn to see Dewey standing there, staring at Gumboot sadly and shaking his head.

I turn back to Gumboot. He's quiet now, still as a rock. "Gumboot?" I say, rubbing his arm. "Gum?" But he appears to have drifted into a deep sleep.

"Dewey, you will tell the sheriff what you heard, won't you?" I ask. "Help me clear Ben."

Dewey turns and disappears without a word.

CHAPTER 38

"Sheriff, my name is Molly Binfet and I'm here about a murder."

The man I'm addressing appears to be in his mid-thirties, about six feet tall and real husky. He seems young, much too young to be a sheriff, and he isn't even wearing a uniform, he's wearing Dockers slacks and a long-sleeved shirt in a muted plaid. At least his sleeves are rolled up halfway to his elbows, signifying a work ethic. Otherwise, it looks as if he's been out shopping at Wal-Mart with his family instead of conducting sheriff duties.

"Please, call me Troy. Have a seat," he says, motioning to one of two tan plastic armchairs on the opposite side of his cluttered desk. "Now, what's this about a murder?"

"It happened about twenty years ago near Snowshoe."

"We've had a few strange murders up there over the years."

When the murder I'm here to talk about happened, this sheriff named Troy was probably in high school. Then I realize I'm not around young people that often. There aren't any youngsters, that is people under forty, living in Snowshoe, and while we have a few at work, we don't have many.

"I'm here to talk about the murder in 1975, the one they call The Bacon Rind Murder, the one where someone stuffed bacon in a guy's shirt and tied him to a tree for the wild animals."

"Oh, that one. I remember. That's the year we beat Bozeman High in football and went on to the state championships. We all followed the trial of the guy they suspected. And since I've been in office, I've looked into the case a time or two. I'll have Lydia bring the file." He buzzes the front desk and makes his request, then continues. "Seems to me the victim was a member of one of those first environmental groups. You a reporter looking for a scoop?"

"Actually, I have a scoop for you," I say. "Last night I heard someone confess to the murder. He's ninety-two, he's a friend of mine, and he's in the hospital."

"No kidding?" he asks. "I mean about the confession?"

"Shouldn't you be writing this down?"

"Ma'am, you have my full attention. We'll write the specifics down on paper in a while. Why don't you just tell me what he told you."

I continue. "He said he only wanted to scare the guy away from a mining claim he was working up Try Again Creek, but things got out of hand. In a way, the death was an accident, not that this excuses what happened."

"No, ma'am, it doesn't."

"Troy, please call me Molly? I'd prefer that."

"Okay, Molly. What's the name of your friend, the one who confessed?"

"Gumboot Charlie, and he's the oldest living inhabitant of Snowshoe."

"But what's his real name?"

Here's the tricky part, I think. Do I tell this sheriff named Troy his name is Baby Shunk? Baby Weigland? What I do say is, "He uses the last name Doherty, but I don't know what's on his birth certificate."

"Could you explain what you mean?"

"It's just that I have reason to believe his real last name, his birth name, might be different from the name Doherty. And while he tells everyone he's originally from Twodot, I think he's from the Helena-Snowshoe area. Not that any of it matters, just that his real name might not be Doherty."

"What do you think his real name might be?"

"Possibly Weigland. He might be the half-uncle of another friend of mine, Ben Weigland, the man who was tried for the murder and acquitted."

"This is all quite a can of worms," Troy says, scratching his dark brown crew cut. "Let's stick to the confession." He begins to tap a pencil on his desk, a nervous habit I find bothersome.

Lydia, a young, plump woman, walks in chewing gum, carrying a fat file frayed on the edges. "You know we have a whole file drawer on this case, Troy, but this is the file on the initial investigation."

"Thanks, Lyd," Troy says. "That's what I need."

I wait while Troy leafs through pages in the file. After a few minutes he looks up and says, "I see where our office did interview a Mr. Charles Doherty of Snowshoe, but he offered no new information, and it's clear we didn't consider him a suspect." He resumes tapping the pencil and says, "Tell me what you have."

So I tell Troy exactly what Gumboot told me, pausing once to ask him to please stop tapping the pencil.

When I finish Troy says, "That's an incredible story. And you're the only one who heard the confession? The reason I ask is this: you mentioned that Ben, the man once accused of the murder, is also your friend."

"Well, I certainly hope you don't think I made all this up just because I'm friends with Ben Weigland!" I say, raising my voice.

"No accusation intended. But it would be helpful to the case if you weren't the only one who heard the confession."

There he goes again, tapping that pencil. I glare at the pencil. He stops the tapping.

"Actually, someone else heard it, too. Dewey Slocum, another Snowshoe resident. He runs the Snowshadow Hot Springs Resort, which makes him almost like the mayor. He heard the confession at the hospital—standing right there at the door of Gum's room. Poor old guy's had nightmares ever since he did it, since the murder happened, I mean." Everything is tumbling out of my mouth, things the sheriff appears not to be interested in, but I continue. "Trouble is, Dewey is even closer friends with Gum than I am, and I know he doesn't want to believe what he heard. He also has a grudge going against Ben." Troy is tapping his pencil again. I glare at it. He stops. I start talking. "Anyway, he *likes* to think Ben killed that guy. I almost think he *enjoys* thinking he did it." I realize I'm venting, but my taxes pay this young man's salary, and I guess I need to say these things. "He also wants the other residents in Snowshoe to believe the same thing. So Ben has lived like an outcast in his own home town all these years. It isn't fair. The judge and jury acquitted him and now here's further proof of his innocence."

"You realize we'll have to prosecute the old man if . . ."

"His name is Gumboot, not *the old man,*" I say.

"Sorry. We'll have to prosecute Gumboot, of course, but it would be helpful if this Dewey Slocum would come in to corroborate your story."

"Like I said, Gumboot is ninety-two. I believe he's suffered enough, and, anyway, he can't live forever—unfortunately. His lungs aren't good. Mostly, I want the victim's family to know the murderer has confessed and I also want Ben's name cleared once and for all, for Ben's sake and for the good of Snowshoe's own residents."

"Well, on the strength of your signed statement regarding his confession, and Mr. Slocum's corroboration, we would have to prosecute Gumboot when he's released from the hospital."

The sheriff is like a dog with a bone, when he gets something in his head. "I'll have to think about it," I say.

Troy looks at his watch and I realize suddenly that it's five o'clock, quitting time for the sheriff. "Tell you what, Molly, if you'll write your name and phone numbers, home and work, on this paper, I'll add some notes for the file. If I don't hear from you in a few days I'll call you to see what you intend to do. We can't do much until I hear from you."

"Thanks, Troy. I do appreciate your time."

"You're welcome. That's why I'm here, and, of course, we do love to wrap up old cases. Too bad in a way it's this one. The case was scheduled to be on television this fall, on *Unsolved Mysteries*. Imagine that. I would have been on national television."

Troy taps his pencil a few times as I rise to leave. I turn to look at him, and smile.

"Sorry," he says, laying the pencil aside.

CHAPTER 39

After visiting with the sheriff named Troy, I'm so confused and troubled I decide not to stop by to see Gumboot on my way home. Last night he seemed to be doing better, at least before his confession. I'll think this thing through and stop to see him tomorrow night. But what will I say to him? "Hi, Gum. I just told the sheriff you committed The Bacon Rind Murder." Is that what I'll say? And what does Gum think should happen now, for heaven's sake? He knows people in Snowshoe still blame Ben for the murder he just confessed to. But then, he's in pain and under sedation, in addition to going through whiskey withdrawal, so I'm sure he's not considering every angle of this situation. Damn. Gumboot's my friend, but now that I know the truth about the murder I can't let Ben keep taking the rap, even if it is just the regulars at the Snowshadow Bar who continue to believe he committed the gruesome crime. And what will Dewey decide to do? Sheriff Troy was right about one thing: this is all quite a can of worms.

Turning onto The Snowshoe Trail, I see lights on over at Laine's house. I shift down to my usual winter crawling speed. After about twenty minutes of peering ahead for the outlines and eyeballs of deer, my truck and I roll, mostly undented, onto my lane. The brothel is dark. Ben must not have worked on the interior today.

Stepping onto my porch, I hear the phone ringing. I turn the black doorknob, flip the switch—no lights. I grope for the phone in the dark, catching it on the fourth ring before the answering machine picks up the call.

"He's gone." It's Dewey's voice, deeper and huskier than normal.

"Who's gone?" I ask. People are always coming and going from the Snowshadow. Why is he telling me this?

"Gum."

"You mean he left the hospital? Where'd he go?"

"Molly. He's left us all. He died about 4:30 this afternoon."

"No," I say, tears streaming down my face. "I can't believe it. He was doing better." I stop speaking. Dewey says nothing. I say, "I'm sorry, Dewey. I know how much he meant to you. And even though I didn't know him for a long time," I say, stopping again, this time to sniffle, "I can hardly stand the thought of never hearing another one of his stories or holding his bony old hand."

"I know," Dewey says. "We'll all have to limp along without him. Funeral's Saturday. I'll have to let you know the time."

"Are you okay?" I ask. "I'll come over if you need the company."

"Nah. I'm fine," he says, not sounding fine. "Just sitting here, playing solitaire."

Then I remember that I'm standing in a dark house. "Dewey, I noticed your lights were on when I went past. And I saw other places all lit up when I came home, but my lights are out."

"That's weird. If everyone else's electricity is working, yours should be, too. You're on the same circuit as the rest of us."

"I have a flashlight or two and some candles. I'll look around, check my breaker box."

"Call me if you need any help," he says.

"Thanks, Dewey. I should be all right. But lights or no lights, I'm going to be sad. What a character Gum was. In his own way, you could even say he was lovable."

"I know one thing for sure, Molly. He really took a shine to you."

Using my flashlight, I check the breaker panel. No fuses blown. No switches in the off position. Yet I have no electricity. A note on the table from Ben says that at about 4:30 his work light went out. He said he'd come back tomorrow. So, after lighting several candles, I feed Chug and Al and heat myself some leftovers on the wood stove. While I eat I think about Gumboot. All of us in Snowshow—we're his family. That is, we *were* his family. Ben might be his one blood relative, but I'm the only one convinced of it. And Ben hardly knew Gumboot. Too bad. Tomorrow morning I'll leave a note for Ben about Gum.

Chug and I take a brief stroll through town in the zero-degree evening, past places lit within, and then head back home to our own dark abode. And when Big Al and I go to bed, I don't need to turn out the lights. Instead, I carry a candle up the stairs. Even my home feels emptier, as if lacking in furniture, with Gumboot gone. My new life, less than a year old, now has a gaping hole in it where a crusty old man used to be, a bright and colorful character who gave our little town of Snowshoe the gift of backbone.

I blow out the candle. "Goodnight, Chug," I yell down to my door guard.

Without the electric blanket's warmth, it takes a while to reach a level of comfort under the covers. Al is content as I stroke his fur. "He's gone, Al. And you know what else? I think it's best not to ponder heaven or hell, in this particular situation." Al purrs like a freight train and drools a little. I should put a bib on him. At least Gumboot lived on his own steam right up until the end. He didn't spend his final hours in a rest home, drooling on a bib. And then it hits me. Dewey said Gumboot died at 4:30, the exact time

Ben said the electricity went out. It's as if The Bluebird House is in mourning.

No bright moon wakes me in the middle of the night. Instead, I awake to something bumping into my bed and a dim, luminous glow, a vertical presence nearby.

"Lempi?"

I hear low crying sounds, but they seem to be coming from far away, from another room, and not from the glowing presence.

"He was your son, wasn't he, Lempi? I'm so sorry."

The glowing in the room becomes dim. I feel the pressure of a hand on my shoulder for a few seconds, and then the form diminishes even further, as if controlled by a dimmer switch. She moves to the top of the stairs, pauses, then descends, taking one deliberate step at a time. I wait and listen. Where is she going? Chug moans, whimpers and sighs. Does she see the ghost and think she's dreaming? The light comes on downstairs, the light that didn't come on earlier when I flipped the switch. I check the bedside lamp. It works. When I go downstairs to switch out the lights, Chug looks up, blinks, and lays her head back down. Back upstairs in bed, I cannot figure out what just happened. What did Lempi's spirit mean? If she intended a message, I don't understand it.

Gum looks different laid out in the casket. His full head of steely gray hair is thin and combed straight back. He's clean shaven and his Adam's apple protrudes unnaturally. Wearing a white shirt and red suspenders, he looks gaunt and sunken and exposed without his hat. Laine places a red carnation on his chest. I hide my treasured piece of mountain goat fur next to his arm so someone unknowing won't see it and think it's a piece of trash. Mountain goats climb around in high, rocky places, and I like to think that's close enough to heaven for some of us, Gum included. Dewey tucks a silver dollar into Gum's folded hand, a hand that had been unlucky at working his own claims. The dollar is one Dewey said he found buried up near some miner's shack when he was a boy. Ben stands and looks at Gumboot a long time, wondering, I suppose, if the weathered old man in the casket could, indeed, be his half-uncle. But I know the truth. The matter of the electricity outage at the brothel clinched it for me. And when I called information in the Twodot area, the operator had no listing for a Doherty family. Then, when I talked to the bartender there, he said he'd never heard of a Doherty family in those parts, and he would know.

All the regulars at the Snowshadow are here at the service, including Shawn, the furnace man's kid, and the man who never talks much, the one with the Fuller Brush eyebrows. I also see several faces from Gumboot's ninety-second birthday party. Dewey looks bleary-eyed, but Laine and I are the only ones who shed tears.

After the service, Ben and I drive home to the brothel. In need of some fresh air, I trade my somber clothes for ski clothing, and we drive to the foot of the gulch where Ben parks his truck. We hike up the shoveled path to his cabin, where he changes into his outdoor clothes and we grab a couple pairs of snowshoes.

The sky is gray and the woods are silent. Although it hasn't snowed in a few days, snow is settled in clumps on the branches. We don't go near laden boughs, with their loads of snow.

"I'll have to invent some snowshoes for Chug," Ben says, looking over his shoulder at the big dog wearing the snowballs on her tummy fur. She's following behind us in our trail so she won't break through the snow so often.

But I'm thinking about other things.

"Ben, when I visited Gumboot in the hospital the night before he died, he confessed to The Bacon Rind Murder."

"I wondered about that a few times, if he might have done it. He was so protective of his claims, so all-fired anxious to strike it rich."

"He didn't mean for the man to die. He didn't get back to him soon enough to untie him. He suffered all those years with the guilt of what he'd done."

"Doesn't make a difference now, unless people know it. The people who've always meant the most to me—my parents and their friends—all know I couldn't have done such a thing. But it would sure be nice if the locals up here knew I wasn't guilty. And Dewey's the worst."

"Dewey heard the confession, too," I say, running out of breath. We're tromping up a steep old road now, and snowshoeing is more work than skiing.

Ben stops. He's not breathing hard at all. "Good," he says. "That's good."

"I told the sheriff, but Dewey said later he wouldn't corroborate what I'd heard. It's because he doesn't want Gum to be remembered that way. It's not about you."

"Lot of good that does me."

"I know." Thinking we've had enough sadness today, I add, "Why don't you come home with me tonight? Maybe we can start a chain of echoes in the canyon, generate some avalanches."

"Well, let's go," Ben says, stepping up the pace as he turns to head back, leaving me to wonder if I'll have enough energy left to live up to my offer.

When we return to the brothel, the answering machine is blinking. I push the button. "Molly, this is Dewey. Say, we're having a toast to Gumboot this evening here at the 'Shadow, starting . . . well, actually we've already started. Hurry over as soon as you can. And bring whoever it is you happen to be with."

Which means he knows I'm with Ben. We were together at the funeral. Someone at the 'Shadow must have mentioned they saw us drive through town together when we went snowshoeing. Interesting. And odd. Dewey just invited Ben, his long-time enemy, to the Snowshadow. Huh.

When Ben and I enter the bar, removing our gloves, everyone sets down his drink in unison and watches us. The bar is full. The place has reached or exceeded its carrying capacity, and all eyes are on Ben and me. *WE RESERVE THE RIGHT TO SERVE REFUSE*, the sign above the cash register reminds me. The moose looks on, head lowered, as if preparing to browse, or to charge someone who has invaded his territory. He sees everything, knows all our secrets.

Laine is standing near Gumboot's stool, empty now except for Gumboot's hat. Everyone is silent. Laine, looking sad and a little lost, moves toward me and hugs me, and then says, "Ben," as she holds out her hand to shake his.

"I know what Molly wants to drink," Dewey says, "but what'll it be for you, Ben?"

Ben seems awkward, out of place, his expression one of suspicion of this scene he finds himself inside. "Lite draft'll be fine," he says, glancing toward his old friend, the furnace man's kid, who nods to Ben. Ben nods back.

"Come over by me," Laine says, leading me, with Ben following, over to where she'd been standing near Gumboot's stool. His bar stool is like the easy chair of a household patriarch. No one else ever sits in the chair, with its invisible *reserved* sign. It's like my grandpa's chair at the ranch on the Big Hole, or the table in the break room where Myra, Gary and I always sit, and the one next to it where my boss and his cronies sit, every single break and every lunch hour.

We take the beers Dewey offers, passed to us by way of Laine, and each take a sip. Ben looks around the room as if he's caged and the men at the bar are his captors. I know he hasn't been here for at least two decades.

The talk at the bar resumes.

"Has the place changed much?" I ask Ben, for something to say.

"Not at all. Same pickled eggs and beef jerky, same bags of peanuts, same guys, only older. Nice moose head, though. That's new since the last time."

Dewey slaps the bar with a wet towel. Crack! Everyone stops talking again. "Now you all know the unfortunate circumstance that brings us together here, and that's the passing of our dear friend and resident storyteller, Mr. Gumboot Charlie. But we have a second reason. The Bacon Rind Murder has been solved. The sheriff's office is not releasing the name of the person who committed the crime, but I just want you to know that Ben Weigland here isn't the guilty party, and he never was. I was wrong about Ben, and I'm sorry as hell about it. Let's give Ben a toast."

Everyone raises his mug or shot glass and says, in various tones of voice, "To Ben." Dewey limps toward us from behind the bar, extends his hand, and says, "Ben, you old son-of-a-gun." They shake hands. "It's good to see you. I'd like us to let bygones be bygones. I apologize for thinking you were guilty of the murder, and I'm sorry for breaking your nose that time."

"And I'm sorry about setting the bear trap you stepped in, Dewey. If I had it to do over again, you know I wouldn't do it."

One by one the men sitting at the bar and those standing wander over to us to shake Ben's hand. "Good to see you, Ben," they say, or "How's the trapping been?" or "Good work you did on that old brothel."

After a while, after most of the handshaking has subsided and mugs and glasses are once again being lifted and tipped toward thirsty mouths, Dewey raises his voice to make another announcement. "I know this doesn't repair all the past hard feelings, but I hereby award Ben Weigland a year's free pass to the hot springs. I'll even throw in a few trips down the luge run."

"Yo, Ben," someone yells. A couple people clap their hands, mugs clink together. I begin to tear up. I can just hear old Gumboot saying, "Be sure to bring an extra pair of drawers." I look at Laine. She hears it, too. We clink our mugs in complete understanding of each other.

"And now," Dewey says, calling out for everyone's attention again. "A great big toast to our friend, Gum, who's gone to happier diggings, where all the diamonds are huge and all the gold nuggets are above average." Cheering, stomping, clinking of glasses. "Gum, you left a great big empty space here at the Snowshadow Hot Springs Resort," Dewey continues. "You hurry back, you hear me?"

The man with the Fuller Brush eyebrows, the man I've never before heard speak, says, "Remember the story Gum told about the time he saved that guy's life in the mine—the powder monkey who set a charge that didn't go off right away so the fool ran back to see why? Gum smelled the fuse burning and ran after the guy, tackled him, picked him up and carried him, running, out of the mine just as the lid blew on the charge. And the guy weighed over two hundred pounds."

Stomping, cheering, clinking glasses.

And while the stories continue late into the night, Ben and I say goodnight to Dewey and Laine, to Gumboot's hat and to everyone else. We steal away to the brothel by the creek, where we try our best to give the wild animals a few stories of their own to tell when they gather at their favorite watering holes around the base of Cinnamon Peak.

CHAPTER 40

In the middle of the night, Ben sits bolt upright in bed and says, "I'm going to the outhouse." Leaping out of bed, he throws on his clothes and runs downstairs to put on his parka and boots. I doze. I vaguely remember him crawling back into bed, cool from his nighttime excursion. Then I fell back to sleep.

In the morning, when I rise and go downstairs to make coffee, I find two old work boots in my kitchen sink—the boots that had been hanging, snow-covered and frozen, on the side of the outhouse. Thawed now, they sit upright, more or less, but wet and warped and split. Part of a nest of an unknown creature pokes out of the toe of one boot.

"Ben?" I yell up the stairs. "Why are these old boots in my sink?"

"I'll be right down."

I hear clothes being pulled on, the sound of large feet coming down the stairs, and I see his big smile. He's up to something. He sits on the couch, as if nothing much is odd about a rotting pair of boots in the kitchen sink.

"I got a wild idea in the night," he says. "In fact, it woke me up. I guess my subconscious has been working on the possible whereabouts of the diamond, trying to supply the words the madam left out when she said, 'Inside . . . hanging on boards . . . Wilbur's.' I had thought her word *inside* meant indoors, but after looking in the hole under the cabin, and searching inside the log building and even the blacksmith shop, I realized it had to mean something else. Then I thought about what the madam might have had of Wilbur's, like hat, clothes, boots—boots! And there they hung. Sure, the diamond might not be inside the old boots. It isn't a safe or secure place to hide something so valuable, but then again she might have considered it temporary. She might have intended to move the diamond to a safer place."

"Well, now I'm curious," I say, "but I'm not putting my hand down inside them."

Ben rises and approaches the sink. He wrestles with the leather laces, aged and stiff but still strong, then pulls the tongue of the boot back. He tips the boot upside down and shakes it over the sink. Dead spiders and chunks of dirt fall out. Ben puts his hand down in the boot. Nothing. The other boot has the nest sticking out of the toe. He loosens that boot's laces, pulls back the tongue and repeats the earlier process. More debris, dirt, dead bugs. But the nest material is lodged in the toe of the boot. Ben begins to pull out twigs, bits of string, a scrap of old paper, hair, moss, another piece of string. But this string is attached to something. Ben pulls harder. Whatever it is, it's caught. He gets out his pocket knife and loosens the object—an old tobacco pouch, its strings pulled tightly together. I hold my breath. Ben fumbles as his big fingers untie the pouch and then he spills an object out into his hand.

"Well, I'll be . . ." he says, "I think this is it." He turns the chunk of raw stone in his hand.

"It's the right size, according to Gumboot—about the size of a bird's egg," I say. Its edges are slightly rounded and one end is fairly clear, like a quartz crystal, reflecting the dim morning light from the window above the sink.

Ben hands it to me, saying, "Here's your diamond."

"But it isn't mine," I say. "It's hers."

Tonight, the first full moon since we found the diamond, I lay the timeless treasure in its old tobacco pouch on the bed stand near my pillow and drift off to sleep. A few hours later, when the moon shines down on the bed and wakes me, like I knew it would, I carefully remove the diamond from its pouch. I turn the gem over and over in my hand. This is no ordinary stone, this diamond given to Lempi by a jealous man who was lucky in his diggings but unlucky in love.

Another aperture to my moonlit world, the window overlooking the creek, displays perfectly repeated patterns of frost on the panes. Reflected light from the snow below is caught and held and released into the room, brilliant as the shine from polished silver, and when it reaches the diamond's luminous end a brilliant, perfect star flashes—a star for Lempi Shunk.

CHAPTER 41

Snow is melting in the high country and Cinnamon Creek is on the rise. That's how the population of Snowshoe, now reduced by one to thirty-seven-odd residents, can tell that spring has returned to our little corner of Gold West Country. We've all checked ourselves for freezer burn. As it turns out, my frostbitten toes are Snowshoe's only climate-related casualties of this past winter, except, of course, for the vehicle collisions with deer and snowbanks.

Dewey has bought a new truck. As an excuse for this springtime act of madness, he tells us, "If my wheels are going to serve as Snowshoe's ambulance, then I damn sure can't be driving a junker. And," he continues, "I know you all don't want your local beer truck breaking down half way to town." There are other ways he rationalizes the purchase. He's convinced that when the story of The Bacon Rind Murder appears on *Unsolved Mysteries*, Snowshoe will be put back on State of Montana maps. Being the *entremanure* that he is, he's convinced traffic will increase, and when it does, the Snowshadow will feed and water the curious. Young Sheriff Troy's photo, along with the news that the murder will be profiled on national television, has hit regional newspapers. Now the sheriff is reportedly walking tall, his chest puffed out. This may be the biggest single thing that's happened to him since he went to the state high school football championships the year the murder happened.

In anticipation, realtors are cruising the canyon and crawling around in the gulches hoping to find some real estate to peddle, but no one is willing to sell. We like things the way they are. We like driving from the fringe of the bell-shaped curve into the bulge that represents, more or less, mainstream society—but we only go there to work or to visit. Then we hurry home to our edge habitat, dodging deer as we drive along The Trail. We don't want the place normalized.

Most of us have made a simple choice to live a life defined by the freedom to be exactly who we are, to live authentically, to get snowed in up to our armpits and shovel our way to the outhouse. Some of us even aspire to the subspecies of humans known as cretins. Others of us are dangerous, and at least one among us once committed a heinous crime. But we're no more dangerous than any other population of humans. Most of us are as gentle as the deer and rabbits out in the woods.

Some residents of Snowshoe remember the old ways, the habits and lives of their great grandfathers who, after the Civil War, rushed to the Rocky Mountains to strike it rich. But most of them failed, resigned themselves to that fact, and adapted their lives to local circumstances. Later, at least one among us would not accept his failure to strike it rich.

We come together in the evenings to share our stories, to celebrate our diversity, our survival. Some of us have become fixtures at the Snowshadow Hot Springs Resort. Some of us have been hunted, stuffed and mounted on the walls—like Dutch, the stuffed moose head lording over the habitat at one end of the bar.

The Snowshadow Hot Springs Resort is a zoo, a wild and crazy warehouse of smells, grunts, and monkeys chattering. Or maybe it's a mental health clinic. Dewey and Dutch both have watched us drink and laugh, and they've listened to our lies. And Dutch now wears Gumboot's old hat, a hat like Jimmy Stewart wore. The doctors are always in. No appointment necessary. Belly up to the bar. Listen to the background music on the jukebox as you reinvent your life in stories, or make your confessions. You will come to believe you are understood, and for many of us, that's nearly as good as the real thing.

At work, the talk of downsizing continues but nothing happens. We no longer pay any attention. We say, "They're just crying wolf." Gary hasn't found the right partner, but continues to entertain us with his brash humor and forthrightness. He reports that he last saw Bradley Binfet in the vicinity of a Republican haunt, accompanied by a woman *not* wearing hiking boots.

And, thanks to the hunter buffoon who mistook an adult llama for *a slow woman elk,* the friends of Myra and Jim are now the proud owners of two llama calves, complete with pedigrees. Chug got to visit them during his recent stay with Myra and Jim while Ben and I flew to Seattle for Easter. This was Ben's first airplane ride and his first brush with a population more numerous than the 1990 census reported for the entire state of Montana. Ben and my chef son, Jeremy, traded recipes and got along splendidly. Ben explained to a fascinated Jeremy how to dress a squirrel, if the need should arise, and then how to cook the squirrel on a stick over an open campfire. Jeremy described in great detail the fine art of flambeau, or how to cook with an open flame in a kitchen. Then we all visited a gourmet kitchen shop and Ben traveled home to Montana with a bag of new kitchen gadgets, including a new set of kitchen knives, a clay garlic roaster, and a spatula that can withstand intense heat, even flames.

Upon our return from Seattle, Ben received word that he had been awarded the property of Mr. Charles Wilbur Weigland, a/k/a Doherty. Based on a search of courthouse records, including Gum's birth certificate and other revelations, Ben turned out to be his only living relative. Dewey had told them of Gumboot's secret, the one he told after his ninety-second birthday party, when he said he knew the madam was, in fact, his mother. Gumboot had told Dewey that the people he lived with across the alley from The Bluebird House had told him about his mother but that he preferred to tell his story about coming here from Twodot after branding gophers.

By the time the film crew for *Unsolved Mysteries* shows up in Snowshoe, Ben will have Gum's place cleaned up, including the years of household trash heaped in the back of the old truck. This won't be a good season for the ravens.

In March, Ben and I traveled on snowshoes into Try Again Meadows to gather red-osier dogwood stems for my twig shutters. Chug came too, and because the surface of the snow had frozen smooth, she didn't sink in. But when she caught sight of a snowshoe rabbit and attempted to investigate, she spun out on the slippery surface and gave up the chase.

Ben and I worked together to build my window shutters. First, we assembled the frames, much like picture frames. On the inside edge of each shutter frame, we routed a groove and I placed the cut-to-length dogwood stems horizontally within the frames. We then glued the pine strip across the top of the shutter. Using small brass hinges, we affixed each shutter to the inside edge of the window frame, one on each side of the window. I can open one side or both. When the shutters are closed, the sunlight filters through the tiny spaces between the stems, creating an intriguing pattern.

On full moon nights, I leave the shutters open as an invitation to the spirit of Lempi Shunk. Other than her brief appearance on the night Gumboot died, I have not experienced the luminous glow of a visit from the madam since my dream of her dying, since she provided the strange clue to the whereabouts of the diamond.

I miss my sister, Lempi. I hope she will return. She would

approve, I believe, of what I did with the diamond. A jeweler in Helena assessed the raw diamond and arranged the sale. The proceeds, over $738,000, were placed in a United Way fund in the name of Lempi Shunk, specifically earmarked to help young women from underprivileged situations gain an education in business and then start their own companies.

Ben and I go to the Snowshadow about once a week to soak in the hot springs and have a beer. We've even taken a few luge runs with Laine and Dewey. The last time we soaked in the hot springs and then went into the bar, Dewey said, "Ben, why don't you have a seat there on Gumboot's old stool?" And Ben did just that.

As usual, whoever is at the 'Shadow clinks their glasses together in a salute to Gumboot Charlie. We all agree that Gumboot wasn't like anyone else we'd ever known, nor anyone else we'll ever meet again. We count ourselves lucky to have known him.

The three of us in Snowshoe who know of Gum's confession have talked about forgiveness, about the importance of forgiving ourselves for things we've done or not done to ourselves and to others. And we've talked about forgiving an old man who committed a terrible crime.

I believe it's all about adaptation, about hearing good music—both manmade and natural—and about following your own poetry. I like to think that even the wild animals have adapted, that they no longer look up in wonder when they hear certain strange, otherworldly sounds originating from the old brothel on the canyon floor next to the creek.

And my year in Snowshoe has proven to me that the Persian poet Rumi had it right when he wrote: *Where there is ruin, there is hope for a treasure.*

A FEW OF BEN WEIGLAND'S

FAVORITE

MOUNTAIN MAN RECIPES

BEN'S MOOSE MEAT SAUERBRATEN

Ingredients:

4 lbs. Moose Meat (rump or boned pot roast)
1/2 cup Gingersnaps, crushed
2 T. Olive or Canola Oil

Marinade Ingredients:

1 cup Cider Vinegar
1 cup Elderberry Wine (or other full-bodied red wine)
2 Onions, sliced
1 Carrot, sliced
1 Stalk Celery, chopped
2 Whole Allspice
4 Whole Cloves
1 T. Salt and 1-1/2 tsp. Pepper

Directions:

In a large, deep dish (with cover), combine all ingredients for marinade. Place moose meat in marinade for three days, turning at least once daily. Remove meat from marinade and dry on paper towels; reserve marinade. Coat meat with 2 T. flour and brown in hot oil. Pour in marinade; simmer covered for 3 hours. Remove meat; can blend juice and vegetables or leave as is. Measure 3-1/2 cups liquid, adding water if needed. Return liquid to pan, mix 2 T. flour with 1/3 cup cold water and 1 T. sugar; stir into liquid. Bring to boil, stirring. Stir in

1/2 cup crushed gingersnaps. Return meat to gravy mixture and simmer covered 20 mins. Serve thinly sliced meat with gravy.

BEN'S CURRIED SWAMP RABBIT

Ingredients:

1-1/4 lb. Muskrat Hams (6–8 hind legs, bone-in)
1 tsp. Salt, 1 tsp. Pepper
2 Cloves Garlic, peeled and finely chopped
1 T. Curry Powder
1 Green Chili, seeded and diced
1 Onion, peeled and diced, and 2 Green Onions, chopped
2 T. Olive or Canola Oil
2 cups Hot Water
2 Potatoes, medium-sized, peeled and diced

Directions:

Place muskrat hams in a large bowl and rub with a mixture of salt, black pepper, garlic, curry powder, chili, onions and green onions. Spread remaining mixture over thighs; cover bowl with plastic wrap and refrigerate overnight. Next day, take a large frying pan and heat oil over medium heat for 1 minute. Scrape onion mixture off meat and set aside. Brown meat in oil. Add 2 cups hot water and any seasonings left in bowl to meat and stir. Cover pan tightly and cook over medium heat for 45 minutes to 1 hour or until meat is tender. Add potatoes and onions and stir well. Cover and cook about 20 minutes or until potatoes are very soft and gravy has thickened.

Note: This recipe also works well with chicken or rabbit.

BEN'S VENISON POT ROAST IN SESAME-SOY SAUCE

Ingredients:

1 Boneless Chuck Venison Roast (About 4 lbs.)
2 tsp. Sesame Oil
1 Cup Water
1/4 Cup Soy Sauce
2 T. Molasses
2 T. Wine Vinegar or Cider Vinegar
2 Green Onions and 2 Garlic Cloves, chopped
1/4 tsp. Cayenne Pepper
2 T. Olive or Canola Oil
2 T. Flour
2 T. Water

Directions:

Combine sesame oil, 1 cup water, soy sauce, molasses, vinegar, green onions, garlic and cayenne pepper in a bowl. Pour over meat in a large bowl; cover and chill half a day, turning meat several times to season evenly. When ready to cook, remove meat from the marinade. Pat meat dry with paper towels. Brown in oil in a Dutch oven over medium heat. Pour marinade over meat; cover and simmer for 3 hours, turning meat once or twice. Meat should be very tender. Remove to a heated platter and keep hot while making gravy. To make gravy, pour pan liquid into a measuring cup or bowl. Add water to make 2 cups. Return liquid to pan and heat to boiling. Blend flour with 2 T. Water; stir into hot liquid and cook, stirring constantly, until gravy is thick; simmer for 3 minutes. Carve meat into thin slices and serve with gravy.

BEN'S SPICED MOOSE STRIPS

Ingredients:

1–1/2 lbs. Moose Steak, cut approx. 1/4" thick (or other red meat, wild or domestic)
2 T. Olive Oil
1 Garlic Clove, crushed in a garlic press
1/2 Onion, chopped
1/2 tsp. Salt
1/8 tsp. Cayenne Pepper
1/8 tsp. Chili Powder
1/8 tsp. Cinnamon
1/8 tsp. Celery Seed
1 T. Prepared Mustard (like Edna's Honey Fire Mustard)
1 Beef Bouillon Cube, dissolved in 1 cup boiling water

Directions:

Brown strips of meat in oil in a large skillet. Turn the browned meat into a covered cooking pan. Saute garlic and onion in remaining oil. With slotted spoon, remove onion and garlic from frying pan and place in medium sized bowl. To onion mixture, add all remaining ingredients, stir well, and pour over meat strips. Stir together, cover, and cook on a low heat for 2 to 3 hours. In the cool seasons up on Cinnamon Peak, I cook this dish on my wood stove. If you have electricity, a crock pot works well. Moose strips can also be baked in a casserole dish in the oven for 2 hours at 300 degrees.

EDNA WEIGLAND'S HONEY FIRE MUSTARD

Ingredients:
1 cup plus 2 T. Dry Mustard
1 cup Orange Juice
1/4 cup Lemon Juice
2 tsp. Grated Orange Rind
1 tsp. Grated Lemon Rind
1/2 cup Honey
1/2 tsp. Cinnamon
2 T. Olive or Canola Oil

Directions:

Place the dry mustard in the top of a double boiler. Add the orange and lemon juice a little at a time, stirring after each addition to keep the mustard from lumping. Add the orange and lemon rind. Heat, covered, over simmering water for 15 minutes, scraping the sides of the pan occasionally with a spatula. Stir in the honey, cinnamon and oil. Transfer to glass jars and refrigerate. Check the consistency after 1 day and thin with a little water if necessary. Makes 2 cups.

Note: Serve this pungent mustard as a condiment with all meats, including moose, elk, venison, swamp rabbit, and the occasional squirrel. You can also add it to sauces or stews.

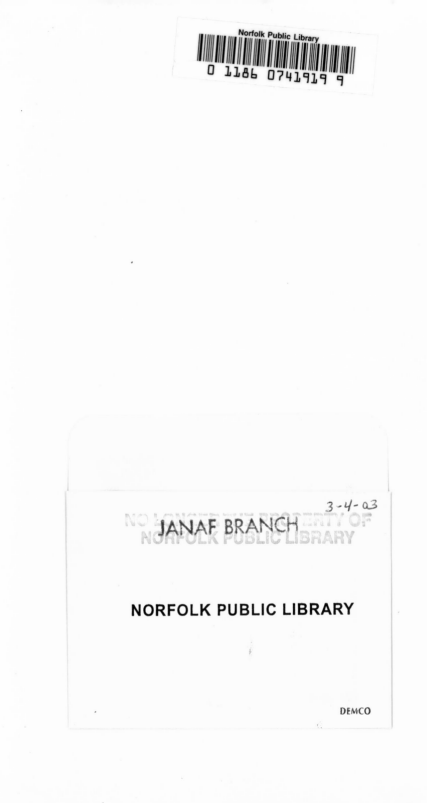